P9-DBO-195

DISCARD

the Secret Ingredient

NANCY NAIGLE

USA TODAY BESTSELLING AUTHOR

Hallmark
PUBLISHING

Cary Area Public Library
1606 Three Oaks Road
Cary, IL 60013

The Secret Ingredient
Copyright @ 2018 Nancy Naigle

All rights reserved. Except for use in any review, the reproduction or utilization of this work in whole or in part in any form by any electronic, mechanical or other means, now known or hereinafter invented, including xerography, photocopying and recording, or in any information storage or retrieval system, is forbidden without the written permission of the publisher.

This is a work of fiction. Names, characters, places and incidents are either the product of the author's imagination or are used fictitiously, and any resemblance to actual persons, living or dead, business establishments, events or locales is entirely coincidental.

Print ISBN: 978-1-947892-37-8
Ebook ISBN: 978-1-947892-46-0

Hallmark
PUBLISHING

www.hallmarkpublishing.com

Table of Contents

Chapter One

KELLY McINTYRE DIDN'T CARE IF the town of Bailey's Fork, North Carolina was too small in some folks' eyes. It was big enough to have kept the Main Street Cafe open through four generations of McIntyres. It also had bragging rights for the winningest high school football team in the region for ten years running and held the honor of the largest loblolly pine in both Carolinas, and that suited her fine.

The fact that she and Andrew York had professed their love by carving their initials in the bark of that tree had made Kelly McIntyre almost famous...for a little while.

Kelly straightened her short black-and-white apron and retied its red sash over her blue jeans. She lifted the tall glass dome from the cake people came from miles around to get and sliced a wedge, letting it fall over right into the center of the shiny red plate. Today's flavor—Southern Seven-layer Caramel. Her specialty. For that, she could still feel a little famous.

"Here you go." Kelly placed the plate in front of Fuzzy Johnston. "Mrs. Johnston out of town again?"

His eyes twinkled. "She'd never let me have this." He sank his fork into the frosting, then lifted it to his mouth. "Only live once, don't you know?"

"Your secret is safe with me," she teased. "You *are* going to eat some real food too though, aren't you?"

He nodded while swallowing the rich cake, then chased it with a sip of coffee. "I'll have the chicken-fried steak, please."

She jotted the order on her pad. "Do I need to even ask if you want mashed potatoes and gravy?"

"Nope." He grinned, looking quite pleased with himself. Fuzzy owned the biggest chicken farm around, and rumor had it his wife cooked chicken six ways to Sunday, which was why when she was out of town, Fuzzy always ended up here in the cafe for something a little different. "And fried okra."

"I'll put this right in." She tucked her pad into her apron pocket and headed to the kitchen. "Fuzzy's usual." Kelly pushed the ticket onto the clip and spun it.

Andrew snapped the order up and then stage whispered from the pass-through, "For someone who complains that his wife won't fix him anything but chicken, you'd think he might switch it up when he got the chance."

She loved that twinkle in Andrew's green eyes. His light brown hair was damp, which made that one piece of hair fall forward, giving him a tough-guy look. But she knew the ooey-gooey sweet side of him. "He did switch it up. He had cake as an appetizer." She spun away with only a quick glance back, knowing Andrew would pick up on the playful jab.

Andrew leaned forward at the pass-through. "He *loves* my chicken-fried steak and gravy."

"He ate a big slice of *my* cake, first," she challenged.

"Saving the best for last," he said with a playful smirk.

She turned and propped a hand on her hip. "I seem to remember helping you get that chicken-fried steak recipe just right." Kelly had helped him with as many recipes as he'd helped her. It seemed like there was nothing they couldn't perfect together.

Andrew straightened, his white apron splattered with grease and barbecue sauce. "Did I tell you that you look real pretty today?"

She swept a loose tendril of hair behind her ear. "Now you have." She never tired of hearing him say that. With a smile on her face, she turned, and then looked over her shoulder. "Thank you." He still made her heart race. She swept her thumb against the band of the diamond engagement ring on her left hand.

"Hey," he called after her. "Mom texted me. She and Dad are coming in for dinner tonight."

Kelly walked back over to him. "Great." They'd hardly ever come in since Andrew had started work at the cafe. "What's up?"

"They want to celebrate. Mom said it's a surprise. Something about my great aunt."

"That's the one who lives in France, right?"

"We haven't seen her in a couple of years. Not since the last time Dawn and I went for the summer. Maybe she's coming for a visit," he said. "Mom would love that. Will you save some cake for them? They love your chocolate cake."

"Of course. I'll put two slices aside right now. I can't let my future in-laws down. How would that look?"

"Very bad."

"My thoughts exactly." She placed two slices in the cooler to hold for the Yorks.

"Thanks, beautiful." He blew her a kiss, then got to work on the order.

I'm the luckiest girl in the world. She and Andrew had known each other since grade school, but it wasn't until high school when he'd landed a job bussing tables here at the cafe that the two of them had started dating. He loved to cook, and she loved to bake, so they spent nearly all of their extra time in the kitchen of the Main Street Cafe making up recipes and testing out ideas. They never tired of it, or each other.

The dinner crowd started to roll in, and the noise level grew exponentially. She pulled another order from the call window. With three plates balanced up each arm, she made it across the diner and dropped them off at table fourteen. "Can I get you anything else?" Everyone was already digging in, so she whisked back into the kitchen to pick up the next order.

Andrew tapped the bell at the window and shoved two more plates of the daily special under the heat lamp, giving her a wink before turning back to the cooktop. Kelly's dad barked an order, and Andrew hopped to it without a single grumble. Andrew loved being in the kitchen as much as he loved her, and she loved watching him cook.

Kelly spotted the Yorks as they walked in. There was no mistaking Andrew's father. Except for slight graying at the temples, father and son looked just alike. Tall, athletic, with wide lean-on-me shoulders, light brown hair and green eyes. His mom wore her signature cowboy boots, jeans and pearls with that ever-present smile and an air of kindness you could sense a mile away.

"Good evening. How are y'all doing tonight?" They weren't big talkers most of the time.

Mr. York gave her a nod.

Mrs. York said, "It's so good to see you. We're doing great."

"Follow me. I'll get you seated." She grabbed two menus as she passed the register.

"Thank you, Kelly," Mrs. York said with a smile.

"I might recommend the savory fried pork tenderloin," she said as she seated them in a booth. The pork tenderloin wasn't only the special on tonight's menu, but it was one of her favorites of Andrew's recipes. When Andrew's dad tasted that, he'd have to finally admit his boy really did have a future as a chef, something he hadn't been supportive of.

"Works for me," Mr. York said.

Andrew's mom scoured the menu, which was funny because

she always ordered whatever her husband was having. "Let's keep it simple. I'll have the same."

"Great. I'll be right back with your sweet teas." She walked over to the kitchen window and waved toward Andrew. "This is your parents' order."

Andrew gave her a half smile.

"Wait right there." He handed a dish through the window. "Appetizer. Not on the menu. For my folks."

"This looks delicious." She took the platter. "You're so thoughtful. I love you for that, you know."

"I do what I can." He swept at his brow.

Were the beads of sweat on his forehead from the heat of the kitchen or his parents' arrival? She couldn't blame him for being nervous; she was too.

The trio platter had Andrew's homemade pimento cheese, a heaping serving of made-from-scratch hushpuppies, and a spicy bean salsa that he'd been tweaking for over two weeks. "We might have to add this to our future menus." Whenever they perfected a recipe, she'd laminate it and put it in their binder full of recipes they'd use in the restaurant they'd someday own together. This looked worthy of the appetizer section.

He nodded toward the dining room. "If Dad likes it, it'll please anyone."

"They'll love it. Don't you worry." She zipped by her other tables to deliver the appetizer.

His dad raised his head. "We didn't order that."

"On the house," she said as cheerfully as possible. "I think you'll like it."

He scowled and muttered something about not ruining his dinner with filler that she pretended to ignore. Mrs. York dove right into the platter.

Thankfully, when she brought out his dinner, he seemed much

more ready to indulge. "How did you enjoy the appetizers?" she asked.

"Fabulous!" Mrs. York said.

Mr. York glanced at the near-empty dish. "Never was one much for hushpuppies, but everything on that plate was good. Probably won't be able to finish my dinner now."

"No worries. We can box your leftovers if needed."

The cafe was busy, but she kept an extra-close eye on their table to be sure to get their dessert to them before they asked for it. When she did, Mr. York didn't even complain.

"Can I get anything else for you two tonight?" she asked.

"No," Mr. York said quickly, then rubbed his stomach.

Mrs. York placed her hand atop her husband's across the table and softly said, "Not a thing, darling. Thank you so much. That was the best cake. So moist. And all those layers? It had to take hours to prepare. You're an amazing baker."

"She is, isn't she?" Kelly heard Andrew say behind her.

She turned and reached for his hand. "Hey."

His blue button-down shirt was wrinkled from where the apron had been tied against it for hours in the steamy kitchen. "My special girl." He pulled her in close.

She resisted the urge to kiss him right there in front of his parents. "Thank you." As she held his gaze, she knew he was thinking the same thing at that moment.

Kelly turned back to his parents. "I'm so glad you enjoyed it." A customer across the way was waving her down. "I need to get their check to them. Excuse me." She left, but she had one ear cast toward their table. Call it female intuition, but every nerve in her body was on alert. Something was up.

She heard his mother's giggle, followed by, "Tell him, honey."

"I thought you wanted to tell him. Aunt Claire is *your* aunt." His voice was impatient.

"What's going on?" Andrew asked.

"Aunt Claire called tonight," his mother said. "You know how excited she's been about your cooking and all. Well, she's lined up the opportunity for you to go to Paris to study under one of the best pastry chefs in the world."

"What?" Andrew's voice carried across the cafe. Kelly glanced over. He looked flat-out dumbfounded. "But I'm not a baker. Kelly is the baker. I'm a chef. There's a difference, Mom."

"You're no chef, just a short-order cook. But maybe you'll be as good as Kelly when you get back," his dad said. "With any luck."

Kelly gulped. What was wrong with that man? Insulting his own son like that? Andrew had a natural talent in the kitchen. It was something to be proud of. Andrew had expressed his disappointment in his father not appreciating his career choice, but it wasn't until today that she realized how much he disapproved. Her heart ached for Andrew.

"You'll be able to stay at Aunt Claire's while you're there," his mother said. "The owner of the school is renting the carriage house for the executive pastry chef teaching this special curriculum. I have no idea what this is costing her, but she's covering every dime. It's a once-in-a-lifetime opportunity."

Andrew pulled up a chair to the end of the booth. "Wow."

"Unless you've got second thoughts about the whole cooking thing," his dad said. "You can always come back and work at the shop with me."

"I have a job, Dad." He fiddled with the bottom of his shirt. "And Kelly is here."

Kelly tucked herself out of their view. Ever since Andrew had refused to work with his father in the family business, his dad had hated all of Andrew's ideas. Truth be told, Andrew was an awesome mechanic, but he didn't enjoy doing that kind of work. After a long day turning wrenches, he'd been filthy and in a foul mood. When he was in the kitchen, his whole demeanor changed.

Andrew's mom pressed her hand on his arm. "I need to let

Aunt Claire know if you're coming. The Pastry and Baking Program begins the first week of July."

"So soon? Kelly and I had plans this summer." He tugged at his shirt collar.

"I'm sure those plans can wait. You two have your whole lives ahead of you. The program runs from July to December. Only twenty students get in. Aunt Claire pulled some serious strings."

"It does sound like a great opportunity…" He leaned back in the chair, looking down at his hands. "But I don't want to be a baker. It would be a big waste of time and money."

"We'd never be able to send you to something like this." His mom sounded almost apologetic. "Aunt Claire says that if you do well, there could be other scholarship opportunities too."

Kelly could see how torn he was. He pressed his fingers into the palm of his hand, the way he did when he was deep in thought. Paris was so far, but if she were faced with this decision, she'd jump at it.

"You'll be home by Christmas," his mother added gently, as if she'd read his mind.

"I need to talk to Kelly," he said.

Mr. York peered over the top of his glasses at Andrew. "You can make your own decisions, son."

Kelly flinched. Those words were like a stab to the heart. Did his father really think she'd ever stand in the way of such a great opportunity for him?

"I will make my own decision. I just want to include Kelly in it. She's my fiancée."

Kelly's heart swelled. At least Andrew knew whose side she was on.

His dad's mouth pulled into a tight line, then he pushed his chair from the table and stood.

Kelly held her breath.

"You two talk it over tonight," his mom said. "We'll see you at the house later. It's the middle of the night over there right now anyway. We can call her tomorrow afternoon and give her your answer." She stood and hugged Andrew.

"Thanks, Mom. This is amazing news. I don't mean to sound unappreciative, but Kelly and I just set a wedding date last week. I'm not going to make a decision this big without her." Andrew's shoulders slumped as if he'd been beaten.

Kelly pulled her hand to her heart. *They don't understand that baking and culinary arts are two entirely different skills.*

His father turned and walked out the door.

Is there anything Andrew could do or say that would make that man happy?

Andrew's mom raised a dismissive hand toward her husband. "I know. Never mind him." She stepped back. "I'm really proud of you. I want you to have the chance to do what you want with your life. Don't let Dad worry you. I'll deal with him." She gathered her purse and rushed outside to catch up with his dad.

His parents' behavior confused Kelly. Mom and Dad had always supported her no matter what she'd chosen to pursue. Last week Andrew had gotten down on one knee and professed his love, never wanting to be apart. They'd set their wedding date for June fourth of the following summer to give them plenty of time to save for and find a house to start their new life together.

Never in a million years did she consider they might be separated for half that time. Even thinking about it made loneliness invade her mood.

Andrew turned his head and saw her standing there. "You heard?"

Right now, the other customers would have to wait. She walked over and took his hand. "I did."

He pulled her into his arms and hugged her.

She didn't envy the position he was in. She tried to relax in his embrace, but every nerve in her body tingled with nervous energy.

He sucked in a deep breath and gave her a squeeze. "I love you."

"I love you too." They'd made so many plans together, and this didn't fit with any of them. If she was this confused, she could only imagine what he was feeling right now. Trying not to sway his opinion, she was careful with her tone.

Pasting a smile on her face, she stepped back. "That's very generous of your great-aunt."

"If you don't want me to go, I won't. It doesn't even make sense. I'm not a baker. I don't want to be. That's your thing." He dropped his head back. "I don't know what to do."

His gentle squeeze of her hands gave her the strength to encourage him, even though it hurt her heart to think about being apart for so long. "I'd never ask you to stay."

The pained look on Andrew's face suddenly softened. "Come with me."

"I can't." She blinked, hoping the tears wouldn't fall. "You know I made that commitment to cover for Mom and Dad while they're on that cruise, but you have to go."

"We're a team." He squeezed her hands. "We're engaged. This is our whole future."

Her throat tightened. "Going to France will only make you a better chef. Think of the things you'll learn. That's good for our future."

Andrew looked up at the ceiling. "Visiting Aunt Claire in France is when I realized I wanted to become a chef. I'd never seen such fancy food. Chefs were like celebrities there."

She'd heard the story a million times, but he always told it with such exuberance that she didn't mind.

His voice became quieter. "It's pretty cool to even have been offered the chance, but I don't—"

"You'd be a fool to turn it down." She spaced the words evenly. She sucked in a deep breath, and with all the control she could muster said, "I'll be right here when you get back. It'll be an even more special Christmas."

"You really think I should go."

"I do." *I don't want you to, but how could I ask you to stay? That would be so selfish.* "We can talk on the phone, and text."

"That training would make a difference in the scholarships I can qualify for here locally."

"Exactly."

The next day he accepted the gracious offer from his great-aunt and began making plans.

And in a few weeks she was standing at the Charlotte airport, choking back tears as she hugged him goodbye, hoping the time would fly.

It had been a lonely Fourth of July, her first in several years without Andrew. But she'd sent him pictures of the fireworks, and he'd texted back even though he'd been sleeping. Over the next weeks he shared recipes and techniques with her, and they often baked the same things and compared notes, but the days dragged on.

It had been fun for Kelly to experiment with the new baking methods Andrew was learning, and her own skills were benefitting from it. A good thing, since she was baking more than ever to get through the weeks.

Summer gave way to fall, and thank goodness for Christmas shopping to keep her busy. December finally rolled around, and on the night of Andrew's certification, she set her alarm at noon to call right after the ceremony.

"Congratulations!" She could hear the excitement in the background.

"Thanks. I'm at the banquet now."

"I miss you like crazy. I can't wait to see you. Eight more days. Finally! I can't believe it. In a way it seems like it's been forever, but at the same time it feels like yesterday that you left."

"I'm glad you said that."

There was a trace of uncertainty in his voice that caught Kelly off guard. "What? You know I miss you. Every single day."

"I meant the part where it seemed like yesterday."

Her heart dropped. Then, what she'd feared most came over the line.

"Kelly, I've been offered a scholarship. Not for pastries and baking, but for real culinary stuff. With the best chefs around. They presented it to me at graduation tonight."

"Oh." It almost took her breath, a verbal sucker punch to the gut. "A scholarship?"

"Full ride. One of the instructors is part of this group of chefs. Francois Dumont. He owns the hottest restaurant in Paris. He was so impressed with me that he sponsored me without telling me."

"That is—"

"Incredible," he finished. "Right?"

"Yes." She forced enthusiasm into her voice. "When do you have to decide?"

"Kelly, come to Paris. We'll get married on June fourth just like we'd planned. Only here instead of in Bailey's Fork. We can save money to help fly our parents over for the wedding. You're going to love it here. The cafes. The food. The bakeries," he rattled on with the enthusiasm of a mariachi band. "You could land a job in a bakery here in a hot second. It's amazing. We'll be so happy."

His words came like missiles, ripping gaping holes in the life she'd dreamed of. She went numb. For the first time in her life, she was truly speechless. *He has to be kidding.*

"I have it all figured out," he went on. "We'll stay in the carriage house here at Aunt Claire's until we get on our feet. I already checked with her. She's fine with it."

Not only was he serious, he had their lives all planned out, and this didn't look anything like what they'd talked about. She'd never in her wildest dreams entertained leaving Bailey's Fork.

"Stop!" She couldn't listen to it another second. "Andrew, I'm not fine with it. I'm not moving. That was never the plan," she said quickly over her pounding heart. A tear slipped down her cheek.

"But I miss you." There was surprise in his tone.

"I miss you too. It's an amazing opportunity for you, but we're going in different directions. I've waited over six months for you. I've been patient. But this is twice you've pushed aside our plans."

"I know, but this—"

"Is not for me," she said. She wouldn't keep him from chasing his own dream, but hers wasn't to work for someone else in a country four thousand miles away from her family. The knot in her chest was so tight she couldn't utter another word.

She wasn't even sure how long she'd been standing there next to the cafe phone when Mom came up and placed a gentle hand on her arm. "What's wrong, honey?"

Kelly gave a choked, desperate laugh, but that didn't fool her heart. Her spirits sank lower. "He's not coming back." Reality swirled around her. She'd had her life planned out—a good life—but now every single thing about that future seemed to be falling away.

"Andrew?"

She turned and looked into her mother's eyes, and the tears fell. She flung out her hands in despair. No way could she utter those words again.

"Oh, Kelly. I'm so sorry." Mom held her close. "Honey, things happen for a reason. You're going to have to trust me on this. I know you're hurt now and you feel like you'll never love another—"

"I won't," Kelly said, because if there was one thing she was completely certain of, it was that she never wanted to feel like this again.

Mom squeezed Kelly's hand in her own and then kissed the top of it. "You will love again. Andrew York can be replaced. Good riddance to him for not knowing how special you are."

Chapter Two
Seven Years Later

FIVE BRIGHT PINK HELIUM BALLOONS bounced in the breeze next to the spiral boxwood topiaries at the entrance of The Cake Factory on the corner of Main and Elm.

When Kelly first opened The Cake Factory, the name had been sort of tongue-in-cheek. The old ribbon factory had sat empty for years after they'd consolidated operations in their facility up north. After months of letter writing, they'd finally agreed to let her lease the small front office space next to her parents' cafe. She'd spent nearly every dime of her savings on the renovation to turn that dusty office into a sparkling and inviting bakery. It was only five hundred square feet and two ovens, with her baking everything herself... hardly a factory.

The following year she'd expanded and re-invested her profits into purchasing the whole factory building. The town had supported her wholeheartedly. They'd even extended tax incentives to help her refurbish that end of Main Street. Bringing jobs to the community and doing her part to sustain the economy in her hometown was her proudest accomplishment yet. Beautifying Main Street was just a bonus.

Now the two-story brick building hummed with activity day

and night, and the smell of fresh baked goods permeated the air—living up to its name.

Inside, she'd decorated the customer-facing area with a combination of crisp pink-and-white stripes, offset with gray-and-white polka dots for a touch of whimsy.

The front door opened, and Missy walked in with her designer handbag swinging from her wrist. A punchy coral color, her purse matched her sweater set and shoes. "What're we celebrating?"

"Our anniversary," Kelly said. "Five years in business today."

"Congratulations!" Missy owned the real estate company located up the block and was a faithful customer. "You know your goodies are my secret weapon."

"You must have an Open House today," Kelly said. "You're in luck. We're having an anniversary special. For every six goodies you buy, I'll give you one free."

"I like the sound of that." Missy stared into the glass case. "I can pick from anything in the case? Even the cake pops?"

"Your choice." Kelly didn't rush her. They'd loaded the case with cupcakes, cookies, brownies and the ever-popular cake pops this morning. She'd been in business long enough to know not to rush her customers. The longer they ogled the goods, the more they left with.

Sara, dressed in The Cake Factory's signature black-and-white tiny polka dot apron with black-and-gray striped sash and straps, stopped at the counter. "I'm getting ready to place the order for shipping supplies. Do you have anything to add?"

"Everything I need is already on the list. Thanks."

When Kelly had opened the online business, she'd hired Sara to help with the storefront and manage the shipping department. She now handled the entire inventory and reordering of supplies too.

"Okay, I know what I want," Missy announced.

Kelly turned back to the case and pulled on a pair of plastic gloves.

"I'm going with cookies this time. Two dozen." Her bracelets jingled as she pointed out items. "I'll do six each of the chocolate-filled butter cookies with chocolate sprinkles, the key lime spritzer cookies, oatmeal date, and chocolate chip."

Kelly took out a large box and started stacking cookies with a pair of tongs, separating each flavor with a square of wax paper. "How about your free ones?"

"Can I have all four in the chocolate-filled butter cookies?"

"You sure can. Those are my favorite too." Kelly sealed the box with a glossy pink-and-black label and rang up the purchase.

"You'd better throw in a red velvet cake pop for me. I can't resist those."

Kelly pulled one out of the case. "In the box?"

"Yes, or I'll eat it before I get there." Missy swiped her debit card. "Are you going to make those lemon blackberry cakes again anytime soon? I swear that was the best dessert I've had in my life. I thought I might order one for someone special on Valentine's Day."

"That cake is not the same with frozen berries. I've tried it a dozen ways, and it just doesn't work." Kelly handed Missy her receipt. "We usually have fully ripe berries mid-July to late August, so I'm afraid you'll have to wait until summer for that. But I have some wonderful new cakes for Valentine's Day you can sample."

"I can't wait. I'm in a hurry this morning, but I'll definitely be back in tomorrow."

"Excellent. See you then."

A makeshift door chime made from vintage tin measuring spoons and baubles tinkled against the glass front of the white wooden framed door as Missy left.

Kelly rearranged the cookies in the case. By the end of the day, this would be empty. It always was. Rather than risk leftovers, she promised bakery fresh products until they were gone. Then she simply turned the open sign to closed for the day. It seemed to work, and if anyone really wanted to be sure they didn't miss out, they ordered ahead; her team was great at ensuring those requests always got filled.

Customers came through the door at a steady pace all morning.

Sara had to go back to the bakery to fill an order of thirty cupcakes for a school class party. "It's been a really good day," she said to Kelly as she came back with the order. "We're going to be sold out before one at this pace."

"Sooner than that," Bettie, who worked down at the library, said. "I'll take the rest of the cookies and any stragglers you've got in the case. Miss Erma's got a cold. She didn't make the treats for this month's book club meeting tonight."

"Oh, no." Kelly grabbed a box and started filling it. "I hope she's feeling better soon. You're in luck though, there's a nice, random assortment of things left."

"Thank goodness." Bettie paid for her order and headed for the door. "Hungry readers are no fun. Thanks for rescuing me."

"Our pleasure," Kelly called after her. She tugged on her apron strings. "That's it. Earliest we've closed since Christmas. Is there a pre-Valentine's sweet tooth challenge going on someone forgot to tell me about? We're usually slow right until the week of Valentine's." She walked over to the door and flipped the sign to closed. "Not that I'm complaining."

"Me neither." Sara wiped down the counter. "It's such a pretty day. You should take the rest of the day off. I can cover for you. Didn't Johnny Ray ask you out to lunch today?"

"He did." Kelly untied her apron. "But I said no. Besides, I know just the guy I want to spend the day with."

"Don't tell me. Gray?" Sara rolled her eyes. "Really?"

"He's great. Don't be so judgmental. He's always happy to see me and has never let me down." Kelly grabbed her keys from the hook and headed for the door. "And he's very cute."

Chapter Three

ANDREW GOT OUT OF THE bright yellow Mustang. It was only a rental, a splurge for sure, but if he was going to drive from North Carolina to New York next week he might as well do it in style.

He strolled up the walkway of the ranch house where he'd grown up. The faded shutters could use a fresh coat of paint. His room had been the last one at the far left of the house. He'd climbed out that window many a night in high school to meet up with friends at the old barn down near the river. Not just friends. Kelly too. The thought of the way things had ended between him and Kelly made him uncomfortable. Maybe coming back to Bailey's Fork wasn't the best idea. He ran a finger under his collar.

It's only for a couple of days.

He'd stick close to home—that way he wouldn't run into Kelly, which was good, because how do you tell someone you're sincerely sorry after you've let this much time pass?

Seeing his parents after all this time would be hard enough, but family was family and he intended to do the right thing by them, even if he dreaded it a little.

He closed his eyes and took in a long breath, praying Dad

wouldn't be the one to answer the door, then pressed the doorbell and waited.

His heart ticked off the seconds, each one thrumming in his head.

Finally, he heard footsteps, and the door swung open. Relief flooded through him.

"Hi, Mom." Andrew spread his arms out, and for a second he thought he might have to catch her.

She wobbled, blinked, and then screamed. "Andrew!" She clung to his neck, then pushed him away. "Let me look at you."

"It's so good to see you." The warmth of her voice made all those fears of coming back home fade. She looked older, and a little tired, but then maybe she didn't look any different at all. His memory had faded a bit over the past few years. One thing was the same. That look of approval in her eyes. He wished he hadn't stayed away so long now.

"What are you doing here? Come in." She took two quick steps inside and then turned around. "I was afraid you might never come back. I'm so happy to see you." She slapped her thigh. "I can't even believe it."

Her blue eyes sparkled, wet with tears.

He followed her inside, closing the door behind him. The smell of cilantro and spices hung in the air, and the memories flooded back. "Taco Tuesday."

"Of course."

"I haven't had tacos like yours in way too long."

"Then you're in for a treat. Nothing fancy like you're used to now, though."

"Nothing compares to your home cooking."

"Good. You keep reminding yourself of that." She stopped and turned, staring at him. "I can't believe you're really here. I know I keep saying it, but I just can't believe it. Why didn't you let me know you were coming?"

"I wanted to surprise you." It was only a half lie. If he'd tacked this visit to the back end of his trip to New York, he'd been afraid it would look like an afterthought.

"I'm surprised." She cocked her head. "Is everything okay? Oh my gosh! How long can you stay?" Tears fell to her cheeks. "I'm sorry. It doesn't even matter. You're here now."

He comforted her with a hug. "I'm doing great. I have business up north next week. A friend of mine is opening a new restaurant there. I'll be helping him with the grand opening."

"How exciting!"

"It is. My mind has been reeling with possibilities." A true statement. He'd been in dessert recipe mode for thirty-six hours straight now. "There's no way I was traveling this close to home and not coming to see you. How are things here? Where's Dad?"

"Oh, honey, he's in Pennsylvania for the annual farm equipment show with Jeff."

Andrew's brother-in-law, Jeff, had stepped into the role Dad had always hoped Andrew would fill. He'd hoped Dad might lighten up once Dawn's husband started working in the family business, but instead it seemed to add salt to the wound.

Mom's lips pulled into a tight line. "Kind of wish I'd known you were coming so he wouldn't think we planned this for while he's gone. You know how he is."

"Well, you didn't know, and I didn't know he'd be gone." He couldn't win when it came to Dad. He was sure either way he'd have something snarky to say about the timing. "When will he be back?"

"On Sunday night."

"Perfect. I'll be in town until Monday night. That'll give us enough time to visit and maybe not get into an argument."

"You two are so much alike. That's why you butt heads so much."

"I'm nothing like him. I can safely say that I'll be okay with whatever career choices my kids make and not hold it against them."

"I think he's finally over that." She sat down in her favorite easy chair. "We're both very proud of you."

"Thanks, Mom." She was the one who was proud, and that was enough. He'd come to terms with that a long time ago.

"You've matured. Filled out. You're not a lanky boy anymore."

He hadn't been out of high school but a few years when he'd left town. "I work out. Have to, with all the rich foods I'm always tasting."

"You've turned into a handsome man. You look a lot like my daddy did at your age."

"Really? I've never seen pictures of Pop when he was young."

She got up and walked over to the bookcase and came back lugging a thick green photo album over to the couch. She sat next to him and started flipping through the pages. "Oh my gosh, this is my mom and dad when they got married. Look how much you look like your grandfather. He's younger than you here."

He leaned in. They had the same coloring, light brown hair and light eyes. "Were his eyes green too?"

"Yes. Just like mine. Momma's eyes were blue."

"I remember that."

Mom flipped through the pages. Pictures dangled from the little paper corners where the glue had lost its stick over time. "This is the picture I was thinking of. Look at this."

Even their hair was similar. Same cleft chin too. "Yeah. I'd almost think that was me if the picture quality weren't so old."

His mom laughed. "True. You'll be showing your kids pictures of us on your phone." She slapped the heavy padded cover of the album closed. "Not in one of these." She hugged the album to her chest. "I can't believe you're sitting here. Can we call your sister? She should be on her way home from the new YMCA. Did you know she's teaching yoga there now?"

"I did. She told me all about it when we talked at Christmas a few weeks ago. Yeah, let's call her." When he first moved, he and

Dawn had talked all the time, but as time went by they'd both gotten busy and the calls had turned into quick texts or emails, and then just the obligatory holiday calls.

Mom picked up her phone and swept her finger across the screen, poking the glass as if it required all the force of a manual typewriter.

"Can you see me?" she yelled loud enough for the folks in Town Square to hear.

"Hi, Mom. I just got home. Why are you FaceTiming me?"

"I have something to show you." She motioned for him, then grabbed his arm and tugged him in close. "Look what the cat dragged in!"

"Andrew? Andrew!" Her scream was louder than Mom's voice. "What are you doing here? Oh my gosh. I'm on my way over. Don't you move a muscle. Ten minutes. I'll be there."

"I'll be here. Don't speed. You know Sheriff Range would love to give you a ticket."

"Don't think so." She lowered her head. "He died three years ago."

"I hadn't heard." He suddenly regretted not staying in touch. What else had he missed?

"On a brighter note, your old buddy Sam Foxwell is the new sheriff."

"No way. They'll let anyone wear a badge in this town." Sam had been one mischievous kid. It was hard to think of him as a man of the law. "Don't make me call and warn him that you're speeding."

"You wouldn't dare."

"You're right. See you in a few."

"I'm so excited. I love you, Andrew. I'll be right there."

His mom ended the call. "I'm sorry your dad is missing this."

"I should give him a quick call before Dawn gets here," Andrew said. "I don't want the news to get to him before I talk to him."

"I'll let you do that while I put together a little snack for us. You have to be famished."

"I am," he said. "It's been a long day, and it's late on Paris time."

"Oh, dear. That's right." She swept out of the room.

He could hear Mom rummaging through the refrigerator and cabinets. A comforting kind of ruckus that felt like home. He pulled up his father's cell phone number.

The call went straight to voice mail. He could picture Dad pressing the button to silence the call when he saw his number.

His throat ached with defeat as he left a message. "Hi, Dad. It's me. Andrew. I'm in Bailey's Fork. I'd hoped to surprise you, but I guess the surprise is on me. I didn't know you were traveling, but I'll be here until Monday. I look forward to seeing you Sunday." He hesitated, then said, "Love you, Dad." He disconnected the call.

Mom came back in the room with a tray full of stuff. "Sweet tea, chips and salsa that I canned last summer, and some cookies from the church bake sale."

"Sounds good."

"We should invite everyone over. They'll be so excited to catch up with you."

"No." He could see her wheels turning. "Let's keep this visit low-key. I won't be here that long and I want to spend time with you, not be pulled in ten directions. A nice, quiet visit with family. That's all I want." Besides, he only had a few more days to get his body on an east coast time clock before he had to do the best baking of his career. And baking wasn't his real talent. He needed some quiet time to brainstorm and plenty of rest.

"Of course, dear," she said, patting his leg. "Whatever you think."

The front door slammed, and Dawn ran into the room. "You're really here." She hugged him and then punched him in the arm. "How dare you come back home and not even call first. Did you rent that Mustang?"

"Yeah."

"Total waste of money. I could've picked you up."

"It's over an hour drive from RDU to here. You're busy. Plus I needed a car. I'm heading to New York from here."

"When?"

"I have to be there next Tuesday, so I'll be leaving Monday at the latest."

She gave him that what-for look, and he was ready for an earful, but instead she threw her hands in the air. "Well, you're here now, and you look amazing. This whole chef thing is really working for you."

"You look great too." Her hair was longer, and a little darker than his now. "How's Jeff doing?"

"He's good. Cussing you when Dad gets on his nerves."

He could only imagine. "I guess I owe him a beer...or two."

"You might just want to buy a keg." Dawn snickered. "Count on him collecting on that."

The decision to not go into business with his father had opened the spot for Jeff. It was something Dawn had pushed for, when Jeff hadn't gotten a job out of college as fast as she'd have liked. Jeff had thought it was a lucky break, but it had come with a price. Working for your father-in-law was probably even worse than working for your dad.

They sat around the coffee table catching up for over an hour, until Andrew could barely hold his head up.

"I'm sorry. It's great to see you two, but I'm beat. I'm still on Paris time. I need to go check in at the hotel and turn in."

"Andrew Lee York, you are *not* staying at a hotel." His mother looked horrified.

"Look, I don't want to be a bother. This will be easier."

"Call and cancel that reservation right now. You can stay in your old room. It's the guest room now. It's all ready to go. Not a bother at all."

He knew better than to argue when Mom had that look in her eye. "Fine. I'll go get my stuff."

"Glad you remembered that look," Dawn whispered to him as he walked by. "Can't argue with her when she's like that."

"Oh, I recognized it."

"I'll come with you." Dawn followed him outside. "I'm so happy you're here, but I have to ask. Are you going to come back after you do this thing in New York? Maybe for a little while, at least?"

He let out a sigh. "Can we talk about this tomorrow?"

She smiled. "At least that wasn't a no."

"Don't read more into it. I'm just tired, and I have a sweet job to go back home to."

"Home?" She pulled her hands to her hips and raised a finger. "Home is here. Where your family is."

He regretted the slip.

He hitched his bag on his shoulder and went back inside. "Goodnight, Mom. Love you. You too, sis. I'll see you both in the morning."

His room was now a girly blue with lots of flowers and ruffles. He was too tired to even care. He stretched out across the bed to the familiar sound of Dawn and Mom talking in the living room. *It does feel like home.*

Chapter Four

"**G**OOD MORNING, MOM," ANDREW SAID as he walked into the kitchen.

"You're up early this morning."

Andrew poured himself a cup of coffee. "I need to get back on an east coast schedule."

"That's got to be exhausting changing time zones like that, but you're still young. You should be able to bounce right back."

He shook his head. "Have to admit, there are a lot of days I'm not feeling so young anymore."

"You're probably working too hard. Every time I talk to you, all you talk about is work. Don't you do anything for fun anymore?"

"I don't have much time for anything else. Ever since Francois gave me the signature restaurant, it seems like I do everything. Hire, fire, prepare the menus, and cook. It's exhausting. Last week I got stuck finding a new company to do the table linens."

"Why on earth would you have to do that? Seems like they'd have someone to handle that."

"Francois fires people faster than they can learn the jobs. I had to fill the gap to keep things going."

"He's lucky to have you. I guess that's a small price to pay to be the chef at one of the most famous restaurants in France."

There was a time when he'd thought that too. "I do love being a chef." Only it wasn't as fun as it used to be. Having to follow Francois' recipes to the very letter was getting old. He yearned for the days when he could create something new in the kitchen for fun. Things like ordering linens and playing mediator between Francois and the employees, or soothing egos when Francois popped in on one of his surprise visits only to wield fury on Andrew's team, was exhausting. He needed a psychology degree, not a culinary one. Not one to complain himself, he let Mom's comment go.

"Dawn texted me earlier. She wants me to come over and see all the renovations they've done at the house."

"It's beautiful." Her smile broadened in approval. "I'm so glad you're making time to spend with her. She's really missed you. We all have."

"I've missed you too." He grabbed his keys from the counter where he'd left them last night.

"Do you remember how to get there?"

"Things couldn't have changed that much."

"You might be surprised. If you have one of those fancy GPS in that car, you might want to use it."

"I'll call if I get lost," he said, joking.

"I'll see you later."

He drove down the long lane that led to his folks' house, then through the center of town.

The Main Street Cafe was bustling with customers. His first and only job in this town had been there.

It was where he'd fallen in love with cooking, and Kelly.

As he got closer, he noticed the cafe had tables out front now, not so much unlike a bistro back in France. A nice addition.

The old factory building next to it had been empty for as many years as he could remember, but now the brick facade had been spruced up with a new glossy white exterior extending both sides of the corner, boasting glossy white painted pillars. It brought a cheery brightness this end of the street had always needed.

He read the bright pink scripted letters over the door. The Cake Factory.

Andrew swallowed hard. Mixed feelings surged through him—pride, envy, and denial.

Dawn had told him Kelly had opened her own bakery. Pink had always been her favorite color, and this was right next door to her folks' cafe. This had to be it.

He leaned forward, trying to get a better look. It was a big place.

Mom and Dawn had tried to keep him up-to-date about what was going on with Kelly over the years, but he'd stopped them mid-sentence every time. It had been his choice not to come home seven years ago. He had to live with the consequences.

But in his mind she still worked at the family restaurant while selling her baked goods out of a tiny shop in town. Seeing this fancy storefront had caught him off guard. As wrong as it was, seeing her succeed…without him…gnawed at him.

Where would we be right now if I'd made a different decision seven years ago? Married. They'd had a wedding date. An inner torment had his mind reeling, making him question his decisions. They'd once dreamed of their own restaurant and bakery.

He slowed down, taking in all the changes from the anonymity of his rental car. There were a few new businesses. A gym, a used bookstore, and a clothing boutique. A frozen yogurt shop sat right next to a new dry cleaner where the old arcade used to be. He'd pounded flippers in that place for hours a day until he was old enough to drive.

Main Street had gotten an upgrade since he'd been gone, with shiny black lampposts and new benches between the storefronts. Planters of brightly colored pansies and evergreens adorned every corner. It seemed brighter, and more upscale than the small town he remembered.

Across the street, a woman made her way through the crosswalk with the fattest little dog he'd ever seen on a harness with a sparkly leash. The lumbering animal didn't seem to be in much of a hurry as they crossed while he sat at the red light.

The woman turned and headed down the alley road behind the row of shops.

Pretty flags lined Main Street in green and gold with the new Bailey's Fork pine tree logo on them. He'd once carved initials in that tree. AY + KM with a big heart around it.

Bailey's Fork Flower & Gift had new awnings and a fresh coat of turquoise paint. He thought to stop and get Mom some flowers. She'd always loved flowers, but there was no way could he get in and out of the flower shop without Mrs. Chalmers spreading the word that he was back in town. It was hard to keep a secret in a town the size of Bailey's Fork.

Just past Town Square, a brand-new row of office buildings filled the block where the old skating rink had once been. What did the local kids do now that it and the arcade were both gone? There'd never been all that much to do here in the first place.

He made a last-minute right-hand turn. Mom was right. Things had changed. The turn to Dawn's had snuck up on him with all the new businesses on this corner.

He had to check the address twice when he got to Dawn's house. The small starter home she and Jeff had bought the year they'd gotten married wasn't even recognizable now. They'd gone up a story and had even added a garage.

She ran out onto the wraparound porch as he pulled into the driveway.

"This place looks great," he said, getting out of the car.

"Come in. You've got to see everything."

An hour later, he'd seen the whole house and even toured Jeff's man cave.

"This is pretty cool," Andrew said. The garage was as neat as an auto parts store. In the middle of the two-bay garage sat a '34 Ford nearing the finishing stages of restoration.

"That's his pride and joy," she said. "Sometimes I think he'd rather spend time with ol' Bessie here than me."

"She's a beauty."

"He says she'll be ready to drive by this summer. I might forgive him then."

"Women." Andrew shook his head.

"Speaking of which, how's your love life?"

He thought before he answered. "Varied."

"Don't you think it's time you start thinking about settling down?"

"Haven't met the right kind of girl." Not that he'd really been looking.

"Life happens fast. You'd better slow down, or you'll miss out on what it has to offer."

"Easier said than done in this 24/7 world we live in." He followed Dawn to the back patio. The sun was warm on this side of the house. It was a gorgeous day for February.

"Fine. I know you're not going to listen to me anyway. So, what's your schedule while you're here? Anything you want to do? People you want to see?"

"There's not enough time to visit. I'll have to do that on another trip, but maybe we could do a little horseback riding. That's one thing I haven't done since I've been away."

"You're on. That'll make Mom happy too. It's hard for us to get all four horses ridden as much as she'd like them to be. Want to go out to lunch?"

"Didn't I just say I didn't want to see anyone? Sure as heck if I go into town, everyone will know I'm here and I won't get a minute's piece."

"Oh? Well, with Jeff out of town, I haven't been doing much

cooking. Why don't we pick up a pizza? No one will know you in that low-key car you're driving."

It was definitely eye-catching.

"You can stay in the car, then we can go over to the old barn and have a picnic. It'll be nice."

"That sounds good."

Dawn gathered a sheet and some paper towels to take with them.

They were able to get their pizza and get out of town without being noticed.

When Andrew drove past the McIntyres' house, a twinge of something soared through him. Guilt? Sorrow? He'd done a pretty good job ignoring those old feelings, but being right here—practically in her front yard—made it a little harder.

He glanced over toward Dawn, who was smiling gently at him. "You okay?" she asked.

"Sure." He remembered this stretch of road. He'd travelled this path what seemed like a million times to meet up with Kelly.

"Do you know where you are?"

"I do." The tallest loblolly pine in North Carolina was on the left. "This was halfway between Mom and Dad's house and Kelly McIntyre's. We used to meet here."

"I guess you do remember that. You did community service for a whole summer to make up for defacing that tree."

"All in the name of love." He laughed, although it hadn't been funny at the time. He'd had to do community service and pay a big fine. "Every time I walked or rode Doc down here to meet Kelly, I'd hum that old Diamond Rio song, 'Meet in The Middle.'"

"I loved that song."

"Me too. In the song there were seven hundred fence posts to the middle. There weren't that many on this walk, but I'd lay odds that I've been down this path every bit of seven hundred times."

"Y'all were really good together."

He pulled up to the old barn in the curve. "We were." The creek ran right behind it, and as kids, he and Dawn had picnicked here often. He was thankful to arrive so they could change the subject.

They ate pizza and skipped rocks on the creek like they had as kids. It was a relaxing afternoon. He hadn't realized how tense he was, but boy could he tell the difference now that he wasn't.

Dawn tucked the trash into the pizza box. "We'd better get back to Mom's. She'll be mad if I keep you all to myself, especially while Dad's out of town. I like to help her with the horses at night when Dad's not around."

"Sounds good." Andrew led the way back to the car, and they headed home. Nightfall came early this time of year, and the sun was already dipping low beyond the horizon when he pulled into the driveway.

"We should've saved her some pizza. Let's throw the box away out here so she doesn't know."

He put the trash in the bin and slammed the lid.

Dawn pointed down the hill. "Mom must already be down there. The barn lights are on." She cupped her hands to her mouth and hollered, "Mom!"

"I'll check inside." Andrew went inside, then came right back out. "She's not up here."

"She's not answering. That's not like her."

"I'm sure she's fine." He caught the look of worry on Dawn's face. "I'll race you down."

Dawn took off down the hill, but he caught up with her easily. She stopped and yelled again, "Mom?"

Andrew turned and ran backward, waiting for her to catch up. "Slowpoke."

"I can't run anymore." She stopped and bent over with her hands on her knees.

"What's wrong, Ms. Yoga Teacher? Are you getting old?" He ran a circle around her.

"Real funny." She leaped onto his back, and he ran to the barn with her piggyback style.

"Hey, Mom. Need some help?" Andrew called out as they got to the barn, but she still didn't answer. Then again, she didn't cry out for help either. "She's probably behind the barn," he said, hoping to calm Dawn.

He swung open the barn door, but he never expected to see this.

Chapter Five

A HUGE WELCOME HOME BANNER IN big red letters, with a chef's hat over the H, hung across the front of the first three stalls, and the barn was filled with people cheering.

It only took a moment for it to register that Dawn had tricked him into getting down here to the barn for this surprise.

He spotted his mom in the crowd. "How did you do all of this?"

"I had help," she said, making her way through the crowd to his side. "I know you said you wanted a quiet visit, but we couldn't let everyone miss out on your visit back, son. I hope you'll forgive us."

He gave her a hug then started making the rounds, handshaking, hugging, and backslapping friends.

His best friends, Sam and Jason, had set up their guitars and amps in the corner and started playing "Take the Long Way Home."

"Real funny, guys," Andrew called out to them with a joking laugh, but he was genuinely surprised by the turnout. As much as he thought he hadn't wanted to see anyone but his immediate family, his heart filled with joy as he recognized friends he hadn't seen in years. "This is crazy."

"Quit being a stranger then," Sam shouted into the mic.

"Yes, it has been too long," he shouted back. "I've missed y'all." But honestly, he hadn't realized it until this minute.

"How's France?" someone hollered from across the way.

"France is beautiful," Andrew responded, not even sure who had asked.

"We wouldn't know," Sam said. "Didn't even get a postcard from the world traveler."

"Guilty." *What kind of friend am I?*

"You should post pictures on Facebook or something."

"I'm not on any social media." He regretted the admission when it was met with a series of groans.

"Get with the program, man. How are we supposed to live vicariously through you if you don't tell us anything?"

"I'll do better," he said. "Be sure I get your number before you leave."

Dawn came in with a big smile. "Surprise!"

"I'm going to get you," he said. "But thanks for an awesome day. And this. I know you were in cahoots with Mom. This is great. It's awesome to see everyone."

"I hoped it would be. Hey, I'm dying of thirst. I'm going to grab something. What do you want?"

"Bottle of water for starters. Thanks." Three six-foot tables were covered in black tablecloths on the other side of the barn. Food was spread out like a potluck. Nice of everyone to chip in on no notice.

Then, as he scanned to the right, he noticed the beautiful display of desserts. Trays of pastries, cupcakes on a three-tier tower, and cakes on raised cake plates like the ones the Main Street Diner used. "I can't believe this."

Dawn brought him a bottle of water.

Behind that table, Kelly stood there staring at him with those chocolate-brown eyes.

The ruckus seemed to fall away as he focused in on her.

"What is she doing here?"

"I ordered desserts from her," Dawn said. "Besides, you can't come home and not see Kelly."

"She hates me. I'm sure I'm the last person she wants to see."

Dawn shrugged. "She's here, isn't she?" Then she whisked away.

Kelly hadn't changed a bit. Wearing a crisp white blouse under a fancy black-and-white apron, her dark hair hung down past her shoulders. Stacking bracelets on her left arm jingled as she dropped her gaze and began to nervously fuss with the cupcakes.

He moved toward her, but his cousin caught him by the elbow. "I was shocked when your mom called and said you were in town for a couple of days. How've you been?"

"Great." He turned back toward Kelly. Each time he laid eyes on her, the pull was stronger, even though she looked like she was ready to run. "Terrific. It's great to see you, cuz. Umm, I need to grab something. I'll be right back."

He headed straight toward Kelly. The noise around him couldn't drown out the thud of his heart.

With each step, he asked himself why he was doing this. Hadn't he said the whole flight here that he was going to avoid Kelly McIntyre at all costs? But his legs kept moving, one foot in front of the other.

A pretty brunette tugged on his arm. "Welcome back. It's so good to see you." She looked familiar but he couldn't place her.

"You too. Thanks for coming." But his attention remained on Kelly. He was afraid the next time he looked she'd be gone and he'd realize it was all in his imagination.

He was within shouting distance of her when the guys started playing their old song.

Her eyes widened, and he wondered if she had the same tingle of recognition of a hundred memories flooding back between them. He glanced over to Jason and Sam, who were giving him a thumbs up. They stood on stage, nodding, then Sam pointed to Dawn. She must've requested the song.

"Hey, Kelly," he said to her, but then he lost all train of thought. Nothing came out. In a desperate attempt not to lose the moment entirely, he pointed to the table full of desserts. "So, you baked all of this?" *That was so lame. Of course she had.*

"I did." She gave him a closed-mouth smile. "Your sister placed the order. I had no idea it was for you, or that you were back in town until—well, until you walked in." Her jaw pulsed, like she was gritting her teeth.

She hadn't come by choice. Now he felt like a jerk. He began to sweat. "Surprised me too. I hadn't expected to visit with anyone while I was here. You know, just not enough time." He found it hard to pull together a sentence. He pressed his fingers into the palm of his hand. "I guess they remembered our song."

"Oh?" She acted surprised, but she wasn't that good of an actress. "Yeah. Right."

"Want to dance?"

She took a giant step backward. "No, thank you. I'm working. I'm not a guest." She rearranged a plate of cookies that had already met with hungry hands. "I know your parents have to be thrilled you're back for a visit. I don't know how they kept it a secret. That's got to be a first for Bailey's Fork."

"Yes, well, I got into town last night. I was trying to surprise them, but it turns out the surprise was on me. Dad's out of town."

"Oh, no." She looked skeptical. "You didn't know he was gone?"

"No. I didn't." But she looked only half convinced. "Does seem convenient though, doesn't it?"

"It does." Her smile was polite.

He wasn't sure if she was nervous or still mad at him.

"You and your dad have had some tough times over the years. I hope things are getting easier between you two."

"I haven't talked to him much since I've been gone."

Her eyes narrowed. "That's been a long time."

"Won't be long now. Dad'll be home Sunday."

"That's good." She wouldn't make eye contact with him.

He stepped into her view. "You know…" He hesitated, almost

afraid to bring it up, but it was hanging over them anyway. "I really wanted you to come to France."

"Don't, Andrew." She straightened as if garnering strength. "This is my home. You knew that. I could never live anywhere else."

"Not even for a little while?"

"Don't think I didn't consider it. But it didn't end up being for a little while, did it? It's been years." She rubbed her hand up her arm. "Don't make our past all my fault. That's not how it played out."

"Maybe things would've turned out different if—"

"Don't play the 'what if' game with me either." There was an edge to her tone. "It's a dangerous one. You chose your path. I followed mine, and I'm very happy with where my journey has taken me."

"You're right. I'm sorry. There's no changing the past, but we were engaged. We were best friends. Can't we at least catch up?" Desperate to lighten the mood, he said, "I heard the cafe expanded to the building next door and you have a bakery there. That's great."

"Not exactly. I opened my *own* business next to the cafe. It started small."

"Nothing wrong with that," he added.

"At first I was just doing local stuff in a tiny five-hundred-square-foot space, but then I took a chance and started the online store. After that, business grew like kudzu. I have two shifts running year-round to keep up with orders. I own the whole building now. We gutted the old ribbon factory and turned it into a bakery."

He set back on his heels. "That's a huge undertaking."

"It was, but we've got great people with lots of talent around here. It's been good for the whole town."

"That's great." He stood there staring at her, still thinking of her as the young lady he'd left behind but impressed and amazed by the businesswoman who stood in front of him now. "Congratulations. I'm truly happy for you. I rode down Main Street when I came in yesterday. I didn't realize all of that was yours. You've really classed the street up."

"Thank you, but that wasn't all me. Once I bought the factory, everyone started working together. I used my first quarter earnings to add the white facade over the corner with the columns and awnings. Then the Scouts made all those flower boxes their project a few years ago, and all those benches, they were donated through a fundraiser the senior class at the high school worked on."

"It makes a big difference. You've been an inspiration."

She blushed. "I don't know about that, but it's been pretty neat to have the whole town working to improve Bailey's Fork. But enough about me. I'm sure your restaurant in France is much fancier than my factory. French and all that."

An acute sense of failure flooded over him. "Well, I don't exactly have my own restaurant." His own accomplishments seemed like a cop-out now. The two of them had dreamed of nothing but owning a restaurant and bakery of their own.

"Oh? I'm sorry. I just assumed—"

"Right. Yeah, but things work differently in the culinary world over there. I work for Francois Dumont. He owns six of the finest restaurants in the country. He's the chef who awarded me that first scholarship to culinary school. He's famous worldwide."

She stood there staring at him. "You work for him?"

"I'm the executive chef of Dumont. His flagship restaurant. Rooted in family history."

"His family. Not yours. I'm sure I should be impressed," she said. "It all sounds very fancy, but I'll be honest, all I'm hearing is that you left me to go to school so you could open the restaurant of your own dreams someday." She brow arched. "But really you just left me to go to school and never came back."

She didn't even know what Dumont was, clearly. "It's an honor to work for Francois." But that was a lie. Working for Francois was a pain.

"Well, then I'm really happy for you. You've made it a long way from Bailey's Fork."

He'd thought so when he'd left France, but now, after seeing her again and hearing about her success, he was second-guessing his decisions. They'd had big plans together.

"There's nothing wrong with Bailey's Fork," Andrew offered.

"You don't really mean that." She stared into his eyes. "This town wasn't enough to keep you here or to bring you home."

Quiet hung between them.

His plans had shifted and changed like the dunes of the Outer Banks during hurricane season. Once he'd gotten to Paris, he'd started to believe that he could only reach his dream by staying close to the best chefs, but somehow Kelly had managed to exceed her lofty goals right here in their own backyard and taken that success nationwide.

She was right. He didn't have a leg to stand on. He'd made his choice.

"I wasn't enough," she added softly.

"Stop. Don't say that." He reached for her arm. She'd always been enough. That he'd made her feel that way gnawed at him. "We were young."

She raised her shoulder and smiled, her lip slightly quivering the way it did when she was upset. "It's true. I wasn't enough. Our dreams together, my dreams, they weren't big enough for you." She took a staggered breath. "And it's history."

"It wasn't an easy decision. You said yourself it was a once-in-a-lifetime opportunity." But that didn't change anything. It had happened. No matter how sorry he was, he wasn't going to fix that. He'd not only left town, he'd left scars on her heart.

"I know I said it, and I promise you I meant it. You know I'd have never stood between you and your dreams."

"You were always so kind." He wished he'd had this conversation with her seven years ago. "I'm not saying I made the right decision. I'm sorry how it all turned out."

"Don't be. You should be very proud of yourself. I'm sorry for the snippy remark. I really am proud of you. You always were an amazing cook. I always knew you'd be an even better chef. Dumont is lucky to have you."

"I don't want to leave with all this baggage between us," he said. "I'm so sorry I hurt you. I wished you'd come with me, and that things had played out differently, but you're right. There's no way to know how that would have turned out either." He took her hand, and all of those old feelings came swelling back.

Her hand became clammy and she stiffened under his touch. Her eyes darted away.

"I want to hear about your life. What you've been up to. What's next."

Her lips parted. "It's not the time."

"I'm only here for a few days."

"My point exactly." Her lashes fluttered.

His sister stepped between them.

"Hey, you two." Dawn's enthusiasm contrasted noticeably to the current conversation. "I see you're catching up. That's awesome! Andrew, you've got to see The Cake Factory. She's done such great things. And not just for herself—for the whole town."

"Thank you," Kelly said politely. "I'm going to go…" she started moving toward the door, "…to the van to get the rest of the cakes."

"I can help," Andrew said.

"No. I've got this," Kelly said sharply, then turned to Dawn with a gentle smile. "I can help cut and serve them if you need me to."

"Oh, please do," Dawn insisted. "I'd make a heaping mess out of those pretty cakes."

Andrew wasn't sure whether he wanted to hug Dawn or throttle her. But seeing Kelly, being this close to her again, had stirred up a lot of unexpected feelings that were making his trip back to Bailey's Fork very complicated.

Sam and Jason announced a break and came down and grabbed him.

"It's great to see you, man," Sam said.

"You too. Thanks for coming, and playing," Andrew said. "You two sound great up there."

Jason thumped Andrew on the back. "If you weren't such a stranger, you'd know Sam and I play almost every weekend all over the state. Last summer, we did an east coast tour. It was a blast."

Sam nodded. "Benefits of being teachers. Summers off. Just like being a kid."

"Teachers. Both of you?"

They nodded. "Sam teaches high school. I've got seventh graders and coach baseball," said Jason.

"Very cool. Man, I bet some of those old teachers of ours about fell out when you two became teachers. You were the class clown, Jason!"

"I know, right?" Jason picked up a cupcake from the table. "Believe me. I get my share of payback from the kids. Some are worse than we were."

"I bet."

"Do you remember Ted? He's a lawyer. And goody-two-shoes Mike Larkin? He went to jail."

"Jail? For what?" Andrew could hardly believe it.

"Embezzlement. He had this high-paying job with some company up in northern Virginia and he got caught stealing, like, hundreds of thousands of dollars over a two-year period. It was crazy."

"Wow, I always thought he seemed too goody-two-shoes to be for real."

Sam said, "You didn't like him because he asked Kelly to the prom."

"You're right." A smile ruffled his mouth. "That's true. Everyone knew the two of us were going together. Who did he think he was, asking *my* girl?" He glanced over in her direction, but she was busy with the desserts.

"It was a wild promposal. And that was before promposals were even a thing. Balloons. Confetti."

"A doggone tiara," he added, but he'd be lying if he didn't admit he'd been pretty jealous of the guy's efforts at the time.

"It was kind of a spectacle," Sam agreed, "but he definitely gave it his best effort."

"He probably lifted that tiara from his mom. His first embezzlement."

"Maybe." Sam leaned against Jason, laughing. "Kelly never seemed the tiara type."

"No. She wasn't. She didn't need props to look pretty or get attention." He'd never met anyone else like her. "She didn't seem too happy to see me." Had he said that out loud? For years now he'd shut Dawn up every time she'd tried to tell him about Kelly, but now…being back in Bailey's Fork…he wanted to know.

"She's pretty focused on her career," Jason said. "Just like you. She never married."

Sam punched Andrew in the arm. "You broke her heart, man."

They'd been so good together, but he'd burned that bridge. He could have handled that so much better, but he'd been young and his head had been filled with the allure of European cuisine. He may have gotten a little big for his britches with Aunt Claire pumping his head full of ideas and using him to basically cater a string of events under the guise of him building a reputation. Not that he'd minded. He loved cooking in her huge kitchen. Plus, he didn't have a room full of other young chefs vying for attention or screwing up his hard work with a messy plating or garnish gone wrong.

"She opened her bakery the summer after you left," Sam said. "Then she expanded. She does online sales of her cakes now too, and she employs, like, sixty to a hundred people depending on the season."

"Are you kidding me?"

"No. We were playing the Azalea Festival and the headliner had stopped in her shop and made a comment on stage about her. Then he posted something on social media and it went viral, man. She had shifts working 24/7 for weeks trying catch up on orders. She's been big business ever since."

"She always made the best cakes."

Jason crossed one foot over the other. "Her company does a lot more than cakes now. Cakes, cookies, pastries. She's won a couple of awards for her recipes. I can't remember what all the hubbub was about, but it was on the front page of the paper and all."

Of course it was. Everything was front-page news in Bailey's Fork. A string of woulda-coulda-shouldas paraded through his brain. He could only imagine what they might have built together. "I can't believe she's doing all that from right here in Bailey's Fork." A whole factory. It was mind-blowing. Although, she was the most enterprising woman he'd ever known. He shouldn't be surprised that she was living out the dream they'd made together.

He'd built quite a reputation for himself, but he was still working for other people and mostly cooking their dishes or their spin on his dish. It was hard to compete with the men he'd learned from. He was loyal to a fault, or was he just losing his competitive edge? Could he have been as successful as Kelly if he'd stayed in Bailey's Fork seven years ago?

"Things are growing around here," Sam rambled on. "The Y is new. There's a big industrial park on the east side of town. Old Mr. Blackwell finally sold off his farmland, and the county took the opportunity to lure a few big companies to town with tax credits and all. It's done wonders for the property values, and there's plenty of work."

"It's been way too long." Sam man-hugged him. "You can't stay away so long."

"Never hurts to relive the past," Jason said. "I don't care what folks say. Old times are good times."

"Yeah. It's good," Andrew agreed.

"Do you have a sexy French maiden hidden away back in Paris?" Jason asked.

"No. I'm too busy working to let anything get serious."

"Living the dream, huh? Dream job and no nagging wife." Sam shook his head. "Must be nice."

The pretty brunette came over, and Andrew finally made the connection. She was Jenny Marshall. She and Sam had dated all through high school. "He doesn't mean that, Andrew." She kissed Sam on the cheek. "He loves being married as much as I do. Did he tell you we have three-year-old twin boys?"

"No." He hugged Jenny. "Congratulations."

"Sharing your life with someone is the best. I can't imagine my life without Sam," she said. "Don't knock it."

"I'm glad you two are so happy. As for me? We'll see." He wasn't in a hurry to go running down the wedding path again. Especially since he hadn't made it past the engagement stage the first time.

For the next hour it was as if he was in a do-si-do, swinging between old friends and family across the barn. It was a good thing there wasn't a pop quiz on who he'd spoken to or the news they'd shared, because his mind was only on one thing. One person. The woman at the dessert table who'd once held his heart in the palm of her hand. How he could've picked career over love made no sense to him at all now.

Chapter Six

THE DESSERTS WERE POPULAR, AND Kelly was so thankful that there wasn't much she had to pack up before she could leave the party. Luckily, there were still plenty of partygoers vying for Andrew's attention when she slid out the back door to leave.

Her hands shook as she got in the company van. She could kick herself for offering to serve the cake. *What was I thinking?* Well, that was easy; she'd expected Dawn to insist they could handle it themselves, but she hadn't.

Kelly drove straight over to The Cake Factory. Sara's car was still in the back lot. She'd hoped she'd be there.

"Good evening, Miss McIntyre." One of her night shift bakers held the door open for her.

"Thank you." She slipped by him, hoping he couldn't tell how frantic she was at the moment. She stormed straight to Sara's office in the shipping department.

Sara sat at her desk working at her computer.

Kelly rapped twice on the door and stepped inside. "Did you know?"

Sara got up. "I swear I didn't know until a little while ago.

Dawn never mentioned Andrew when she called and placed that order. I promise I would've told you had I known."

"Why would Dawn surprise me like that?" Her hands shook. "I wasn't prepared to see him. I was caught completely off guard."

"Are you okay?" Sara got up and came around to her side. "I'm so sorry. I came in to get the timesheets done for tomorrow, and a couple of the workers were talking about having come from the party and how great it was to see Andrew there. It was too late to warn you."

"What was she thinking?" Kelly turned her back on Sara and sighed.

Sara got up and closed the door. "Did you two talk?"

"Me and Dawn? Or me and Andrew?"

"Andrew. Of course."

Kelly nodded. "Sort of, but I can't be thinking about that. He's one big, fat distraction." Why after all this time did he still get under her skin?

"How did it feel to see him again?"

"Shocking. Heartbreaking. Maddening." She stared at the ceiling. "Stupid. Why did it even bother me?"

"It's not stupid. What you're feeling is just...nostalgia. And surprise. I mean, who wants to see an ex? Pleasant or otherwise. I mean, without the right outfit or makeup, that's never good."

Kelly laughed. Sara was so great at helping her maintain perspective. "You're probably right."

"Why don't you go home for the night?"

"No," Kelly insisted. "I'm going to do some baking. That's the only thing that calms me."

"I'll be here for another hour or so if you need me."

"I've got that groom's cake to work on, but quite honestly I feel so frazzled I'm almost afraid to mess with it. I think I'll make some small specialty cakes." She wrung her hands. "He's only going to be in town a few days. I'll just avoid him until he disappears again."

An hour later she was pulling mini cake layers out of the oven to cool when her mom walked in. "How's it going?"

"Hey, Mom. Good. I'm experimenting with a few new flavors. I'm trying to mimic a caramel macchiato for a wedding cake flavor. We'll see how that tastes."

"I'm sure it will be wonderful," Mom said. "Everything you make always is."

"Thank you for always encouraging me. I love you. You're the best mother a girl could ask for."

"I'm very proud of you, honey. It's easy to encourage you, because everything you bake is amazing."

"You might be a little biased, though," Kelly said with mock resignation.

"Completely. Like any mother should be." Her mom leaned a hip against the refrigerated case. "One of these days we'll be tasting cake for your wedding. I'm looking forward to that day."

"Don't hold your breath." Kelly snorted. "I'm not sure there's a perfect mate out there for me."

"You've been out with Kirby several times, and there's Michael."

"We're really just friends."

"Michael fixed your wiring."

"That's the only spark we've got."

"You're not trying hard enough."

"Trust me. I'm good. I've got Gray. He's plenty for me."

"A pet pig is not a replacement for a husband. Or grandchildren."

"I beg to differ. Weren't you the one who told me Andrew was replaceable in the first place?"

"I may have spoken in haste," she said. "I was trying to make you feel better, and it worked. So don't hold that against me. Besides, I heard he's back in town. Did you know that?"

So that was the reason for Mom's drop-in visit. She should've known.

Kelly had finally shed the anxiety from running into him earlier, and now Mom was bringing him up. Emotions swirled around her, and her hands began to sweat...again. "I know. They ordered desserts for the party they threw for him."

"From you?"

Kelly nodded.

Mom placed her hand on Kelly's arm. "So you saw him? Are you okay?"

"I did. I thought I was going to fall out right there in their barn when I saw him walk in, though." She still couldn't believe it.

"I bet. How'd he look?"

She wanted to say awful. But that was far from the truth. "Handsome as ever, Mom. Actually, even better looking than before. He's a grown man now." She stopped herself from going on. "I don't want to talk about him. It was hard to see him again."

Her mom let out a long breath. "Honey, maybe it was hard to see him because you've never gotten over him."

"No." Kelly raised a finger in the air, daring her mother to say it again. "Just no. I'm over him and I'll never go through that again."

Expecting an argument, Kelly was surprised when her mom simply turned on her heel and left.

She resisted the urge to run after her. *Great. Now I've hurt her feelings. It wasn't enough that I'm upset, now I'm dragging everyone else down with me too?*

She shoved the cakes into the case and without even a walk-through of the bakery or a goodbye, she went home to feed Gray.

The drive home was only a few blocks. The old craftsman-style house with its open porches, overhanging beams, and rafters welcomed her even when she couldn't have the hanging baskets overflowing with pretty flowers. The thick columns with the stone supports on the front porch were her favorite part. The decorative lights had come on as the sun went down; those usually gave the house a fairytale look that made her happy, but tonight emptiness filled her.

She parked in front of the carriage-style garage door and hitched her canvas bag on her shoulder. As usual, she had a treat for Gray tucked in the front pocket. She twisted the key in the lock and hung her purse on the hook by the front door. As soon as she pushed the door closed, behind her she heard Gray's hooves scurrying against the tiles in the mudroom, followed by his high-pitched snorty-squeak welcome.

At least this little guy brought her joy and love every day. He was way more reliable than any other man she'd met anyway.

"Hey Gray. How's my best buddy?" She peered over the bottom half of the Dutch door.

He danced around, doing a little hippity hop with his front feet up off the ground, but really it was like his nose did all the work.

"That's my boy. Dance for momma."

She opened the door and stepped inside the mudroom and sat on the floor with him.

When Gray had started growing, she'd had an addition built to the house to accommodate him. Her contractor had come up with the perfect solution. Putting a mudroom off the back end of the house allowed Gray to come and go all day while she was away without keeping him in the house. From the mudroom, a doggy door led to a covered play area with a sandbox.

Every Sunday she spent time using her old bulb planter to hide treats in his yard area. It gave him something to do. She'd learned early on that a bored pig was a destructive pig, and that wasn't good for anyone.

"Look at that face." She put her hands on his cheeks. His snout was dirty. He'd most definitely done some rooting around today. She grabbed a towel to wash his face, but like any little boy he tried to wiggle away.

"Now that you're all cleaned up, let's do our tricks."

Gray sat down. Then stood and spun around.

She held up her hand. "Wait a minute." Sometimes Gray got so excited that he started before she gave him the command. "Okay. Now sit." He did, one ear flopping low over his eye. He looked so stinking cute when it did that.

She handed him a treat. "Now spin around."

Gray spun in a circle and waited for his reward.

"Good boy. Last treat, then I'll fix your dinner." He gobbled the treat, then ran to the corner of the mudroom and came back carrying his little blue wire basket. That meant he wanted to play their version of basketball. She took the basket and sat on the floor with him. "Okay, but just for a few minutes. Go get your ball."

Gray raced across the room, skidding to a stop, then came back with the beanbag ball in his mouth. He dropped it into the basket and then sat with his nose in the air.

"Aren't you proud of yourself." She grabbed the ball from the basket and tossed it across the room.

Gray sped across the room again, oinking and snorting all the way with his tiny feet scampering for all he was worth. He grabbed the ball and came back, dumping the ball into the basket again.

"Good job, cutie pie. By the way, I saw your namesake. He's cute too." She got up. "He thinks he's a better cook than me, but you love my cooking, don't you? Come get some dinner."

Gray followed her. She heated up a cup of mixed vegetables in the microwave, and then stirred them into a cup of pig chow pellets.

She carried the bowl back into the mudroom and put his dish on his place mat. He sat next to the bowl, waiting patiently for the command. "Get it!"

Then Gray leaped to his feet and pigged out.

She stood at the door and watched him eat. Gray finished his dinner and then exited through the doggy door to the back porch and then out to the yard. She closed the Dutch door. He'd come in when he was ready. It had been so tempting to let him in other parts of the house when he was little, but a pig could wreak havoc on things with that snout. She was glad now that she'd stuck to her guns on creating a little pig-proof space of his own.

She skipped dinner for herself, choosing to lay on the couch and go through the big stack of magazines that had piled up over the holidays. One by one, she flipped through them, tearing out interesting recipes, flavor combinations, and decoration ideas, then setting them aside for the recycle bin.

But her thoughts kept going back to that party. Andrew was the last person she'd expected to see. After seven years, she'd colored him gone for good. What bothered her more than seeing him was how off kilter she felt about it.

If anyone had asked her a week ago about Andrew, she'd have said she was long over all of that, but now she wasn't so sure, and that wasn't fair.

It was only eight thirty, so she took a long, hot bath then went to her bedroom. She slid beneath the crisp white sheets to dream about all she'd accomplished without him.

I'm living the dream. He was only a tiny piece of my past that helped build my passion for baking. A short-term purpose, that's all he ever was.

She closed her eyes, repeating that to herself and picturing all the projects she'd worked on since he'd been gone.

Only sleep wasn't coming.

She was frustrated, and bothered. Rather than fight it, she got up and got dressed and went back to her happy place—The Cake Factory.

Last Christmas, the factory workers had pooled their resources and had a sign made for her that read Cake Factory Boss Parking Only and posted it in the parking space right next to the back door. The letters were a wild mix of stripes and polka dots, just like the storefront decor. Black and white with hot-pink accents, and a little cupcake crown over the O in Boss. It still made her smile every time she parked here.

The sweet aroma of cake hung in the air. The sky held the twinkle of a million promising stars. She wished on one as she stood at the back door, because a girl could never have too much luck.

With the swipe of her card key, she entered through the back factory entrance. The whir and chug of the equipment was soothing. Employees talked as they finished their baking for the night, raising a hand in a friendly hello as she walked through.

If she wasn't going to get any rest, she might as well be productive. She had that groom's cake to bake, and that would keep her busy for hours. If that didn't make her feel better…nothing would.

Chapter Seven

ANDREW STOOD AT THE EDGE of the driveway with his mom and Dawn, watching the last few people leave. It had been a great party, but it was after midnight.

"Thank you for going to all this trouble. I'd wanted to just lay low and slide out of town unnoticed, but I'm glad I didn't miss out on seeing everyone. I had a great time," he said to them.

It had been cool talking about his accomplishments since he'd been gone. Kind of made him feel like less of a failure when they'd seemed so impressed. No one but Kelly had even asked about him having a restaurant of his own. Then again, that had been their dream. A long, long time ago.

"I'm so glad you enjoyed it," Mom said. "I was afraid you'd get mad, but Dawn was going to do it with or without me, so I figured I'd better help. Thank her for everything."

Andrew was glad they'd surprised him. It was good to rekindle those old friendships. He felt whole and fulfilled in a way that he'd forgotten. All of his friends back in Paris were actually more of the work acquaintance variety. This was different. "I love you, Mom." He hugged her, then stood next to her with his arm around her. "Thanks to both of you."

"Yes. Thanks, girls," the deep voice came from the other end of the barn.

"Dad!" Dawn spun around. "You did make it."

Andrew turned to see his father standing there dressed in his usual flannel shirt and khakis. He seemed smaller than Andrew remembered.

"Tried to get here sooner," he said as walked toward them. "Sorry I missed the party."

Andrew pushed his hand toward him. Seven years rushed back to the day he'd called home to say he was staying in Paris to take advantage of the scholarship he'd been awarded. There hadn't been a congratulations from his father. Instead, Dad had said he couldn't believe after six months of playing "Suzy Easy Bake Oven," he hadn't wised up. Even after all this time the memory was as raw and painful as it had been that Christmas. A hard Christmas in more ways than one.

Dad shook his hand, then yanked him in for a hug. "Good to see you, son."

Emotion swept through him. He'd been worried about the day they'd reunite. Unsure of how it would all turn out. Never expecting this.

"It's great to see you too, Dad. Thanks for coming back early. I didn't expect you to cut your trip short. I mean…I should have called first."

"Jeff can cover that show," Dad said. "I go every year. Not every year I see you anymore."

"That was a long drive for you." Andrew noticed how weary his father looked, or maybe it was just that his hair was completely gray now.

"Nine hours. Took eleven though. It was snowing to beat the band up there."

"I'm glad you're home safe," Mom said, pushing her arm around his waist. "I was getting worried."

Dad scoffed. "You know better than to worry about me."

"I'm pooped," Mom said. "I'll clean the rest of this up tomorrow."

"Don't worry about it," Dawn said. "I'll come over after my yoga class tomorrow and clean up. There's really not much left to do but gather up the trash. I'll drive the truck and take it up to the dump for you."

Andrew said, "I'll help."

"Deal." She kissed him on the cheek. "Love you, brother."

"I love you too. Thanks again."

Dad cuffed his shoulder. "Okay if we wait until tomorrow to catch up?"

"Yes, sir. That sounds good."

"I'm going to the shop, but maybe you could come by at lunch time."

"Count on it," Andrew said, feeling acceptance from his father for the very first time. At least he was trying.

He watched as his parents walked up to the house arm-in-arm. The party had been good. This whole day had been pretty awesome. He stretched and rubbed his stomach. It had been a long time since he'd eaten so much junk food, but it had been totally worth it.

He headed to the house. Dad had stopped to get his duffel bag out of the truck. They walked inside at the same time, and Dad headed straight to the bedroom.

Mom stopped at the telephone table where the light on the circa 1990 answering machine flashed. She pressed the button to play it. "Hey honey, pick up the phone. Where are you? You're probably in the barn with those horses. I just wanted to let you know we're headed home. I wanted to surprise you and make it home for the party, but the weather's slowing us down. I'm glad Andrew's home for a visit. About time. See you tonight."

If Mom hadn't been standing right there, Andrew would've rewound that tape to listen to that message again. Dad sounded genuinely happy to see him. He was astonished at how much satisfaction that gave him.

"See? We both love you," she said, as if reading his mind

"Thanks. That was really nice to hear." He was suddenly buoyed with energy. "I might go for a drive and try to unwind. Do you mind?"

"Not at all, but I don't know where you'll go. It's after midnight. There's nothing open around here."

He knew that good and well. "Just a quiet drive."

"Watch out for deer."

"I'll be careful."

"Happy thoughts and sweet dreams when you do turn in. I'm going to bed right now." She went down the hall and closed her bedroom door behind her.

He stood there for a minute, then headed outside to his rental car and eased out of the driveway. The roads back to town were dark. There were no streetlights; only the occasional yard light near someone's house shone through the darkness.

Pressing the button to open the convertible top, he found the night sounds soothing. At the stop sign, the territorial hoots of owls, probably nesting high in the huge pin oak trees here, echoed through the leafless winter woods. It was an eerie, solemn sound that made him suddenly feel very alone.

On Main Street, at least the road was amply lit with the new decorative street lamps, even though everything was closed. You'd think by now someone would have opened a restaurant or pub that stayed open late.

He pulled along the curb in front of the Main Street Cafe. He'd cut his teeth on the basics of cooking here. It was here he'd fallen in love with the creativity of cooking, and found the drive to want to not only cook, but also build menus and define his own tastes and recipes through hours and hours together with Kelly. Mr. McIntyre had given him a chance when he'd been barely old enough to bus tables. There were times when he'd felt closer to the McIntyre family than his own.

Andrew's rental car was the only one on the block. He shut down the engine and got out.

He walked over to the big front window of the diner and peered inside. Cupping his hands beside his eyes, he could see the tables were still set up in the same way they always had been. Even the old cash register with the NC GROWN sticker on the side of it, and the red-and-white checkered tablecloths were the same. A glass domed cake plate sat at the edge of the counter. A couple of slices of a seven-layer cake were all that was left. Kelly had probably baked it. When they'd worked here together, for her parents, she'd baked all of the desserts early each morning, and waited tables every night.

After closing, they'd clean up, close out the till, and then share a snack and wind down for the night. It wasn't often that she'd make a seven-layer chocolate cake that there'd be a piece left, but if there ever was, he'd bargain anything for it. He could almost taste it now.

They had the same work ethic. Aside from how beautiful she was, it had been one of the first things that had attracted him to her.

Back then, the night air hadn't been filled with the smell of fresh-baked goods though. The whir of equipment carried into the night.

He meandered over toward The Cake Factory. The cafe might look like time had stood still, but this building was a whole other story. It had been a crumbling, dirty brick building when he'd lived here. Grandpa had worked in the ribbon factory, and a Christmas didn't go by that Mom didn't repeat the stories about how she used to be able to buy a whole spool of wide ribbon for just a quarter to make Christmas bows. He didn't even really know how good a deal that was, but Mom had spoken of it like it was the best memory ever.

Lights shone through the second-floor windows of the building now. Kelly had mentioned that she ran two shifts.

The pillars that flanked the front door were welcoming, so much so that he couldn't stop himself from walking over. A whimsical sign hung in the front window. CLOSED in curly black letters with hot-pink polka dots.

Through the window facing Main, he could see inside.

He could imagine Kelly working there. All the pink. It was her favorite color, and the stripes and polka dots were a weird combination but it worked. It looked like a fun place to bring your kids to pick out a treat. The window that faced the side street held a display of cakes. He went around the corner to get a better look.

A five-tier wedding cake in shimmery ice blue flaunting white details rose from the center of the display. Every single scroll and dot was precise, and it was frosted, not fondant. Not an easy cake to perfect, but this was just that…perfection. Next to it, a shiny Tiffany blue box with a glossy white ribbon looked so real you might expect to find a place setting of china from your wedding registry inside. On the other side, a superhero cake in primary colors had Spider-Man rappelling down one side of a tower and Superman soaring above. Clever.

He stared at the display, impressed by all she'd accomplished. *I knew her when this was just a dream.*

Suddenly, every light in the bakery illuminated and he was standing there in a stream of light, like he was on center stage. He hesitated one second too long. Before he could move, the door straight across from where he stood opened and Kelly walked through it.

Chapter Eight

ANDREW DIDN'T MOVE A MUSCLE, hoping to not draw attention. He stood there in front of her store window in that stream of light, wondering if he could make a run for it and not be noticed. Or maybe pretend to saunter by like it was a coincidence.

That seemed risky, but before he could decide what to do, he heard it...the spine-tingling scream.

He waved and tried to act like he was supposed to be there.

Kelly leaned in momentarily then pressed her hand to her heart and walked over to the door. She twisted the lock from the inside and stepped out onto the stoop between the tall, glossy white pillars.

"What are you doing here?" She clung to the edge of the door as if she might run back inside. "You scared me half to death!"

He pasted a smile on his face, determined to make the best of it. Being a goof was better than being a stalker! "I was trying to pass time. I'm a bit of an insomniac."

"There's nothing to do here after hours. Still," she said.

"What are you doing here?" He took a couple of steps closer to her. "Is there a problem with the late shift?"

"No." She seemed to relax a little, letting the door swing closed. "I've got managers who have that completely under control."

"Are you an insomniac too?"

"No. I'm usually a champion sleeper. Not tonight though. I have a groom's cake to bake. I want it to be really special. I thought I might as well come down and see what I could come up with that was fantastic enough for this guy."

"I used to be pretty good at helping you come up with designs."

"I remember."

"Want some help?" Worst-case scenario she said no, but he found himself really hoping she wouldn't.

"No thank you. I've got this. You ought to get home and get some rest."

"Aw, come on. Afraid I'll steal your ideas?"

She raised a brow. "Maybe."

"I might be able to show you a thing or two. I've trained under—"

She shook her head and rolled her eyes. "I know. I know."

"I didn't mean it like that. I didn't say anything was wrong with being self-taught."

"You didn't have to." She cleared her throat. "And I happen to know firsthand that it wasn't good enough for you."

"That's not fair. You know I've always thought you have amazing talent when it comes to baking." And he meant it. She had to believe that. "I remember when you'd read that the hardest dessert to make was a chocolate soufflé. You worked on that skill until you nailed it."

She broke into a grin. "You ate chocolate soufflé fails for a week."

"I wasn't mad about it. Even the flops were pretty fantastic. That's my point. You figure things out. You're a natural. I always wished I could do that. It took years of training for me to learn that."

She looked away.

"Look," he said, feeling a little desperate. He didn't know how to break through the wall she'd put up between them, but it was now or never. He pushed past the lump in his throat. "I know I hurt you. I regret it, and I'm so sorry that my bad choices hurt you. Can you ever forgive me?"

Her shoulders lifted slightly, but she didn't say no.

Even though they were standing not five feet away from one another, it felt as if they were miles apart.

"I'd like to spend some time with you." He proceeded carefully. "Let me help you tonight. It'll be fun." If she'd let him stick around, then he'd even postpone his departure until Tuesday morning if he had to. He'd have to drive straight through, but he could still get there on time—maybe not as fresh as he'd planned, but then, he hadn't planned to step right back into those feelings he'd once shared with Kelly either, and here they were tumbling upon him again. "Come on. Please let me help."

"Andrew York, are you begging?"

He lifted his hands in the air. "It appears there's a first for everything." He was half tempted to actually drop to his knees for comedic effect.

She pulled her hand up on her hip and fixed her gaze on him. Then a flash of humor crossed her face. "How am I supposed to say no to that?"

"You're not." He walked over to her. "I can't wait to see what you've done with this place. It's impressive even from out here."

"Fine. Come on in." She opened the door to let him in. "But I'm not sure I forgive you."

"Fair enough."

She gave him the tour of not only the bakery storefront, which she was very proud of, but she took him out to the factory floor and showed him around there too.

"You're amazing." He was so proud of what she'd done here. She'd surpassed everything they'd dreamed of, or maybe he'd never seen the vision the way she had. "I can't believe you've done all of this. Alone."

"Didn't have much choice. My partner ran off."

He dropped his chin to his chest. He had. There was no arguing it. He'd left her waiting.

She regarded him with somber curiosity. "You couldn't even come home and talk to me about it that Christmas. I'd waited for months. Counted down each and every day—one by one. I missed you so much." The words caught. "And then you didn't even really give us a chance."

"You're right. I was selfish. I should've come home and told you. I think deep down I knew if I came home, I'd never go back." At the time he couldn't bear to think he might have been stuck in this one-horse town flipping burgers at the cafe when there was so much more out in the world. Then again, she proved bigger things could be done right here.

"Thanks for at least being honest with me."

"I really am sorry."

"It's okay." She paused, glancing around. "What doesn't kill us makes us stronger, right?" She turned and walked off of the factory floor and back into the bakery. "Come on."

He jogged to catch up with her. "Yes. I suppose you're proof." She'd never looked as beautiful as she did this moment. "Thanks for the tour. How about I repay the kindness with a day out tomorrow?"

"I can't. I'm too busy. Even if I wanted to, I couldn't possibly. I've got a stack of orders to work on." Taking the clipboard down, she flipped the pages. "See?" Then she marched into the bakery kitchen.

Much smaller than the factory, it was still impressive. "I thought you had two shifts of people working for you to handle things. You can't get away for just a couple of hours?"

"I've got a lot to do."

He wasn't convinced there wasn't some way they could work this out. "What's the biggest thing on your plate right now?"

"I promised to do the groom's cake for Rusty. The cake is my gift to him. I can't very well hand it off to someone else to do."

"Rusty Addams?"

"Yes. He's marrying a real nice girl from Georgia. They're getting married down at the river at his parents' place this week. An evening wedding."

"Let me help you. It'll be like old times."

A melancholy frown flitted across her face. "I don't think that's a good idea."

"Oh, come on. Let's have some fun." He stepped closer to her. "We were young. I didn't handle the situation very well. I said I was sorry. Look at you now. I practically did you a favor. You've blown your goals right out of the water."

"A favor?" She glared at him. "You always had a way of twisting things around. I worked hard for this."

"I didn't mean it that way. I can see that you worked hard, and it's truly impressive. Can we please call a truce?" He crouched down to get eye-to-eye with her. "Please?"

She turned her head.

He dipped to the side, not letting her get out of his view. "Come on. Let me help you with the groom's cake. What are you going to make?"

"I'm not even sure yet."

"I'll do the grunt work. Wash pans. Whatever. Pay for my mistakes." He clapped his hands together. "Even more reason to let me help."

"Why?" Theirs eyes held.

"Why not? I know him. It could be fun. Come on. I've already caught up with Mom and Dawn, and you know there's no other nightlife in this town. Throw this old friend a favor."

"I guess Bailey's Fork isn't busy enough for a guy who hangs out with the rich and famous in Paris."

"It's not like that. The only thing I do with the rich and famous is cook for them. I work. A lot. Like, all the time."

"I know how that is. I can bet you wouldn't want it any other way either, though."

"You're right. From the looks of things with you here in your bakery in the middle of the night, you're the same way."

"Guilty as charged."

"It's our passion. So let's cook together." He moved through the kitchen. "This is nice. Top of the line." He flipped through a book of laminated recipes. "How about you make a red velvet cake? You always made the best red velvet around."

She threw her hand into the air like a traffic cop. "Whoa. Hold on right there. If you're going to help, you have to stay within the few guidelines I have from the customer."

She agreed to let me help! "Sure thing."

Kelly picked up the order sheet. "He likes chocolate, peanut butter, and caramel. No mint. No fruit. No pastel colors. No cupcakes. No frilly stuff."

"He really said all that? More like a list of what he doesn't want."

"Men. Go figure."

He held his tongue.

"Yep. See? It's right here." She turned the page around for Andrew to read. "Actually," she continued, "I think the six-tier wedding cake has him a little freaked out. It's pretty fancy. And very frilly."

"Fair enough." He'd probably feel the same way.

"So, I'm making it up to him with an amazing groom's cake. I'm thinking chocolate with peanut butter center. I've done tons of themed groom's cakes, but I want this one to be special."

"A theme?" Andrew chewed his bottom lip as he pondered. "He loved fishing. What if we made a big fishing lure? We could do edible metallic hooks."

"For a bachelor party, maybe, but this is their wedding. It needs to be a *little* classy," she said.

"Okay, fine, but seriously, how much has Rusty changed? Because the Rusty I remember is about the furthest thing from classy I've ever known."

Kelly pulled her apron over her head and put her hands on her hips. "He's Dr. Addams now. He's kind of a lot classy, actually. You haven't kept up at all, have you?"

"No. I haven't." It hadn't been entirely intentional. He'd been busy. "But you don't miss what you don't know about."

The way she was looking at him, he knew that she was going to say like me, but she held her tongue. Instead, she said, "I guess that's one way to look at things." Kelly turned her back to him and began pacing the floor.

"Think mode," he said in a sing-songy way like he used to back in the day.

"Some things will never change," she admitted as she made two more passes across the kitchen. "I've got it." She snapped her fingers. "I'll do a simple square layer cake. Chocolate with peanut butter filling. He does still love fishing, but we'll do a simple watercolor blue fondant and a fish leaping out of the top."

"I can help make this magnificent with some sugar work." He grabbed a piece of paper and sketched it out. "Edible sugar glass for the water. Like it's splashing up. It'll look like that fish just jumped in the air. That would be cool."

"I've never done sugar glass."

"I can teach you. It's amazing. You'll love it. It'll change your life."

"I like my life just fine, thank you," she said, but she'd said it playfully. "I'll make the chocolate cake with peanut butter centers and a simple chocolate crumb coat."

"You could do a smooth pearlescent fondant wrap. Save the real blue for the sugar glass. That wouldn't be too hard, would it?"

He knew it wouldn't be. If it was one thing this woman knew, it was baking, but he wanted to collaborate with her, not just make suggestions.

"Easy, and you're right. I think this is going to work."

The energy in the room shifted. She was getting excited about the project too. "It's going to be amazing," he said.

"I love it. Maybe a few edible reeds." She waved her hands in gentle strokes above an imaginary cake. "A couple of cattails? Just for balance?"

"Yeah, and I'm thinking a wide-mouthed bass." He held his hands up to show the approximate size that seemed right for the cake.

"That's exactly what I was thinking. I've done dozens of them. I made a cake mold for fish a few years ago." She grabbed a notebook from the shelf. "Here are some pictures. I use it all the time, then I use sculpting chocolate to give it a little texture before airbrushing it."

He stepped in tight, peering over her shoulder as she flipped the plastic-coated pages of the binder. "Oh yeah, that looks real. He's going to love it."

"I hope so. Let's do this." She turned and raised her hand to high-five him like they'd always done when a plan had come together.

And just like before, his hand met hers. He gently laced his fingers between hers. For that second, him leaving to go to Paris never happened and that perfect feeling was back. Things had once been so good.

She tugged her hand back. "We'd better get started."

"Right. Yes." He'd almost blown it. He was glad he hadn't totally spooked her off. If he'd tugged her in after lacing his fingers through hers, then spun her…she'd have surely freaked. "I haven't been this stoked about a project in a while." He was excited to be actually creating something from no plan. It was exhausting following the rules of a world-renowned menu of someone else's design. Besides, it would be good practice for him. "Thanks for letting me help."

"This doesn't necessarily mean I'm going to have time to play or go off with you tomorrow. You know that, right?"

"I don't even care. We're here now."

"Then let's get to work." She grabbed an apron from a drawer and tossed it to him. "Here." She put hers on.

He glanced at the feminine design, then shrugged and put it on without a complaint.

"With all the sugar glass, are you sure we can we pull this off before you leave town?"

"We'll finish it tonight if you're up to it," he said. "Piece of cake."

"Don't tell me," Kelly said as she slid the chocolate cake recipe in front of him. "No pun intended?"

"Make no mistake," he said. "Everything I do is intentional."

Chapter Nine

I T WAS A LITTLE AWKWARD being in the kitchen with Andrew again, but once they got to work, their rhythm came right back and those worries fell away. He preheated the oven, gathered the dry ingredients, and put them in the mixer while she started the process of working the wet ingredients together.

"Do you mind getting the pans prepared?" she asked.

"Not at all," Andrew said.

She was half surprised that he didn't mind taking on the menial task. "They're on the second rack over there. The square ones. Three."

He tapped a drumbeat on the bottom of the pans as he went to the other end of the huge worktable to butter and flour them. "Why three?"

"It's the groom's cake. It can't outshine the wedding cake, but it still needs to have enough size to it to be a focal point too. I'm thinking of doing two dark chocolate fudge layers and a white chocolate layer. The contrast will look pretty when it's cut, plus I can use the leftover white chocolate cake mix for the fish."

"Sounds like a great plan."

She was surprised at how smoothly it was going. He'd taken her instructions and completed each task without complaint. He was actually very helpful.

"So it's really weird being back in town," he said. "I left and didn't keep up with anyone, so in my head everything here stayed the same. But seeing everyone at the party tonight, I realized everyone has moved on and things have changed a whole lot."

"Main Street Cafe hasn't changed."

"Not true. There's outdoor seating now. Nice touch, I have to say."

"Well, that's the only change."

"Thank goodness. The café is a landmark. If it wasn't here, I wouldn't believe I was home."

She turned on the mixer. "Where is home now for you? Paris? Or do you still consider Bailey's Fork home?"

"I don't know." His face clouded with uneasiness. "Both?"

"No. It has to be one or the other," she said, standing her ground.

He stopped, and for a moment she wasn't sure he was going to respond. "Does it?"

"Yeah. I think it does," she said as she stirred. Then she stopped. "You know what? I'm sorry. That's really none of my business. Let's change the subject."

"Okay. That works for me." He wiped his hands on a towel and tucked it into the ties of his apron. "Do you want me to work on the chocolate or the peanut butter frosting?"

"The chocolate, please."

"Great."

It wouldn't kill her to let him run with the chocolate frosting. It was just for the crumb coat anyway. The fondant would hide any flaws, and if there was one thing she knew she could trust it was that whatever he made would taste good. She could never, would never, deny his talent or palate, but his comment about everything being intentional still gnawed at her. What did he want from her?

They tag-teamed putting the cakes in the oven.

"I'm not sure I've really saved you any time," he said, glancing at the clock, "but this is going to be one heckuva cake."

Enthusiasm coursed through her veins. "I can't wait to see it all come together."

"Let's get the sugar work going."

She clapped her hands. She couldn't help herself. It was exciting to learn a new technique.

"I promise you it's not as hard as everyone makes it seem." Andrew took over, grabbing pans and taking control of the stove. "I'll teach you how to *not* make every rookie mistake I made the first two years I tried to work with it."

"Two years?" She stepped up next to him at the stove.

"Yeah, but you're a natural. I know I can teach you better than I was taught."

She hoped so, because if this didn't turn out, she was going to be in a real pinch to make another cake in time to deliver.

For the next hour they worked on making the sugar glass shoulder-to-shoulder. He imparted every tip he'd learned, and he was right—it was surprisingly easier than she'd expected, at least with his help. He even showed her some tricks with coloring the mixture and pulling the sugar to give it an even more realistic texture.

As she used a set of tongs to pull the sugar, he reached around her and guided her hands. His gentle touch caught her off-guard. She tried to push aside the old feelings that were rushing back and focus on the task, but it wasn't easy.

The longer they experimented, the easier it became, and the banter she'd always loved between them came back too.

"Wouldn't it be neat if we could really get it to look like a real splash? Almost 3D?" She placed a finger against her lips.

"I know that look. You're getting ready to come up with something really good."

She mused. "I think the hot sugar would stick on heavy foil wrap or we could shape a mold to get that rounded splash look."

"I've got an idea. I've never done it, but I've heard of it. Do you have some balloons?"

"I do." She retrieved a bag of twisting balloons from the cabinet. "Pick your color."

"Red for me. Pink for you."

"He remembers," she said softly.

He leaned in close and whispered into her ear, "Believe me. I haven't forgotten a thing."

She flinched, turning toward him, and his lips were so close to hers. *Don't kiss me.* Her heart turned over in response, and darn if her hand wasn't shaking. Her brain was saying no, but in the moment it might have been so nice. *Stay focused.*

She pushed the balloon over the nozzle, hoping Andrew wouldn't notice her trembling and get the wrong idea.

He filled the balloon and tugged the end to tie the knot, then filled one more and tied the two together, making a circle smaller than the size of the cake, but big enough for the sculpted fish to jump through.

"That's what'll keep the hot sugar from bursting the balloons when we pour the mixture over it to form the rounded splash." He looked up and made a funny face. "Hopefully."

She grabbed a bottle of coconut oil. "Might as well hedge all of our bets. Maybe this will help keep it from sticking." She poured a generous amount over the water balloon.

"Good idea."

She capped the oil bottle and set it aside. "This is turning into a science project. All we're missing is those goofy goggles like we had to wear in lab class."

"I hated those things, but you were pretty cute in them." He helped her at the stove until they got the mixture just right. "Want to do the honors?"

"Let me watch and learn," she said. "What's plan B if it doesn't work?"

"It'll work." He took the pan of hot, sticky sugar and splashed it all at one time into the center of the circle they'd made with the balloons.

The thick mess clung to the balloon and dripped over the rounded shape.

"I honestly can't believe this is going to work." There'd been a time when they'd spend all day creating in the kitchen. She'd almost forgotten how much fun that was.

"Be ready to be amazed. It's going to look awesome."

"Meanwhile, I'll do what I do best." She removed the cake from the fish molds and covered it in sculpting chocolate. It didn't take her long to carve the fins and scales into the chocolate. She'd done these dozens of times. Then she took the drab brown fish over to the table where her airbrush was hooked up. In just a few minutes she was set and airbrushing layers of edible colors. First base colors of browns and greens, then on to the shimmering colors that would make the fish really come alive.

"It looks like taxidermy instead of cake," he said. "Nobody's going to want to eat it."

"That's what I'm going for." Looks too good to eat was her favorite compliment.

"Rusty is going to love this. I love it." Andrew sat down on the stool right next to her. "I forgot how much I enjoy watching you work. Better than TV. I have to admit, even if we hadn't done the glass work, that fish is an amazing topper."

"Are you worried the splash isn't going to work?"

"Not at all."

"Time will tell," she said with a smirk. Tilting her head to one side, she stole a slanted glance his way.

"It always does." He leaned in closer.

His breath was warm on her neck. Quickly she re-coiled the

airbrush hose and stepped to the other counter, putting some distance between them. This was fun, but that was all it could be.

"Umm." Andrew jumped up from the stool. "Why don't we work on those cattails you mentioned?" He stayed where he was and started another batch of sugar glass, this time in a goldish-green. "Here, take over."

She stirred and watched the temperature like he'd taught her. "You're right. This is easy once you understand the timing of it all. I think the key is how much time you have to work with it before it gets past the pliant stage. It would have taken me forever to figure that out. I love this."

"I knew you would." His hand grazed hers again.

She sucked in a quick breath just as the timer went off on the oven. She gave him a quick smile and zipped over to the oven to get the cakes out.

"I'll get those." He grabbed the oven door.

"Okay, thanks."

"You try your hand at some sugar ribbons with what's left there." He set the cakes on the cooling rack.

"I'm going to make the cattails with this green we made." She poured the liquid out onto the marble pad, then rolled it into a sausage-shaped pod. As it cooled, she stretched it a bit more, changing the color and striations a bit at the same time. "This turned out better than I'd hoped. I love it." She slowly poured the green leaves and shaped them.

Andrew reached over her with a pair of long tweezers she usually used to place edibles on wedding cakes. "May I?"

She had no idea what he planned to do. "Why not?" Why was he being so nice? She wanted so badly to not be nice to him, but all the things she'd liked best about him hadn't changed at all. Just like old times.

He reached around her, his chin close to her shoulder, then picked up the pointed end of the cattail leaf and folded it over, holding it at an angle for a moment to keep it from flattening into itself.

"That looks amazing."

"Wait until we stand a few up together."

"I see what you mean."

"If you'll mix up another batch of caramel sugar, I'll show you how to blow the shapes for the cattails."

She didn't hesitate. She mixed the ingredients and took it straight to the temperature like he'd said, and trusted the thermometer for the right time to pull it and then add the colors.

"You're a fast learner."

"Thanks." She went through each step, even the part where she warmed the sugar in the oven to 275 degrees. That made so much sense now.

She finished the amber-colored sugar and handed it off to Andrew, who worked on blowing the sugar glass, much like a real glass blower, into long, tubular shapes for the cattails, then attached them to solid sugar glass rods he'd rolled out of the leftover mix earlier.

She took note as she finished up the chocolate crumb coat and laid the iridescent fondant over the cake.

"Okay, time for the big test." She moved the mesh rack where they'd poured the sugar over the balloons to the sink. She popped the balloons and let the water run into the sink, then carried the rack back over to the counter and lifted the blue glass. "This is amazing. It seriously looks like blue water splashing up. Crazy!" She positioned it on the far-right edge of the finished cake.

"The size is perfect."

"It is. Can you bring the fish over? He'd better fit." That would be her luck. She didn't want to have to remake that now that the water had turned out so great.

Andrew positioned the fish in the center of the water sculpture and pressed the dowel into the cake. "It's absolutely perfect."

She clapped her hands, jumping and hugging his arm. "It's awesome. We can put the cattails right over here on the other side."

"Yep." Andrew handed her the glass pieces.

She set them in place carefully.

"What do you think?" He smiled. He already knew the answer.

"Thanks for your help. The sugar work makes it."

"It's easy once you get a little practice. Took me forever to get it right. We once had a guy from Japan come and demonstrate actual candy glass sculpting. It was amazing what he could do."

"I can imagine you'd have to work really quickly."

"Yes, the master pastry chef said that before he ever picked up the first piece of soft sugar glass, he had to know exactly what he was making. Once that stuff begins to harden, you have to be done."

"I bet that was inspiring to watch." In awe, she realized what a wonderful experience it must have been over there. Learning and doing so many things. Being exposed to things she hadn't even heard of. It had been an amazing opportunity for him, and he'd taken it seriously.

"I can't even explain how cool it was," he said. "You'd have loved it. You'll find lots of uses for it. It's great on gingerbread house projects for the holidays."

"Wouldn't that be awesome?"

"You can light them up. You wouldn't believe the gingerbread competitions over there."

"I get it. Paris is known for their culinary expertise, but you do realize there are wonderful chefs and cuisine right here in America. We have them here in North Carolina too. Asheville has a wonderful one."

"I'm sorry. You're right. It's just all I've focused on for seven years."

"Don't I know it." She clasped her hand across her own mouth.

"Sorry, I didn't mean to get snappy with you again. I don't know why I keep doing that."

He shrugged, then without a word he moved the pots to the sink and started cleaning up.

She let him as she made the final details on the cake. "Thanks for helping clean up. I'll get the rest of this in the morning."

"It is morning," he said.

She noticed the clock. "Oh gosh. I need to get home and fix Gray's breakfast. Thanks for your help. What a great night."

"Yeah. Like old times, but wait...who is Gray? I didn't. I mean..." He stared at her, his brows pulling together. "So...you're seeing someone?"

Chapter Ten

KELLY HAD HALF A MIND to let him believe she had a boyfriend. "No." She couldn't let him languish, although he probably still deserved to. "I'm not seeing anyone. Gray is my pet pig. I got him after you left."

"A pig?"

"Yes. A pig. As in oink-oink. It's a long story."

He touched her elbow. "I've got to see this. Can I come with you?"

It had turned out to be a fun night, just like he'd promised, but coming to her house? She wasn't sure about that.

"I'll drive you over, and then when we get back I'll be out of your hair." He tilted his head. "Wait. You don't really have a pig, do you? You're just giving me a hard time."

"Oh, I most certainly *do* have a pig."

"Then prove it."

She felt alive again with him, but he'd just be leaving again. She didn't want to get her hopes up. Her head knew this was just a friendly reunion, but her heart wasn't to be trusted. But what was the harm of letting him see Gray? The pig was named after him, for goodness' sake.

"Fine, but I'm driving." She headed out of the bakery before he could argue.

"Okay." He ran to catch up with her before he got lost in the maze as she cut through the factory to the parking lot. "Wait up!"

She got in the car, and he jumped into the passenger seat. "Buckle up," she said as she revved the engine and took off.

"That's our tree," he said. "I saw that it made it to the new town sign. Tallest loblolly in the state."

"Yep. Sure did." She pulled into the driveway. "Tallest in both Carolinas, to be exact." *This was a bad idea. What was I thinking?* She kept her eyes straight ahead.

"How tall is that thing anyway? Any idea?"

She knew exactly. She'd been there the day the team had come out and measured it. "One hundred sixty-four feet tall and just shy of five feet around last time they measured."

He twisted in his seat as she cruised by the tree. "Hey. There's a birdhouse over the spot where we'd carved our initials. Who would cover up a declaration of love like that?" He turned back with a look of bewilderment.

"Me." She flashed him an unapologetic smile. "I own the place now."

"You live *here*?" He looked confused. Or maybe he thought she was kidding.

"Yep."

"And you covered up our initials on the tallest loblolly pine in all of North Carolina?"

"Yep."

"Man, you *were* mad at me."

"Kind of still am." She regretted saying it, because that alluded to her caring at all. *Too late now.* She parked in front of the house.

"It wasn't easy for me either. You know I never meant for things to end up the way they did."

"But they did. Game over." She opened the car door and got out. "Coming to meet Gray or not?"

He jumped out of the car. "Coming." He ran around the car to catch up with her. "I'm kind of hungry. Think we could grab something to eat after?"

She headed straight to the front door. "I have chili in the crockpot."

"I always loved your chili."

"Then you should like it now. It hasn't changed a bit." She opened the front door and walked inside with Andrew on her heels.

"Wow, this place is great."

"Thank you. I did some renovations, but the house was in pretty good shape for being empty for so long. Amazing the difference some paint and refinishing the floors made, but I hired someone to knock out some walls to give me the kitchen I wanted."

"I love what you've done with it. It looks just like you," he said.

She blinked, unsure if it was a compliment or not. "I look like a house?"

"No. Stop. You know what I meant. The colors. The style. Comfortable. Pretty." He spoke slowly. Cautiously. "Real pretty."

Unlike the bakery, her kitchen at home had deep cherry cabinetry with black granite countertops and the prettiest cobalt blue tile backsplash he'd ever seen—more like glasswork than tile.

"Awesome kitchen," he remarked. "I could totally cook in here." He ran his hand across the hefty burners of her Viking range. "My favorite range. Like the Range Rover of the kitchen."

"Thanks. It was a splurge."

"I bet." He walked through the kitchen nodding. "It's kind of funny that you live here. I mean, with the tree with our initials right in the front yard and how we always met up here."

"It just happened to be up for sale at the right time. Don't read anything more into it. This house was where we met because it was the center point between our two houses. I bought it because it was an amazing deal. Too good to pass up."

She took two cobalt-blue soup mugs down from the cabinet and scooped chili into them with a shiny metal ladle.

"That smells so good." Andrew took the bowl she handed him. "I think my stomach just growled a thank you."

"Better wait until you taste it, Chef." Their conversation must've woken Gray, because she heard him scurry in the mudroom.

Andrew stopped in his tracks. "That was *not* my stomach."

"That," she said, "was Gray." She hurried down the hall to the utility room door and let Gray wander into the kitchen.

"Holy cow. Pig. Whatever. You really *do* have a pig. That was *you* I saw walking..." he gestured to Gray, "...this *thing* near Main Street when I got to town. I thought he was way too fat to be a dog."

"Had to be me. There's not another one like this around town."

"Probably not too many anywhere."

She reached down to pet Gray on the head. "You'd be surprised. Micro pigs are a thing here now."

Gray accepted the attention, but only for a moment. He raced over to Andrew and nudged his leg with his snout. Andrew dropped right to the floor and started petting him. Gray ran off and came back with one of his toys, showing off for Andrew. The pig was giving Andrew a hometown hero's welcome. *Traitor.*

"He's smarter than a dog!" He squeaked the toy and watched Gray pounce around with excitement. "He is too cool. So, why is this guy named Gray when he's clearly black and pink?"

"It's a long story." Thankfully Gray dropped his ball and ran behind her to get breakfast. "Come on, Gray." She let Gray out back, then they sat down at the table and ate chili. "I rarely let him in this part of the house."

"This chili is just as good as I remember." He shoved another bite into his mouth.

"Is it making you sweat yet?"

"In a good way," he said. "Someday I'll have to make you some of my jalapeno cheddar corn muffins. They'd go perfect with this."

Live in the moment. He'll be gone before I know it. "That sounds delicious." She had no doubt they would be, but she needed to keep her guard up. Sharing new memories would only make those old ones harder to keep tucked away where they belonged.

As soon as they finished, she put their bowls in the dishwasher, and then grabbed her keys. "Let's get you back. I've got other things I need to take care of this morning."

They were quiet on the short ride back to Main Street.

"Thanks for letting me help tonight, and for letting me tag along to feed the pig. The chili brought back some great memories. It's been a really good night."

She resigned herself to roll with the evening. "I'm glad too."

She pulled behind his rental car. He sat there, quiet, and she hoped he wasn't thinking about kissing her. *That would be a mistake.* To break the mood, she blurted out, "A convertible. In the winter? With the top down?"

"Seemed like a fun idea at the time." He shrugged. "I want to see you again."

It was what she'd wanted to hear for so long, but now that he'd said it, it scared the dickens out of her. Her heart pounded so hard she could hear the beats. Her body was telling her to run from trouble. She fidgeted, grappling for a response. "Maybe next time you come to town you'll give me some notice."

"But I'm here now." His words were warm. "You haven't changed a bit." He touched her face with the tips of his fingers.

A ripple of excitement ran through her. "Neither have you." She wanted so badly at that moment for him to say he'd be staying, but she knew that wasn't going to happen. "You'll be leaving soon." The words rolled out like an accusation.

He lowered his head. "So this is it?"

"I guess so."

He pulled his hands together. "Can we stay in touch? I've missed this. I didn't even realize how much I've missed this, but I do."

She was so tired, and her defenses were down. She knew better. Her heart should know better than to set herself up for another huge letdown. *Be strong.* "Andrew, you've had seven years to not miss me. I think it's time we just say goodbye and close that door."

A part of her felt so brave for having the guts to say that. She'd wished she'd said it seven years ago when he'd first left for France, but now that she had…a new emptiness filled her heart. She wished she could take the words back. "I can't let you break my heart again. We're better off being old friends. At least now we're not enemies." Only the truth was, no matter how much she'd tried to convince herself that she was over Andrew, her heart was still broken from all those years ago.

He opened his mouth, and then closed it. Without a word, he opened the door and got out of the car. Without looking back, he climbed behind the wheel of his car and sped off down Main Street.

Chapter Eleven

ANDREW PAUSED WITH HIS HAND on the front door of his parents' house. It was still early, and there was no way he could sleep now. He turned and sat down on the top step of the front porch.

As much as it hurt to walk away from Kelly, he didn't want to say the wrong thing and push her further away either. Walking away had seemed to be the best option, and as awful as that should have made him feel…it didn't really. Happiness filled him when he was near her.

Even still rallying from the jet lag and being up all night, he was ready to conquer anything.

He'd played the role of student in France and had followed the path that had unfolded for him, and he'd excelled. But that was nothing compared to how he'd felt standing next to Kelly, creating for the sheer joy of doing it…that was real.

Is it the creativity I've missed? Or Kelly?

It had been so easy to be with her again. Her laugh still tickled him. He loved the way she pursed her lips when she was thinking, and her sheer delight in the finished product—as if it had been luck, rather than her talent.

He wished now that he'd gone in for that kiss last night when they'd been working the pliable sugar. It had taken everything he had not to put his lips to hers. He was sure she'd felt the same connection too, or at least something.

But he'd hurt her, and there was no making up for that in one night of walking down memory lane. That much he knew.

The door opened behind him, and he spun around.

"Your bed wasn't slept in last night." Mom stepped out on the front porch. "Where have you been?"

Why do I feel like I'm sixteen and caught sneaking in after curfew all over again? The thought made him chuckle. "I told you I was going to take a ride."

"And you're just getting home now? Where'd you go? Georgia?"

"Nope. Main Street."

Mom cocked her head. "There's nothing to do there in the middle of the night."

"Ran into Kelly."

"Oh? In that case, I guess you're right on time." She gave him a crooked grin. "I've got coffee made. I'll pour us both a cup."

"I'll come inside."

He sidled up to the counter next to her and took one of the mugs. "Did Dad already go to work?"

"Oh, yeah. You can still set a clock by him. Up at five. Out of the house at five-thirty on the dot."

Andrew found that amusing, since not one clock in the kitchen read the same.

She slid a steaming mug of coffee in front of him. "You're meeting him for lunch today, aren't you?"

"Yes, I'll probably take a nap before I head over."

She placed her hands on her hips. "Are you going to small talk me all morning?"

"What do you mean?" he said, but he knew exactly what she was eluding to.

"Are you going to tell me what you were up to all night with Kelly or not?"

He leaned his elbows on the counter. The news of them being together had probably beaten him home. The small town pipeline was swift, if not accurate. "We made a groom's cake together. It was fun."

"For Rusty Addams and his fiancé, I bet," she said. "He's marrying a real nice girl. He brought her to church a few weeks back."

He took another long sip of coffee. "Yep. Kelly said he's a doctor now. Hard to imagine."

"A good one, from what I hear." She moseyed closer. "Kelly's a good one too. Y'all were baking *all* night long?"

"It's a big cake."

"There had to be some talking. Maybe good memories to think about together," she prompted.

"Sure."

"I don't guess I should go hoping you might stick around and see where that goes, should I?"

"No." He finished off his coffee and put the empty mug in the dishwasher. "If you ask Kelly, I think she'll tell you that bridge was burned to a crisp. No fixing it." Only he wasn't convinced that was the case.

"Let me tell you this. If you still love that girl, don't lose her again. Women don't take kindly to getting their hearts broken." She stepped right in front of him and poked her finger in his chest. "You might have a long row to hoe to earn back her trust, but it can be done. If it was real love all those years ago, it's still there. I promise you that. Loving your work is not the same as having love in your life. If you love that girl...fight to get her back."

Why muddy things up when he'd be back in France in just a week or so? Kelly had made it perfectly clear that her heart was still in Bailey's Fork. How could he leave an executive chef position behind? For love? That sounded crazy. But his emotions were in turmoil. Anxiety and excitement fought for position. What would things be like back here in Bailey's Fork? Could he open his own restaurant? He'd done it for Francois Dumont several times now. Suddenly nothing in his life seemed clear.

"I'm going to sleep on that." He walked back to his old bedroom and climbed into the queen-size bed. Between the trip back, time zone changes, and being up all night baking with Kelly, every bone in his body ached for sleep, but all he could think about was her.

He'd left a wake of heartache behind when he'd left Bailey's Fork. He wasn't proud of that.

He set the alarm on his phone to be sure he wouldn't miss lunch with his father. At least that was one thing he could definitely reconcile while he was home.

He closed his eyes. Kelly had succeeded. She'd done exactly what she'd dreamed of and more and hadn't changed a bit in the process. The way she looked. Smelled. Moved in that kitchen. The banter. They'd always loved picking on each other. And she could still dish it out. He punched his pillow and nestled down into the feathery softness.

When his alarm rang, he was more tired than when he'd laid down. He forced himself out of bed and pulled the faded green York Equipment Company T-shirt out of his bag. The thing had seen better days, but he'd packed it for this reason. Kind of an olive branch to Dad. He might not be working at his side, but he was proud of the family business and he wanted him to know that.

He went to the kitchen and drank two glasses of water, still feeling dehydrated from the travel and lack of sleep, then headed over to Dad's shop. Fidgeting with the satellite radio in search of something he could sing to, he finally brought up an old Brooks and Dunn song from his phone to the radio. Singing was supposed to ease anxiety, but he couldn't even keep his mind on the words to his favorite song on the short drive.

The dusty parking lot was filled with equipment and customers' pickup trucks.

Walking toward the door, Andrew squared his shoulders, trying to appear relaxed and non-confrontational.

Dad looked up, and when he noticed the T-shirt Andrew was wearing Dad smiled with approval.

"Don't know how you kept up with that shirt all these years."

He glanced down at the faded, once navy-blue shirt. It had definitely seen better days. "It's family."

"Yes it is," Dad said with a smile.

"The shop is pretty busy right now. Are you still up for lunch? We can make it another day if we need to."

"Wouldn't miss it." He shouted to the back. "Heading out, guys."

Dad came toward him, and they walked outside together.

"I can drive," Andrew said. "Where do you want to eat? Hot dogs at Tucker's?" They'd been Dad's favorites for as long as he could remember. Chili and onions, no mustard.

"No. I'll drive. I know just the spot."

Andrew climbed into the passenger seat of Dad's old pickup truck.

Dad cranked the diesel engine and pulled out onto the main road. Old country music flooded the cab of the truck. Andrew was thankful to not have to fill the ride with conversation.

They were clear on the other side of town before Andrew put together where they were headed. "Are we going to Parker's Farm and Grill for lunch?"

Dad nodded and smiled. "Been a long time since we've been there together."

"It has." It had been their father-son lunch spot. "I hope they still have that amazing pimento cheese Mrs. Parker used to make." They'd made lots of good memories over Parker's home cooking. Parker's Farm and Grill had served farm-to-table before it was even a thing.

But when they pulled into the parking lot, Andrew didn't even recognize the place. It used to be in a repurposed tobacco barn, a small one, still carrying the aroma of the drying leaves that it had once stored. But now it had doubled in size, and the parking lot, formerly shell sand, was shiny black asphalt with bright yellow lines marking the parking spaces.

"This place has changed," Andrew said, and he wasn't sure he liked it as much. The old place had charm. Now it was like every other chain restaurant.

"Things change over time. Sometimes for the better."

Sometimes not.

They were seated at a table near a window that overlooked the pastures. At least the Black Angus still meandered through the field, picking at the dwindling green as they made their way to the pond for a drink.

A waitress brought them ice water in mason jars and set two clipboards down on the table. "Today's menu," she said. "I'll give you boys some time to mull it over."

Dad said, "I'll have sweet tea to get started."

"Sure, honey. Anything else to drink for you?" she asked Andrew.

"I'm good with the water, thank you." He mulled over the menu. Some of the same old home-cooked meals, but there were some new dishes too.

Dad didn't even open his menu. "Do you know what you're going to have?"

He was tempted to try one of their new dishes, but instead he stuck to what they'd always had when they'd come together. "I think I'll stick with the Thursday special. The pimento cheese Angus burger."

"Can't go wrong with that," Dad agreed.

The waitress came up to the table. "Two pimento cheese Angus burgers, I take it?"

"Yes, ma'am."

"And fries for you, I know," she said to his dad.

"I'll try your sweet potato fries." Andrew handed the clipboard to her.

"Good choice."

A few people came over to talk while they ate, and each time Dad introduced him. "This is my son. He's home for a visit from France. He's a professional chef."

Andrew swelled with pride. All he'd ever wanted was for Dad to be proud of him, and this was the first time he'd experienced that.

Their burgers came out, and they were just as good as he'd remembered. "Dad, this is an awesome lunch. Thanks."

"I owe you a lot more than a lunch. I'm sorry I was so hard on you. For a long time I took your career choice so personal, and then I felt like the only reason you went to France was to get away from me."

That had certainly played into it.

"I'm sorry it took me so long to realize how ridiculous I was being, son."

Andrew had no idea what had changed Dad's mindset, but he was grateful. "I understand. I could have handled things better too."

"But you made the right decision, didn't you? I mean, you're happy."

"I love my cooking. This job isn't always what I'd like, but it's a good job and I've learned so much about the business."

"Still thinking you might open your own restaurant one day?"

"Yes, sir. I still want to do that. I've been saving money. Trying to plan and be prepared. Most restaurants fail in the first three to five years. I'm not going to let that happen, so I'm taking my time to ensure I'm financially *and* professionally ready."

"I'm really proud of you, son. Aunt Claire can't say enough things about the man you've become."

"Thank you." He could hardly believe how much those words meant to him. He'd spent the last years just blocking out all the negativity he'd left behind, and he'd never even considered he and Dad may come together on this one day.

"When do you leave to go up north?"

"Monday night. I'll probably drive halfway and get a hotel."

"It's not that bad of a drive if it's not snowing, but they're forecasting snow and ice the next week or so."

"Not looking forward to that."

"How long will you be up there?"

"About a week."

"Maybe you'll consider coming back down for a few days before you head back." He got up and dropped cash on the table to cover the bill.

The statement stunned Andrew. In a good way. The smile on his face came all the way from his heart. He scrambled from the table to catch up.

Dad opened the door. "I have one more thing to show you before we go back to the shop, if you have time."

"I've got all the time you'd like." Andrew followed him outside to the car.

Dad drove across town. "Have you heard about the new industrial park?"

"Yeah, I heard the county was giving incentives to pull in new companies and jobs."

"That's right. Population has grown faster the last two years than it has in the last ten. It's good all the way around." Dad turned into a parking lot in front of a hand-painted sign boasting fresh strawberries in season. Wide-open fields had been tilled and rowed, already prepping for the early March planting. About five hundred feet off the road, a huge Dutch barn looked to be empty. The red paint had faded, but the roof appeared to be brand-new.

"Why are we stopping here?"

Dad got out of the truck and closed the door.

Andrew followed suit, crossing in front of the truck.

Dad shoved his hands in his pockets looking out over the land. "I own this property."

"You do?"

He nodded. "My dad bought it years and years ago. He'd wanted me to farm it."

"Looks like good land. Are you farming strawberries now?"

"No. I lease it to a guy for just enough to offset the taxes on it."

Andrew wasn't really sure what the point of this visit was. "Nice barn."

"Roof blew off it last fall in the hurricane. Insurance covered the new roof. That thing is built to stand for all time. They don't build them like that anymore."

"I bet."

"You know I didn't go into farming like my father wanted me to. Instead I started my equipment business. I'd always had a love for anything with a motor. I was taking apart Mom's appliances before I knew how to put them back together. I was on restriction a lot back then." He laughed as if remembering the memories fondly. "Your grandfather gave me this land the year you were born, hoping that I'd change my mind. I never did a thing with it."

The realization that Dad hadn't followed in his father's footsteps had never resonated with him before. Gramps had died when Andrew was in grade school. He barely remembered him. Had Dad and Gramps gone through the same rift? They said trouble followed generations.

"Son, if you were to come back and wanted to open a restaurant, you could build one here. Remodel that old barn. There's plenty of room to expand."

His jaw dropped. "A lot of room."

"As much parking as you want. You could probably run some grass-fed cattle on the rest of it. There's eighty acres in total. I know all that farm-to-table stuff is popular here. Not sure how things are in your part of the world."

"Farm-to-table is popular everywhere. Dad, I—"

"Don't answer." He raised his hand. "Good or bad, don't say a word. I just wanted to plant the seed today before you leave. While you're here in town and can really consider it." He pointed down the road. "We're sitting just a mile and a half from the new industrial park. Plenty of lunch traffic could come from there. And we're only a short distance from just about anyone in Bailey's Fork. It used to be out in the sticks, but now…it's a pretty good location. You could probably turn this into something special."

"I'm—"

"Nope. Not a word. Just keep it under your hat for a while. We'll talk about it another time. There's no expiration date on the offer. It's sitting there. Ready if you ever want it."

Andrew swallowed. "Thank you."

"You're welcome." He turned and opened the door of the truck. "Are you ready to roll?"

He stopped and looked back out over the property and where the barn sat. The roll of the land against the clear blue sky seemed like a promise of a bountiful harvest. "Yeah, I'm coming."

They rode back to Dad's shop in silence.

Andrew was overwhelmed by the afternoon. By his whole trip home, in fact. Nothing had gone as he'd thought it would. Had he become so hardened and cynical in such a short time away that he'd lost the hope in his heart?

You reap what you sow. Don't tire of doing good, because in time you'll be rewarded. The words his mother had said so many times when they were young had been her answer to everything, and at the time he'd thought it silly. For the first time in his life he truly understood what she meant. Those words he could have recited now finally resonated with him.

This morning, after being up all night, he'd left to meet his father but hadn't steadied himself for a battle. Instead, for the first time he'd come expecting, and hoping, for the best.

For the first time in nearly ten years, they'd had a pleasant day and both of them were giving a little to make it all work.

He'd hoped to dodge Kelly, but letting that opportunity happen when it was presented had turned out to be an incredible part of the visit too.

Today seemed like the best day of his life.

Andrew hoped he had enough good fortune left to win the Four Square Valentine's Day Bake-Off like he'd hoped. He'd do his best and let the right thing come his way, but he'd already be going home better than he'd arrived.

Chapter Twelve

KELLY WASN'T SURE HOW GRAY knew the days of the week, but that little pig always knew that on Friday they'd take a long walk since she probably wouldn't come home at lunchtime. That meant she'd take a right off their street and go back into the neighborhood. Being a social guy, he seemed to like these days best of all, raising his snout with an air of confidence, looking for whoever might offer him a hello or a snack. The next morning, Kelly was walking Gray when Mr. Crews hailed her from his front porch.

"Good morning, young lady." He took his porch steps two at a time. He had to be in his seventies, but you'd never know it the way he moved. "TGIF."

Does anyone even use that acronym anymore?

Gray tipped his nose in the air and oinked a greeting.

"Good morning to you," Kelly called out. "How are things going?"

"Can't complain." He shoved his hands into his pockets and rocked back on his heels. "Bought your tickets for the Valentine's steak dinner yet?"

She should've known that overzealous greeting came with an

ulterior motive. "You know I wouldn't miss it. Dad already got tickets for us."

"Perfect." He leaned in, lowering his voice. "Does this mean you've got a date this year?"

"No. I—"

"Oh, I'm sorry. I just assumed with Andrew being back in town that the two of you—"

There wasn't a body in this town that hadn't heard about that. "You assumed incorrectly." The words came out a little more abrupt than she'd meant. Then she wondered. Did Mr. Crews know something she didn't know? *Is Andrew coming back for the Valentine's Day dinner?* Sweat dampened her palms. "He and I are just friends," she said, trying to soften her tone.

"Well, that works out quite nicely, actually. My grandson will be here. I'll introduce you." Mr. Crews beamed. "You'll like him. Smart. Handsome too. Works for Bank of America in Charlotte."

"You must be very proud." She had no doubt he was nice, but she wasn't interested in being fixed up. She wasn't interested in seeing Andrew at the Valentine's Day dinner, either. That would be just a little too much. So far she'd been able to resist falling back into his charms. Maybe she'd just get Dad to get her steak to go this year.

Gray tugged on his leash. "Well, I'd better get moving. Gray doesn't like to get slowed down on his morning walk. I'll see you soon." She waved and let the pig set the pace. He took off in a scamper down the sidewalk as if he was in a hurry to make sure no one else stopped them all the way home.

Once she got Gray settled in for the day, she hopped in her SUV and drove over to The Cake Factory. Usually she'd walk or ride her bike when the weather was pretty like it was today, but she had a cake she needed to personally deliver this afternoon.

She went inside, put on her apron, and got right down to work on the finishing touches on the multi-tier cake for the grand opening of the new bookstore in the next town over. It had been a big undertaking with a lot of design work, including specific book covers. She'd spent several hours on it, starting some of the decorations over a week ago, but these were the projects that made her love her job every day.

The last hour was always her favorite, when everything finally came together. This time, even better than she'd dreamed.

Sara walked in just as Kelly made one last check for imperfections.

"That might be the most creative cake you've made yet," Sara said. "It's gorgeous!"

"Thanks." It had turned out even prettier than what she'd had in mind. She liked being a part of everyone's special moments.

Sara stepped closer. "Those books look so real."

"I hope it gets there in one piece. Dad's going to drive my SUV so I can sit in the back with it. I'm a little nervous. You know how the roads are over to Farmington." Kelly swept her hair behind her ear. "That's an awful road."

"You're right," Sara said. "I hate that drive."

Kelly and Andrew used to drive from Bailey's Fork to Farmington to go to the gourmet kitchen shop and ogle the high-dollar cookware and utensils, then pore through all the specialty food items and ingredients. They could blow a whole paycheck in an afternoon in that place. It had never felt like an extravagance, though, but more like an investment in their future. They'd challenged one another. Keeping their creativity and craft sharp. But on that ride back, it never failed that they'd tease they should've ridden horses instead of driven because of those bumpy back country roads—the only way to get to Farmington from there unless you swung all the way up to Richmond and took the highway over.

"If we have enough time, we might go ahead and take the Richmond route. I sure would hate to mess this cake up after all this work." Making repairs onsite was always nerve-wracking. Plus, that looked bad to the customer. She hadn't been back to that gourmet kitchen shop since Andrew had left town. At least now enough time had passed that the memory didn't hurt anymore. Instead, she could enjoy it for what it had been. A wonderful part of her journey as a professional baker. If the cake made it in one piece, maybe she and Dad could stop in and do a little ogling of fancy bakeware together.

She finished the last few touches then went out front to help Sara prep for the early morning rush. Sara started the coffee and Kelly tidied the case, filling the racks with the fresh-baked goods.

The front door opened, and Kelly watched a man back inside. *What is he doing?* Hunched forward, he appeared to be carrying something.

She noticed a black Suburban she'd never seen before parked across the way. "Can I help you?" She moved to the edge of the case to get a better view.

The stranger scooted in, shuffling one step at a time.

"Sir, do you need help?"

Voices carried as the man cleared the doorway and a cluster of people rushed inside, filling the space.

It took her about four seconds to put it together, which was two seconds longer than it took Sara, who was already squealing like she'd been stuck with a pin.

It was Martin Schlipshel. *The* Martin Schlipshel. The handsome host of the Four Square Cooking Show, and one of the world's most amazing pastry chefs himself.

"Kelly McIntyre?"

"Yes, sir!" She wiped her hands on her apron smoothing it as she ran around the counter to shake his hand. "Mr. Schlipshel, it's an honor to have you in my bakery."

"Call me Martin."

Her insides were practically inside out with excitement. "Martin. Yes. Welcome." *Did I just curtsy? Must have been his accent.*

She slowly cast her eyes to the side. The man who'd backed in first carried a movie camera, and it was aimed right at Martin.

"Someone who thinks you're one top baker submitted your name to our competition. We've had an undercover customer come in, and we've even ordered from your online menu to try them for ourselves." He glanced to an older gentleman on his right.

Kelly recognized him as the gray-haired man who'd come in last week. He'd eaten more desserts in one sitting than she'd seen in a long, long time. Only the time the football team had come in after they'd won the state championship had she seen someone devour that many desserts so quickly. She waved to him. "Welcome back."

Martin shoved a red chef's jacket that bore the television show logo on the front left pocket in her direction. "Four Square Cooking Show has selected you to be one of the contestants on our new Valentine's Day Bake-off!"

She gasped, taking in so much air so fast that she almost doubled over. "Oh!" The back of her throat seemed to be closing, and boy, was she going to be mad if she had a heart attack and died right here and now before she got to compete on that show.

"You know the show?"

Kelly struggled to keep her wits about her. "Do I know it? I—"

Sara ran to her side. "We love that show. We even have a TV in the factory. Everyone that works here loves your show."

"I've created new recipes out of some of the challenges you've thrown your contestants. I might add that I think mine would have won." Kelly glanced at the gray-haired man. "I remember how much you liked my 'Avocado Get Home' cupcake."

"Guilty," he said. "I still can't believe there was avocado in that frosting."

"Excellent!" Martin turned his attention back to Kelly. "Then you know our bake-offs are a blind competition. No one can know you're going to be on the show. That means both of you have to keep this a secret."

"We can do that," Kelly said.

"Scout's promise." Sara raised her fingers in a Girl Scout salute.

"Excellent. We'll get this camera put away before we have to swear anyone else to silence, and our gal Jennifer here will go through all the details of the Four Square Valentine's Day Bake-Off with you. You'll have to sign a non-disclosure and be ready to fly out to the studio kitchens on February seventh."

Kelly blanched. "That's so soon."

"A problem?" Martin swiveled his head toward Jennifer.

"Of course not," Kelly and Sara sang out in unison.

They both sucked in a breath at the same time. That wasn't that far off. "How long will I be gone?" Kelly asked.

"Depends on how good you are." Martin's laugh had an evil undertone. "If you win, we'll hold you for a few extra days to do some promo. You'll be back by the eighteenth at the very latest. Call it ten days."

"Let me get y'all something to snack on while Kelly signs those papers." Sara ran behind the counter and started pulling dessert plates and forks out.

"This is a dream come true," Kelly said. "Who nominated me?"

"Can't say, but it was good timing. This year's special Valentine's Day edition has some major sponsors, and the prize money has doubled. We'll film all of the episodes up until the finale. The finale will be filmed in front of a live studio audience on Valentine's Day. First time we've ever done that. It's brilliant, if I do say so myself. All the episodes will air on Valentine's Day. Back to back. A full day of programming and interviews with the contestants."

She wasn't sure she'd heard half of that. All that was echoing in her brain was, *Martin Schlipshel is in my bakery! "Call me Martin."*

"Is there anyone who might be expecting to spend Valentine's Day with you whom we need to find a way to get to New York?"

Her laugh was almost too loud. "No. No plans on Valentine's Day other than baking, and my team here can handle all of that."

"Surprising. You're such a lovely and smart woman," Martin said.

That was awkward. As if being alone on Valentine's Day wasn't bad enough, announcing it kind of sucked. It was like he was looking for her big flaw. "Thank you," she said, trying to sound polite.

"The network is so excited about this. We'll be choosing the winner of the one-hundred-thousand-dollar prize before a live audience."

"One hundred…thousand?"

Martin waved his hands in the air. "You're in the big time now, lady. Enjoy every minute of it. I'll let Jennifer go through all the details with you."

Sara raised her tongs in the air like a dancing lobster in front of the pastry case. "What can I get for you? Everything was just baked this morning."

Martin rubbed his hand across his chin as he stared into the case. "Do you have any of the four-layer caramel and coffee cake with mascarpone?" He smacked his lips. "I haven't stopped thinking about it, and I had the mail-order one. I can only imagine how good it'll be fresh."

"You don't have to imagine." Sarah pulled the cake out of the case and sliced a generous piece, serving it up on a china dessert plate. "Coffee? Milk?"

"Coffee would be delightful. We'll just tuck ourselves in that corner over there to keep things on the down-low," Martin said.

As Kelly led Jennifer over to her office to get the papers signed, she watched Martin, long and lanky, scurry like a giant rat to the corner to devour his cake. It was almost comical.

And all this before seven in the morning. TGIF for sure.

Chapter Thirteen

ANDREW CLIMBED OUT OF BED and wandered out to the kitchen for water. Mom had left a note on the counter.

I'm playing bridge this morning.

Be back before lunch.

So glad you're here.

Love, Mom

The clock in the kitchen read 10:05. He'd slept hard last night. He opened the refrigerator still half in a daze, just like when he'd been back in school.

Only, one glance into the refrigerator brought him back to reality. Where the whole milk used to be was now soymilk, and fake butter. At least the eggs looked normal.

He got lucky with ready-packaged salad spinach that looked halfway decent in the bottom drawer, but the cheese was low-calorie. *Will it even melt?* He read the ingredients. *Cheese food?* He tossed it back in the fridge. The bacon was pre-cooked. It would have to do.

A little more scrounging turned up a jackpot. Someone must have sent them a gift basket for the holidays, because he found a few packs of still-sealed designer cheeses. A reserve apple smoked cheddar and a Sicilian jack cheese. He could work with that.

He texted Dawn.

Good morning, sis. Can I cook you breakfast? Mom's at bridge.

Was just going to call you, she texted back. *Just finished a yoga class. Sweaty but on my way.*

Funny how much being home made him realize he missed spending time with Dawn. That "out of sight, out of mind" thing was true.

Gathering ingredients, he set them on the counter and then grabbed bowls and utensils. Right where they'd always been. He walked into the pantry, and sure enough, the potatoes and onions were right in the old wooden bin Granddad had made for Mom when Andrew had only been six or seven. He remembered because when he saw it he'd thought it was a laying box for the chickens he and Dawn were raising. He'd been so disappointed when they'd told him what it really was.

He sliced two potatoes and some onion and tossed them in olive oil with some spices, then fired up the gas stove. The cast iron skillet sputtered and sizzled as he browned the home fries.

By the time his sister got there, the room was filled with the savory scents of sage, rosemary, thyme, and bacon. He salted and wilted the spinach in a separate pan.

"I come bearing gifts," Dawn said. She plunked a thermos on the counter then raised a carton of half and half in the air like the statue of liberty. "Caffeine."

"Girl, you always were my hero." Andrew shook his head. "I wondered why her coffee wasn't doing the trick. This morning I saw the label. Decaf? What's the point?"

"Exactly!" She took down two mismatched coffee mugs. "How do you take yours?"

"Black, but I'll use that half and half for the omelets."

"Now we're talking." She poured the coffee and leaned against the counter, watching him cook.

"Do you really have to leave on Monday? Or are you just trying to keep the trip short? Ya know…"

"Because Dad and I can't do anything but argue?" Andrew finished her sentence.

"Yeah. That."

"You're not going to believe this, but we're getting along great."

"Really?" Dawn pushed her mug aside and placed her hand on his arm. "That's great, Andrew. I'm so glad. He really has mellowed a lot the last couple of years."

"I probably have too." He pressed his hands against the counter. "I really thought we'd never have a relationship again. I'm glad I was wrong."

"Stay longer. Please."

"I can't. I have to be in New York on the seventh. It's a nine-hour drive, so I have to leave the day before. I can't arrive dead on my feet."

"You came all the way from Paris to help some friend open a restaurant?"

"Yeah, but it's turned out to be so much more. I'm so glad this trip fell into my lap." He wanted to tell her the real reason so badly.

"He must be a good friend. What exactly is it that you're going to do for him?"

He kept his attention on breakfast. Dawn would see right through him if he made eye contact. "I'll do whatever he needs me to do." He poured the egg mixture into the pan, pretending to concentrate on the omelet. She always asked a million questions. It was hard to not tell her the truth.

"This is just so out of character for you. One…to just drop in unannounced. Two…to not have a plan. You always have a plan."

Same old Dawn. Nothing got past her. "Maybe I've loosened up a little."

"Or you're just playing it close to your chest. This restaurateur wouldn't happen to be a woman, would she?"

He laughed out loud. "No. There's no woman waiting for me in New York. End of story."

"Did you meet this chef friend in Paris?"

"I did. We went to culinary school together."

"But unlike you, this guy finished his training and then came back home."

He knew exactly where she was going with that. "He did."

"Why haven't you come back?" Her eyebrow lifted. "The studying I get, but you finished all that years ago. You've proven yourself, and this is home. Don't you remember all the good times we had here?"

"I do. We had a great childhood." He flipped the potatoes in the pan and removed them from the heat.

His phone rang, and he dug it out of his pocket, thankful for the interruption. "Sorry. Have to take this." He turned his back to her and put the phone to his ear. "Yes, sir."

"It's a mess. I fired that good-for-nothing—" Francois, his boss and mentor for the past seven years, was up in arms again.

Andrew backed the phone from his ear. That man had a set of lungs on him. Much worse over the phone where there wasn't a loud kitchen to tone him down. "What happened?"

"He went off menu complètement," Francois said in his own mix of English and French. "Qui pense-t-il être?"

Andrew heard the clatter of pans. François was on another rampage. He hated that he wasn't there to shield his team from Francois' wrath.

"Sneaky. Defiant. Ungrateful. He's sabotaging my business!"

Occasionally Andrew would offer advice, but he'd learned early on Francois didn't want that, and it usually left Andrew in the wake of the angry explosion too. He kept his opinion to himself.

"I fired him on the spot."

Great. Francois was talking about Victor. He'd only been with them a few months, but he was a great asset to the team. He'd warned Victor to stick to the menu.

"Yes, sir. I understand." Thankfully, Francois bid adieu and disconnected the call. No doubt when Andrew got back in town, Francois would want him to rehire him. It wouldn't be the first time.

Andrew turned down the ringer on his phone and set it aside.

"Sorry about that," he said. "What were we saying?" He shook off the remnants of the call. "Oh yeah, opening a restaurant in the United States. It's just different. You wouldn't understand."

Dawn must've picked up on his mood shift. As loud as Francois had screamed and bellowed, she may have even heard the conversation.

"Here's what I do understand. You've earned your stripes. You've done the training. You've proven yourself. If you have dreams, then make them happen. None of us knows what tomorrow will bring."

"That was deep."

She slapped him on the arm. "Shut up. It's sincere. Mom and Dad are getting older. Things are changing. Even this town is changing, even though most of us would've been happy for it to stay the same forever. Maybe you'll bring a little something special and different back here." She cocked her shoulder. "What about your dream of owning a restaurant?"

"I still plan to do that. I've saved quite a bit of money."

"I guess you have. Aunt Claire seems to love having you in the guest house."

"She does put me to work when she has parties, but I don't mind. It's a nice trade-off. I'm just waiting for the right time and opportunity."

"Sometimes you have to make your own opportunities." She leaned in closer. "There are opportunities here too. You can make your dreams happen anywhere. Why not here? Don't say anything. Just tuck it under your toque."

"I don't wear a toque."

"I thought all the famous chefs did," she said, poking him in the ribs as she moved by.

"I'm famous enough to do what I want."

He was so close to telling her why he was really back in the States, but he couldn't. Not after putting his whole career at risk by leaving on such short notice.

"Then come home and do it." Her phone rang. She grabbed it, then raised a finger. "Just a sec," she said, taking the call. "Hey, honey."

Must've been Jeff. Andrew took the opportunity to text a friend in Paris to cover for him with Francois, telling him he was dealing with a family emergency that might take longer than he'd originally planned before he'd get back, and asking him to cover the staff, along with a reminder to stick to the menu.

He'd played it safe by asking for just the first week off, which hadn't gone over all that well as it was. Hopefully, it would all pay off in the end.

"That was Jeff. He said hello, and thanks for coming home so he could do the Ag show without Dad."

"He's welcome," Andrew said.

"And so are you."

"Welcome? For what?" He plated their breakfast.

"I heard you and Kelly spent a little time together. How'd that go for you?"

"It was a little awkward, but it was good. She's a great gal."

"And?"

"And you're nosy." He slid the plate in front of her. "Eat up before it gets cold."

"Fine." She took a bite. "This is really good. I don't know how you made something this tasty out of the fake food Mom has in this house. I never eat over here anymore."

"It was a challenge. But I always did like one." He stabbed a forkful of potatoes. "I guess the challenge today will be finding something to do while Dad's at work and Mom's playing bridge."

"We should go horseback riding. The weather is perfect for it." Dawn ate her breakfast. "I have a couple of errands to run this morning, but I could be back over here by lunchtime."

"Are you just trying to get me to cook for you again?"

"Well, you're the only chef I know. Can't blame a girl for trying."

"I'll fix a lunch to take with us. Does noon mean noon or twelve-thirty?"

She laughed as she pushed away from the table and put her plate in the dishwasher. "It'll be a surprise."

It would be a surprise if she was on time. At least the fresh air might get his mind off Kelly.

Chapter Fourteen

KELLY LED JENNIFER TO HER office, letting her sit down in the leather chair across from Kelly's desk. "Is this really happening?" Kelly clung to the coveted red jacket.

Jennifer smiled broadly as she set her handbag on the desk and pulled out papers from her briefcase. "It certainly is."

"Please make yourself comfortable." Kelly was glad she'd taken the time and spent the money to create an office she could be proud of. The white bookshelves were filled with her favorite cookbooks and cooking magazines. Pictures of award-winning moments dotted the shelves, chronicling her successes. "Can I get you a cup of coffee? A pastry?"

"No, thank you. This won't take long. Basically, you're signing a non-disclosure that says you won't divulge your involvement with the show prior to the airing date, or without express permission from us."

Kelly signed that.

"We'll give you a signing bonus of five thousand dollars. Kind of a good-faith thing. I've got that check right here." She pulled it out of her designer briefcase and slid it across the desk.

"Thank you."

"I'll send you this itinerary in an email too." She flipped the page toward Kelly and started going over it with her. "We ask that you get yourself to the airport to keep the anonymity, but we'll schedule and fund your flight to New York, where we shoot the series. A driver will meet you at the airport. Meals and accommodations during the process. The location where you'll be staying will be undisclosed. You agree to keep it that way. You'll also receive a stipend for as long as you remain in the competition. Once you're eliminated, we'll send you back home."

"Okay. Sounds simple enough."

"You'll arrive in New York on the seventh of February. The first day, we'll get you settled in. A production assistant will be assigned to you. She'll be your lifeline to the outside world, make sure you make it to everything on time, and get you anything you need. The second day, we'll be doing photo shoots, and some preliminary interviews and questionnaires to use during production and for promotion for when the show airs. We go to great lengths to keep the contestants apart to ensure this truly is a blind competition. You'll have to adhere to the itinerary we set."

"I'm fine with that."

"No exceptions. If you break the rules, you'll be eliminated and lose the stipend and owe us that five thousand dollars back."

"I understand," Kelly said. There was no way she was breaking any rules. There was too much at stake.

"You could be home as early as the eleventh, or as late as the eighteenth, but honestly we usually wrap the post-show interviews up in just a day or two. So I think you can count on being home by the seventeenth. I'll need you to sign here agreeing to appear on our network's talk show and we have the right to use any footage for advertising. It's pretty standard."

"I love that show." She read through the document, although really she was just staring at the words. Her thoughts swirled so fast she couldn't even string the sentences together to comprehend much of anything.

"It's a fun show to be a part of." Jennifer smiled gently. "They'll take good care of you while you're there."

"So about eleven days? That's going to be hard to explain. This business is my whole life. I never go anywhere." Suddenly the reality of sneaking away and making sure her friends and loved ones believed she was going somewhere was overwhelming. She'd never even been on a plane before. "How will I convince them?"

Jennifer pulled all the signed papers into a pile. "Well, some people have used the excuse of a sick friend, or going on vacation. This one guy told all his friends he'd been hired as a personal chef on a movie set. Everyone believed him. I'm sure you'll think of something, but it had better be good. If the cat gets out of the bag, you'll lose the bonus and stipend, and depending on the level of exposure, you could end up in court."

She jolted upright at the thought. "I can promise you I won't do that."

"I wasn't worried. I hope you enjoy the process. This could really help your business, not that you need it. You've done extremely well, especially to be in such a small town. We were all really impressed."

"Got to love the Internet," Kelly said. "I have the best of both worlds." But as calm as she might appear on the outside, she was doing aerials and back flips on the inside. *They like me!*

"Have you ever been to New York?"

"I've never been out of Bailey's Fork."

Jennifer's laugh filled the room. "You're in for a treat. Bring your camera. All our production assistants are wonderful, and they know everything about New York. Yours will be with you pretty much night and day. So don't worry. You'll be in good hands, and if there's something you really want to see, let her know. We can try to make that happen. Might even take a camera crew along for some candid interviews of your impressions of the city."

"That would be fun." Kelly led Jennifer out of her office. The rest of the team had already finished and gone. "Can I get you a little something to go?"

Jennifer raised her hand. "I'm gluten-free. And a vegan. No worries."

"Oh, wait a minute." Kelly took a mini cake out of the case. "Gluten-free, dairy, egg, nut- and soy-free vegan. Seriously, it's so delicious. Rich and fluffy all at the same time." She presented the chocolate concoction to Jennifer. The two rich, dark layers enveloped a fluffy layer of rich chocolatey frosting in the center and was topped with a swath of frosting and a raspberry on top. "You have got to try this. I'm quite proud of it. My mother is also a gluten-free toe-the-line vegan. I had to make something that she liked, else she might disown me."

"You do it all! Thank you. I can't wait to try it."

"Great. I'll box it up for you." She tucked the mini cake into a small glossy box. "Not to sound cocky, but I have a feeling you'll be asking me to bring some of these to New York." Several of Kelly's customers regularly bought them and didn't even realize they were vegan or gluten-free.

"I just might," Jennifer said. "As long as it can't be seen as a conflict. Can't schmooze the network people, you know, even if I'm not a judge. How about I just order it myself from your website?"

"Even better. No worries on the bribery. I intend to win this on skill alone."

"I have no doubt you're going to give the others a run for it." Jennifer headed to the door, turning back to wave as she pushed it open.

"Let me know what you think," Kelly called after her.

Kelly stood there next to Sara, neither of them saying a word until Jennifer got into the Suburban parked across the street. When it pulled out of the lot, they joined hands, and both squealed in a happy dance to beat all.

"Oh. My. Goodness! This is crazy. This is real, right?" Kelly's hands shook.

"It's happening! You're going to be on television! We might have to run an extra shift. I'll be ready to schedule it," Sara assured her. "We'd better make a list."

"Yes. A list. We definitely need a list." Then all of her responsibilities and reality came crashing in. Her team could bake the cakes for the cafe, and the factory handled all the online orders anyway. But when it came to her personal life, there was a problem. "Oh, no. Someone will have to take care of Gray."

"I can do that," Sara said. "He's no trouble at all."

"What are you saying? He's nothing but trouble. It's a good thing he's so adorable. And smart. You know Gray is needy as heck in the evenings. You're going to have to spend time with him, and I've never been away. Who knows what trouble he'll get into?"

"Stop worrying. I'll just stay at your place." She squared her shoulders. "I'll be an awesome babysitter. He won't even know the difference."

She frowned. "He'd better know."

"You know what I mean," Sara said.

It wasn't like she had a lot of options. Her parents were busy with the cafe, and she couldn't drop a pig off at the local dog kennel for ten days. Not even a smallish pig.

That whole teacup pig thing had seemed like such a good idea at the time. She'd been so upset after she and Andrew had broken off their engagement that finally after three months of feeling lost and hibernating, her girlfriends had dragged her out for a day of pampering to get her out of her funk.

Over too many mimosas at the Pamper Me Perfectly Day Spa, Kelly's friend Patty had said, "I'm glad you didn't marry Andrew. We might not be here having a girl's day. You don't need him anyway. Good riddance."

Those words had stung. She knew she had to get over it, but

hearing it made it so real. Trying to play it off, she'd lightheartedly shared, "That's exactly what my mom said." She threw a hand in the air dramatically, imitating her mother's more southern drawl. "He doesn't know what he just gave up. That boy can be easily replaced."

"Get a puppy," Sara had suggested.

"I'm allergic." Kelly couldn't imagine a house full of dog hair anyway. Not when she did so much baking at home too.

Lulu raised her glass in the air. "My momma always had me gather all the pictures of the heartbreaking rat, and we did a burn-off." She clicked her long fingers above her head. "Just made him disappear."

"I can't do that. I'd have to burn half of what I own."

"Voodoo doll? My second cousin knows how to do that stuff. Once gave my cheating ex a leg ache he could never explain." She nodded. "I bet he didn't take anyone dancing so soon after that."

Patty shook her head. "I like where we were going with the pet thing. Get a stand-in. A hairless one."

"A fish?" Kelly mocked the idea.

"Not the same," Patty said. "I've got it. Men are pigs anyway. Just get one of those cute little micro pigs."

"Those are so cute!" all of her friends had enthused. And Sara had one up on her phone in less than ten seconds. "Look! So cute."

"Not all men are pigs," their newlywed friend, Vicki, had defended.

"Says the newlywed," Kelly teased. "How is Mr. Perfect anyway?"

"Perfect. Not a pig, but those pigs are adorable, like a little Yorkie, only they don't shed and bark. They have a teacup pig farm over in Boot Creek. It's not that far. I'll drive!" And before she knew it, Vicki had called and made an appointment, and all of them had piled back in her Range Rover and headed to the Teensy Weensy Pig Farm an hour away.

That night Kelly had arrived home with a good dose of girlfriend advice, a perfect mani/pedi in "It's Raining Men" even if it was a little brighter color than she'd normally wear, and had replaced Andrew with a pink-and-black spotted teacup piglet named Gray. "G.R.A.Y." An acronym for Good Riddance Andrew York, aptly named by Patty who, with five small children, had an acronym for everything, as she talked in code around them.

Gray weighed less than a can of soda and literally fit into a teacup the day she brought him home. That was seven years ago though, and now Gray was nearly a foot tall and schlepping around a whopping thirty-eight pounds. She loved that silly pig. He'd been there for her through the good and the bad times without fail.

Leaving Gray behind for the competition wasn't going to be easy. On the other hand, getting out of town while Andrew York was around was a bonus.

"Sara, you can't do everything while I'm gone."

"Why not?" Sara pulled her hand up on her hip. "You covered me for two weeks when I went to Alaska with Dalton."

"That's completely different."

"No, it's not. You can't tell anyone where you're going, and the more people you have covering things, the more lies you have to cover. No offense, but you're the worst liar I know."

That was true. "I'll make this up to you. I promise."

"Just win!" Sara untied her apron and hung it on the peg outside of the office. "Besides, this is the best advertising you could get for The Cake Factory. And they're paying you to do it. It's a win-win for everyone. The whole town will benefit."

Making Bailey's Fork an attractive town to live and work in was important to her. She was proudest of the jobs she'd brought to the community. "I hope I'm not in over my head. You know most of those contestants have fancy culinary degrees and have worked for swanky resorts like the Four Seasons. I'm just a hometown girl who likes to bake." She let out a breath. "It's not about the money. I want to prove myself. It would be validation. I'm tired of apologizing for having learned to bake at my grandma's and daddy's hip."

"And you shouldn't. You should be proud of that, and trust me, there's not one single customer who gives two toots about some cooking degree. You're an amazing baker with original recipes and more God-given talent than those fancy pastry chefs have ever learned. Don't you freak out on me." Sara placed her hands on Kelly's shoulders. "Repeat after me. 'I've got this.'"

"I've got this." Kelly straightened her shoulders. "I've been hoping for this chance my whole adult life. I've totally got this."

"That's my pal." Sara held the clipboard in the air. Right now it read,

Take care of Gray
Stay at Kelly's
Cover Kelly's shifts starting the 7th

"Can you approve payroll for me while I'm gone too?"

"No problem." Sara added it to the list. "I'm putting this in your top drawer. Just add to the list when you think of anything, and I'll divvy up the to-dos and get them done. No worries. Please promise me you'll just concentrate on this amazing opportunity. It's going to be the best Valentine's Day ever. I know it."

"At least I don't have to worry about people talking about me not having a date at the Valentine's Day steak dinner again this year. How am I going to come up with an excuse that will fool my parents?" Kelly had a feeling that might be harder than the competition. "I'm going to have to find a quiet spot to brainstorm on this one."

The chimes clanked against the front door, followed by a friendly, "Yoo-hoo!"

Kelly followed the voice out to the counter. "Dawn?" It was just one surprise after another today. There was no doubt in her mind that Dawn had been playing matchmaker with that huge order for Andrew's surprise party. She wondered what she was up to now. "Hey there. What brings you back twice in one week?"

"I just wanted to stop in and personally thank you for those amazing desserts. They made the party."

"I'm glad you enjoyed them."

"I really hope we can spend more time together again. It's just been too long. I let life get busy, and I regret us not maintaining our friendship. I hope you'll forgive me," Dawn said.

"Forgive you? I let myself get busy too," Kelly said. "It works both ways."

"She works too much," Sara butted in. "I'm always telling her that."

"You still have your horse, don't you?" Dawn folded her arms across her chest.

"Absolutely. Don't ride her near as much as I should, though."

"I'm going horseback riding this afternoon. You should come," Dawn said with enthusiasm. "Nothing long, just a quiet ride through the old creek trail. It's as good as yoga, but a lot less sweating. Better scenery too."

Sara nudged Kelly. "Kelly was just saying she needs some quiet thinking time."

It would be nice to ride with someone, and she did need to come up with some kind of story about being gone. "I haven't been down the creek trail in a while."

"You've got to come. Just an hour or two. It'll be fun," Dawn said.

Kelly looked to Sara, who was practically pushing her out the door. "That sounds good." It would give her a chance to reconnect with Dawn. She needed to spend more time with friends.

"Let's meet where the creek splits off. We'll take it around to the old barn and then we'll go from there. We can make the short loop. In about an hour?" Dawn glanced at her watch. "Actually, make it an hour and a half. That'll give me time to get my stuff together."

"Yeah. That should be plenty of time. See you there."

Dawn left just as Kelly's mom came in the side door. "Was that Dawn I just saw leaving?"

"It was. We're going horseback riding."

"I'm so glad. You two used to be so close. It's good to see you finally taking time for yourself."

"I'm going to try to start doing a lot more of that," she said, hoping the change in scenery would grease her fictional rails to come up with an excuse for going out of town that her folks would believe.

Chapter Fifteen

ANDREW WENT OUT ON THE deck and stretched out on a lawn chair to enjoy the free time. It was chilly, but the air seemed to clear his head. A squirrel scrambled up the big oak tree, and birds chirped at the commotion. He should be thinking about desserts right now, but the only thing sweet on his mind was Kelly McIntyre. He was lucky she hadn't slapped him for being too familiar when they'd been baking together. It had been seven years, after all, and the way he'd left, or rather had never come back, hadn't exactly been a warm departure…but doggone if it didn't seem like no time had passed since they'd been together.

Of course, Kelly wasn't feeling what he was. He'd left her behind to chase his own dreams and never looked back. *Could I have been more selfish?* He could have handled things so much better. Then again, seven years of maturity made that much easier to see now.

Initially he hadn't even really wanted to go to that pastry school, but it had been too good to pass up, especially if it might help him and Kelly meet their lofty goals quicker. Even Kelly had said so.

He'd had every intention of coming back when he'd left Bailey's Fork for Paris. Somewhere in that six-month period of pastry school, he'd started believing that he couldn't reach those goals without the skills he could only get in Paris under those experts' tutelage. He'd never know if that was true or not. It was done now, and there was no changing it.

Leaving her this time would be harder, because he'd have to face her to do it. He wouldn't be 4000 miles away over a telephone. For a fleeting moment he pictured himself going to say goodbye to Kelly, and her asking him to stay. A warm rush flowed through him at the thought. *Would it matter if I stayed?* She had his whole heart and mind in a state of confusion.

He took his phone out of his pocket and scrolled through the contacts. He still had her in the list, although he hadn't dialed that number in seven years. He brought up her number. Maybe he could call to thank her again for last night.

But as he stood there with his finger over the CALL button, he just couldn't do it. It was selfish when in just a couple of days he'd be gone again.

His phone rang and buzzed in his hand. He nearly dropped it trying to answer it. "Hey, sis."

Dawn's chipper voice came over the line. "I'll meet you down at the barn in about an hour?"

"Text me when you're on your way. You're never on time."

"I'll be on time. Trust me." She disconnected the call.

He shoved his phone into his pocket and walked back inside into the kitchen. Mom looked up from the table where she was drinking a cup of coffee and reading a magazine.

"I didn't hear you get back," he said.

"I figured you were still in bed asleep."

"No. I made Dawn breakfast this morning, and she's going to come back over and we're taking the horses out."

"That's a great idea." The color rose in her cheeks.

Seeing her so happy made him feel the same way. "You should come with us."

"Not today. I've got some errands to run."

"I'd say you'd have time to do them later, but you know Dawn. No telling when she'll actually show up."

"Dawn-time," Mom said. "That's one thing that'll never change."

"Do you mind if I rummage through the cabinets and freezer? I thought I'd make lunch to take with us."

"Have at it. There are some of those flash frozen chicken tenders in the freezer, and ingredients for a decent potato salad. Fried chicken and potato salad would make for a good picnic that would fit nicely in the saddlebags. It won't hurt my feelings if you want to leave me a plate," she said with a wink.

"Deal." He got right to work.

While he fried the chicken, Mom made herself comfortable at the island. "It's so nice to watch you cook again."

"Feels good to cook for myself instead of for customers." He never cooked at home. "It'll be nice to get on Doc again. I hope I remember what I'm doing." He rinsed the chicken tenders and dredged them in flour he'd doctored up with the spices Mom had on hand.

"Let me know when you're ready to go down to the barn, and I'll help you get saddled up." She'd been a competitive barrel racer when she'd met Dad. The barn was still her favorite way to spend time.

"That would be great. It's been a while."

"It'll all come right back to you, and Doc is a great horse. He'll treat you right."

"No doubt about that." The chicken sizzled in the oil.

"Your old cowboy boots are in the attic if you want to ride in them. All the boxes are marked."

"Really? I can't believe you didn't toss all that stuff a long time ago."

"Not mine to toss," she said. "Besides, those were nice boots."

"If I'd known I wasn't coming back, I would've taken them with me." He turned the chicken, and then dumped the boiling potatoes in the strainer in the sink.

"That smells so good, and you make it look so easy."

"Practice," he said.

"You've practiced your clean-up skills too. I used to cringe when you cooked here."

"Yeah, that won't fly in a restaurant. That was one of the first things I learned." He laid the fried chicken strips on a paper sack to drain as he finished the potato salad. He took a plate from the cabinet and made a serving for Mom. Pleased with how it all turned out, and with time to spare, he turned to her. "I'm going to go hunt down those boots."

"All your stuff should be on the right-hand side in the attic."

"Thanks, Mom." He went down the hall and pulled the string to the attic stairs. They creaked and groaned. He went to the hall closet where Dad kept the house tools and got what he needed to oil the hinges. One generous squirt, and the stairs were moving without so much as a moan.

Mom came down the hall. "You're an angel. Do you know how long I've been asking your dad to do that?"

"Since I left?"

She laughed. "Not quite that long. But it's been a while. Thank you for doing that."

"You're welcome. Here, you can put this back for me?" He handed her the can as he ascended the stairs.

Waving his arm in the darkness, he finally made contact with the old pull string that operated the single light in the attic, although it wasn't much brighter with it on. The space was cold and smelled of dust.

Along the right wall tucked up near the eave were boxes with his name on it. Andrew Trophies. Andrew Clothes. *Andrew and Kelly?* He paused. *Now why on Earth would Mom save that old junk?* The box next to that one was labeled Andrew Shoes & Boots.

He grabbed that box and sure enough, his old cowboy boots, ostrich skin, were tucked neatly inside with newspaper stuffed in them to hold their shape. They'd been a Christmas present. He slipped one on. They still fit like a glove.

He folded the corners in on the top of the box and slid it back over where he'd found it.

The box with Kelly's name on it taunted him.

He glanced at his watch. He still had a little bit of time before Dawn was supposed to be here, and if things hadn't changed she'd be at least fifteen minutes late.

Walking toward the box, he questioned himself for even being curious. At the fork in the road, he'd made his choice. But rather than turning and going downstairs, he got the box and carried it over under the light. He sat cross-legged beneath it and pulled the tape that secured the top. It had lost its sticky over the years. Inside, his high school yearbooks were on top of a couple of photo albums Mom had made for him. Several spiral notebooks that held some of the first recipes he'd ever created were in the bottom. He flipped through them, impressed by some of the techniques and combinations he'd come up with at such a young age.

He turned to the inside cover of his yearbook. Some of the quotes were so cheesy.

Dude, no one trusts a skinny chef. Eat more junk or you'll go broke. Your brother from another mother, Michael

I expect a chair in your restaurant with my name on it so I'll never go hungry after tasting all your homemade lunches. I'm not tipping you though. Jordan.

Remember me when you're a rich restaurateur. Carla

Andrew, You'd better invite me to the wedding. You're the luckiest guy to have Kelly. She's too good for you. Not going to be the same without you around here. Just one more year for me. David

Andrew— Go all Chef Ramsay on the world! Bobby

I kissed a chef, and I liked it! Here's to our future together. Love, Kelly

Everyone had expected him to marry her, and wished him well on his own restaurant someday. Neither of those things had come true.

How many of them had done what they'd thought they'd do back in high school? Most of them were probably still right here in Bailey's Fork. Kelly's senior picture had a red heart around it. The yearbook was creased, as if he'd stared at that picture a hundred times. He probably had. She looked fresh and natural, and her confidence shone through even in that picture. Thinking about her, he could almost smell the fragrance of citrus and apple from the shampoo she used to use back then.

In the very bottom of the box there was another box. He opened it to find pictures of the two of them on their horses. At prom. A faded black-and-white strip of four pictures from the photo booth from the arcade. In the diner. In the kitchen downstairs making something, but mostly a mess from the looks of things. Four small frames held pressed fresh herbs Kelly had grown for him and framed as a gift on his nineteenth birthday. The actual plants had been behind the diner, where he could snip them for his recipes that day. Yellowed paper held more recipes the two of them had worked on together. Some had more scratch-outs than actual ingredients.

He flipped through them until he got to one all written in purple ink. She'd worked on it for weeks and couldn't get it quite right. He'd thought it was perfect way before this final version, but she was going for something a little richer in taste. They'd spent an entire weekend messing around with this recipe. Finally, they'd added a little extra vanilla and he'd helped her come up with the mascarpone crème fraiche, and they'd made magic. She'd garnished it with thin slivers of almonds. He remembered that day so vividly, the way her hand had delicately sprinkled that final garnish across the top when she'd served it.

It was that day he'd been inspired and confident enough to really believe they would have the restaurant they'd always talked about.

And yet here he was seven years later, and he was still making someone else's recipes in someone else's restaurant.

He dropped the memorabilia back into the box and gave it a swift shove, sending it sliding across the smooth wooden floor of the attic. Enough of that.

Downstairs he changed into a pair of jeans and a long-sleeved T-shirt with his boots, then went to the kitchen to box up the picnic lunch. He grabbed two apples from the fruit bowl for the horses. "You sure I can't talk you into riding with us?"

"You and Dawn will have fun. The creek trail is gorgeous right now."

"We may as well go saddle up the horses so when Dawn finally gets here, we can go." He put their lunch in a bag and walked with Mom down to the barn.

As they neared the barn, the horses frolicked and nickered, happy to see them.

"You already had your breakfast," Mom scolded the horses as she pulled the chain on the gate to get enough slack to unhook it. She waved an arm in the air. "Get on back."

The horses sauntered away as she swung the ten-foot gate open.

Andrew slipped his fingers under Doc's halter, a big bay gelding standing sixteen-three hands. He was tall to get on, but anyone could ride him. A babysitter horse, Mom had always said.

Gentle as could be, Doc dipped his head, letting Mom rub his nose.

"Doc's happy to see you," she said to Andrew.

"Come on, old buddy." He reached up and rubbed the side of his neck. "Best friends forever."

The horse snorted.

To his surprise, Dawn came riding up on her horse, Gabby. "Thought you'd never get here," she teased.

"I thought you were going to call when you got here."

"Thought I'd surprise you instead." She pulled on Gabby's reins and spun the golden palomino in a tight circle. "I'm waiting on you for a change." Gabby tossed her flaxen mane.

"Show-off." Andrew threw the saddle on top of the blanket on Doc's back. The shiny bay used to be a competitive header horse. He'd been retired early after his cowboy got injured. He was a good horse with a less-than-competitive demeanor these days.

It didn't take long to get Doc tacked with Mom's help. He tucked the food into the saddlebags, then put his foot in the stirrup and lifted himself up onto Doc's back.

"You good up there?" she asked.

"Your mothering is showing," he teased. He shifted in the saddle side-to-side. "Fits like a glove." He tugged low on the reins and clicked to move Doc back a few steps, then caught up with Dawn.

"You still look good up there," Mom said. "A natural cowboy."

"Thank you, ma'am," he said in a southern drawl while tipping his imaginary cowboy hat. He let Doc move at his own pace.

"Have fun." She waved as they rode across the field.

When they reached the back gate that led to the creek trail, Andrew dropped down from his saddle and opened the back gate, letting Dawn lope ahead. He was perfectly happy to take it slow and soak in the beauty of the North Carolina landscape again.

He'd forgotten how different things looked from another five feet in the air. The world felt more open from up here in the saddle.

He sucked in a lungful of the fresh, pure air.

Although winter was in full swing, the abundance of evergreens in this area made it still feel lush. He brushed his hand through the thick pine needles that hung heavy from the trees along the trail. The pungent aroma of pine released into the air around him, reminding him of Christmases past. He wiped the sticky residue from the pine tar against the horn bag on the saddle.

Doc snorted. "It's good to be with you again, Doc."

It didn't take long for Andrew to relax. "I've missed this." Andrew loosened his grip on the reins and let Doc pick his own path. As a kid he'd wandered these trails on horseback and on foot, pretending to live off the land and hunt for secret treasures.

Dawn waited for him. "It's nice having you around."

"It's been a good trip. I can't believe it's already half over."

About fifteen minutes of riding through the tall pines and bare hardwoods, the tension in Andrew nearly disappeared. It had been a long time since he'd felt this way. He took in a deep breath and let it out slowly. As he loosened up, Doc did too.

Since it was early February, there were no bugs to contend with, and the mild temperature was like no weather at all. He pushed his sleeves up. The sun was warm against his skin. Birds chirped above, as if asking what he'd been up to all this time, and that was exactly what he was thinking about. He'd accomplished a lot, but a lot of it wasn't what he'd set out to do, either.

Dawn eased her horse down the bank toward the creek. Here the river rock was smooth and the water was never too deep unless they'd had a rainy run of weather. The familiar cluck and clop of the water being sucked from below by the pounding hooves was as soothing as rain on a tin roof, loud and mellow all at the same time.

Water splashed from Gabby's hind legs, sending icy-cold water up Andrew's leg and the side of his face.

"No fair."

"I guess you forgot the rider in the back is the one who gets the wettest."

"Payback is coming," Andrew yelled as he dodged another splash. Then he spurred Doc and blew past her, leaving her in a wake of icy-cold water.

She shrieked. "Okay. We're even."

They pulled the horses up onto the bank.

"You got me good," she said, still laughing.

"I'm not as out of practice as you thought," he teased.

The echo of horse hooves clopping through the creek rose from up the way. "Think that's Mom?"

Dawn shook her head. "No. Wrong direction. She'd be coming from that way."

They waited, not wanting to spook the horse or splash a neighbor.

Andrew twisted around in his saddle, pulling a bottle of water from his saddle bag, when he heard his sister say, "Look who's here." Only her tone seemed a tinge too surprised to be authentic.

When he looked up and saw Kelly riding toward them on a black-and-white paint, he was even more suspicious of his sister's innocence. Then again, if Dawn had arranged for Kelly to show up, he wasn't mad about it. He hadn't had the guts to make the call himself.

"Hey again," he said to Kelly.

He wanted to believe that her pulling back before had been because she was feeling those same old feelings too, but was that disappointment on her face now?

"Hi?" It came out more like a question, and from the way Kelly was looking at Dawn, he'd lay good money that his dear sister was behind this little run-in.

"Andrew made lunch," Dawn said. "Perfect timing."

Kelly looked confused. "Okay."

Dawn turned Gabby and took the lead down the creek trail. Kelly fell in right behind her, and Andrew took up the rear.

As Kelly rode along, her ponytail bouncing from the hole in the back of her ball cap, it was as if time had turned back ten years with that first step into the creek.

He couldn't hear what Dawn was saying to her, but when Kelly laughed, he caught his breath at the familiar sound. Her shoulders lifted, like they always had when she was amused, and he didn't have to see her to picture her smile.

They rode along quietly for about forty-five minutes, and then Dawn turned up the trail toward the old barn.

He dismounted and tied Doc while Dawn and Kelly chatted next to the barn. He unpacked lunch from his saddlebags. Here behind the barn there was just enough wind block to make it feel like a spring day.

"Oh!" Dawn grabbed for her phone. "That vibration always scares me. Let me take this." She held up a finger and turned her back from them, walking away as she spoke into her phone.

"Great ride," Kelly said.

He nodded. "Been a long time since I've ridden."

"You looked comfortable enough."

They'd just sat down under the tree when Dawn came back over. "You're not going to believe this. The plumber is at my house. I totally forgot he was coming today. I need to zip back over there and meet him."

Andrew could read right through that lame excuse. He was sure Kelly could too.

"I'm so sorry." Dawn was already getting back toward Gabby.

"You'd better run. They charge by the hour," Kelly said.

"Sorry again." Dawn made the fastest exit he'd ever seen.

They watched her lope off.

"I have a feeling we've been duped." He offered Kelly some potato salad.

"Thanks." She scooped some on her plate. "Your sister isn't that good of an actress."

"Tell me about it. She's good at fooling me into things, though."

"Apparently, she fooled me too," Kelly said.

She took a bite of the potato salad. "This is good. Very different."

"Thanks." He set his plate aside. "Do you remember the day I carved our initials in that tree?"

"Of course I do. You broke the tip off the pocket knife I'd given you that Christmas."

He'd forgotten that part. "It was after a ride along the creek like this morning."

"I remember. Only it was cold as the dickens. We wore our winter coats." She pulled her feet up under her. "The whole town was so mad about you defacing that tree."

"Because no one can keep a secret around here."

"You shouldn't have told all your buddies."

"They were blabber mouths."

"It turned out to be front-page news," Kelly said.

"Yeah, but in all fairness, even when Mrs. Jones made her husband sleep in the shed it was front-page news."

"True. Besides, how were two teenagers supposed to know that tree was a registered landmark?" Kelly laughed. "There wasn't even a sign next to it back then."

"I kind of knew it was a big deal. That's why it seemed like the perfect way to profess my love."

She plucked a piece of grass and toyed with it.

"I did community service that whole summer because of that, and had to work for Dad part-time for six months to pay back the fine." *It had been worth it.* "Man, that feels like a hundred years ago."

"Feels like just yesterday to me," she said quietly. "Lunch was really good. Not that I'm surprised. You always could whip up an amazing meal." Kelly put her plate in the trash bag and tilted her chin to the sun. "I love winter days like this."

"Me too. I'm sorry Dawn tricked you, but I'm glad we got to spend more time together." He turned over on his side, watching her sitting there with her eyes closed.

"It's been a nice break. I had some help last night, so I had some free time."

He tossed a pebble into her lap. "Must've been a pretty awesome helper."

The rock startled her. She looked at him, amused. "You could say that." She flipped the pebble back toward him.

"I think I will."

"You're too much. Thanks for the lunch."

"You're welcome. It's the least I could do after I ate half of your pot of chili." He reached for her hand, and this time she didn't pull back.

"I've got to head back."

Andrew let his thumb graze the top of her hand. "Can't you stay a little longer? It's a gorgeous day."

"I can't." She took in a deep breath, then withdrew her hand. "Do you remember the way back to your mom's?"

"Yeah, I can get there." *If I'd kept my mouth shut, she'd have probably ridden all the way back home with me.* He stood and extended his hand to help her up.

"Thanks."

"For what?" She brushed the back of her pants.

"For reminding me there's a whole lot more to life than work." Andrew helped her get on her horse.

"You're welcome then."

Andrew coaxed Doc to stand still long enough that he could get a foot in the stirrup. Every time he got his toe in, Doc would take a few steps, leaving Andrew hopping alongside.

"You know I'm out of practice, don't you, old man."

The horse lifted his nose in the air, then Andrew finally got back in the saddle. His muscles warmed to the physical activity, especially after the long plane ride.

He worked the reins to make Doc side pass, which he did with no hesitation, proving Andrew was the only one out of practice. Doc was one jam-up horse.

Finally, Andrew rode over toward Kelly. Their two horses offered familiar snorts.

He looked at her. As beautiful as ever. Still the nicest woman he'd ever known. So much had changed since he left, and the best parts were just the same. *I've got some priorities to get straight.*

Kelly nodded as if she'd read his mind. "Thank your sister for the ride for me," she said, then kicked her heels against her horse and took off in a lope down the road toward her house.

Chapter Sixteen

KELLY STROLLED BACK INTO THE bakery, energized.

Sara carried a tray from the back to the counter. "Hey, you're back. How was the trail ride?"

"Dawn tricked me again. I can't believe I'm that gullible."

"Again?" Sara put the tray down and put her hand on her hip. "Do you mean to tell me Andrew was there?"

"She tricked him too. You should have seen his face when I came up to them in the creek. She took off and left us."

"Oh my gosh. I can't believe she did that. It's almost funny. Are you mad?"

"Not really. I just can't believe I fell for it." She grabbed a towel and wiped a smudge from the glass countertop. "He made lunch too. For her. Not me, but since she left, I got the benefits. It was delicious."

"No surprise there."

"True." She raised her chin, feeling somewhat proud of herself. "I feel good about it. It was really nice, and I've been able to keep it in perspective. Just a friendly ride between friends."

"Are you sure?" Sara didn't look so sure. "Because you look awfully smiley for not making more of it."

"Oh, stop it. It was fun." She swatted Sara with the towel. "I still have way more important things to concentrate on than Andrew York and what happened between us forever ago." She glanced over her shoulder to make sure no one was within earshot. "Like New York to the tune of a hundred thousand dollars."

"Good for you. I'm glad you two had fun."

"We did. Now time to get down to work. If I win—"

Sara interjected. "When you win."

"When I win," she repeated, holding her crossed fingers in the air, "the Four Square Valentine's Day Bake-Off will give us more exposure than the rock star shout-out that first put us on the map. I might even be able to extend full-time positions to some of our part-time decorators."

"That would be wonderful."

"I know." She was proud of the jobs she'd brought to her neighbors. "I'm excited and so nervous all at the same time. I hope I can pull this off."

"This competition—baking something awesome on the fly and integrating random ingredients—is totally in your wheelhouse."

"But the competitors on that show are real pastry chefs."

"I don't care how educated the competition is. You know desserts and you're a quick thinker when it comes to those kinds of challenges. I don't think I've ever missed an episode of Four Square, and trust me, you are every bit as good as the very best I've ever seen on it."

She sucked in a breath of hope. "I hope so." A huge fan of the show for years, there'd been times when she tried recipes based on some of the challenges. Sure, a few of them had been pretty horrible, but for the most part she'd pulled off something terrific. The margarita cupcake with the lime filling and salted frosting, for example. It was one of her biggest sellers.

As long as she could stay relaxed, maybe she had a real shot at taking home the trophy.

"I'm so thankful for you and Calvin. I know this place will

run just fine without me here. I couldn't do it without y'all here to handle everything."

"I wish we could tell him—"

"No. We can't!"

"I know." Sara raised her hands like she was under arrest. "Don't worry. My lips are sealed."

"Thanks." The panic dissipated in a long sigh. "Sorry. I overreacted a little. We can't chance being eliminated. They were very serious about that."

"I promise. Don't worry, we'll take care of everything here."

"I know you will. I'm mostly worried about my parents. What am I going to tell them? I'm running out of town. It's going to have to be one heck of an excuse for leaving town that they won't question it."

"I know. I thought about that last night. You never go anywhere. What if you tell them that you're going to take a vacation? A cruise? Then you'd be able to explain not checking in while you're away."

"They'll never buy that. Especially alone. Plus, it's too sudden."

Sara chewed on the end of her pen, then raised a hand in the air. "I know. Tell them you won a free ticket to a baking convention. I saw something. What was it? The Retail Bakers Association, I think. They're having something in Atlanta this month. It's just far enough away to keep anyone from showing up to check on you."

"That might work." Kelly glanced at the stack of industry magazines on her desk. She grabbed the one from the top and flipped through it, then turned the page back. "The Retail Bakers Association Road Trip." She held up the magazine. "You're right." She read through the advertisement. "Too bad I won't really be going. It looks fun."

"We really should do that sometime. I think it's so cool how they visit the different bakeries and swap ideas for marketing and stuff."

"You're right," Kelly said. "We'll plan one together. Things around here are humming on all cylinders. We should be able to do some things now and again."

"Perfect. See, that wasn't so hard. An excuse and a girls' trip for the future. I'm so ready."

Kelly was relieved to have a plan. "I'm going to go ahead and make the cakes for the cafe and get that out of the way." Main Street Cafe had been her first contract order after she'd made the down payment on this space. Sure, it was her folks' place, but still it was a standing order, and that had helped pay the bills in those early days. No matter how busy she got, she'd never been late delivering on that order. And even though she sold those cakes right here in the bakery, too, people still opted to pay the per-slice price and have it at the cafe with their meals. People were just loyal like that around Bailey's Fork.

"I'm going to go see what we need to restock the front case for the morning rush." Sara went to the front, and Kelly headed to her kitchen in the bakery.

Standing at the stainless-steel counter, Kelly prepped the frosting for her seven-layer banana pudding cake. Seven had always been her lucky number so when it came to layers, she stuck with seven, and that had kind of become her signature. Good thing her lucky number hadn't been something like fifteen.

She placed a cardboard circle on the spinner, then started stacking the super-thin layers of cake on it one at a time, adding a layer of banana frosting between each one until the cake was seven layers tall. The sides and topping were her Zen moment. She'd been doing these cakes for so long that sometimes she didn't even remember frosting them. She added dollops of fluffy whipped frosting, which did double-duty as decoration and size indicators for the girls next door to slice, making sure no customer was short-changed. That had been Dad's idea—a good one. She finished off the cake with good old-fashioned vanilla wafers.

Kelly then put together the chocolate and red velvet cakes, and she was done with her morning routine before it was even morning.

She moved all the finished cakes to the glass top cart to take them to the cafe. The antique cart was from the early 1900s. She and Dad had found it while they'd been at a restaurant auction in South Carolina a couple of years ago.

Her parents were always so supportive. She hated having to lie to them about the contest. They'd understand when they found out, but it still made her feel horrible. She'd tell them first thing in the morning.

She drove home, wondering what kind of crazy life warp she was in where Andrew showed back up, she was selected to be on a cooking show, and she was planning to lie to her parents.

What could possibly happen next?

Chapter Seventeen

WHEN KELLY'S ALARM WENT OFF, Gray was already snorting and shuffling around in the mudroom.

"Good morning," she said over the Dutch door. Gray pranced on the terrazzo tile like a tap dancer that needed practice. She went inside and petted him on the nose. "Are you ready for a walk this morning?"

He spun around.

"Looks like a yes to me." She grabbed his harness from next to the door.

He knew exactly what was going to happen next. He sat and waited patiently for her to put his black-and-white checkered harness on him. She straightened the hot-pink sequined bow tie around his neck, which had been a joke from her girlfriends who'd wanted her to make Gray the logo of her bakery. As much as she loved that pig, that wasn't the look she was going for.

They'd also given her a blinged pooper-scooper, but the joke was on them, because she loved that pooper-scooper and didn't mind carrying the flashy thing around. She led Gray out the front door. They walked around the neighborhood, tossing the newspapers closer to the house where little Johnny had gotten a sloppy arm and not made it past the sidewalk. Which was often.

A few of the neighbors would routinely greet them with a little snack for Gray. The manager at the local Krispy Kreme jogged this same route most mornings and almost always carried a glazed doughnut in his coat pocket for Gray. He loved those doughnuts.

"How are things going for you, Kelly?" Mrs. Fuller asked with a wave. "I've got some leftover popcorn for my little buddy. Hi, Gray!" She waddled over in her robe.

"Good morning." Kelly stopped, and Gray plopped down next to her. Mrs. Fuller must've been watching Hallmark again last night. It seemed she could never finish a bag by herself on movie night.

Mrs. Fuller held the bag in front of his snout, and Gray happily attacked the popcorn.

"I'm glad you stopped me this morning. I was going to let you know that I'll be going out of town next week. My friend Sara will be staying at the house."

"I'm so glad you did," Mrs. Fuller said. "I'd have been concerned seeing a strange car in your driveway."

Kelly found that humorous. She was pretty sure what Mrs. Fuller would have been was excited. Excited to be the one to spread the rumor that she'd had an overnight guest. Yeah, that could've been awkward. "No worries. I'm going on a business trip. She'll be watching Gray for me."

"Well, you have a wonderful time. You work way too much. You deserve some down time."

"Thank you, but speaking of work...I need to get to it." Kelly patted her thigh. "Come on, Gray. Time to go inside so I can get to work."

Gray bounced to his feet and led the way to the walkway that led to the backyard. She took him inside through the back and put his harness and leash away. A quick rubdown to get any mud from between his hooves and off that low dragging belly, and then he was ready to eat. She fed him, then headed to work. Dad's car was already parked behind the cafe. Mom would straggle in a little later, as usual.

She had a light morning ahead, except for convincing her parents she was going out of town for fun, and she was looking forward to having the free time to focus on the cooking show.

As soon as she got to the bakery, she wheeled the cart of cakes over to the Main Street Cafe.

She took a deep breath and hoped for the best. "Hey, Dad. I've got your cakes."

"Thanks, Kelly. Let me help you with those." He lifted the seven-layer cake from the cart and moved it to the empty cake stand on the counter. In his signature Main Street Cafe short-sleeved T-shirt and khakis, he looked more like he owned the hardware store than the cafe, but everyone knew and loved CB McIntyre. CB stood for cornbread – a nickname he'd gotten in college in Northern Virginia, and it had stuck. "They look perfect. As always."

"Thanks, Daddy."

"I was thinking about throwing a surprise party for your mother on Valentine's Day."

But I'll be gone. Unless I get eliminated in the first round. That would be awful. "Why then?"

"It's the anniversary of our very first I Love You's."

"Dad, are you getting sentimental in your old age?"

He looked insulted. "Are you calling me old?"

"Well, older...ish." She'd heard the story a million times; just her luck Dad would go all mushy when she wouldn't be in town, and it wasn't like she could tell him either.

"What do you think about me renting the gazebo in Town Square?" he continued with excitement.

"It might be cold."

"Good point."

"You know everyone will have their own plans on Valentine's Day, and there's the steak dinner the night before. I'm not sure it's great timing."

"That could present a problem."

144

Thank goodness. Besides, I don't want to miss something like that.

"It would be a bigger surprise if you did it another time. Plus, you know hard she is to surprise."

"That's true. We need to come up with a better plan."

Mom walked into the room. "What do you two have your heads together about?"

"Talking about you." Kelly stated the obvious, hoping it would work like reverse psychology.

"Yeah, yeah. Like I believe that," Mom said.

Dad busied himself with the cakes and then pulled money out of the cash drawer for her. "Here you go. We'll need an extra red velvet cake tomorrow."

"I'll add it to the list." She would add some decorative hearts and Cupid to help remind guys that Valentine's Day was just around the corner. It'd give her an excuse to practice something unique for the bake-off too.

Her mom leaned in close. "Do you have any special Valentine's plans this year, Kelly?"

"Well." She widened her stance, hoping her knees wouldn't buckle. "Actually, I have some news."

Her heart river-danced in her chest. "I have the chance to go on an RBA Road Trip event." She swallowed, trying to keep from blowing her own cover.

"The Retail Bakers Association trips? That's wonderful."

"Yes. I'm really looking forward to it." Kelly hoped Mom didn't notice her bottom lip quivered as she spoke. "It's short notice. I entered a recipe in the quarterly contest. They're paying for my airfare and everything. I can't believe I won. I never win anything." *Why am I adding all this to the lie? I'm going to put my foot right in it.* "I leave on Tuesday."

"Kelly! That's wonderful. Congratulations." Mom and Dad both hugged her.

"We're so proud of you," Dad said.

Cary Area Public Library
1606 Three Oaks Road
Cary, IL 60013

"It's too bad you're leaving when Andrew just got into town," Mom said.

They were more concerned about Andrew than the fact that she was doing something totally out of character. At least it was playing to her favor.

"He's not sticking around long anyway. I heard he's helping a friend open a restaurant up in New York." A surprising feeling of disappointment fell upon her. How long would it be before she saw him again after that? If ever?

Mom pressed her lips together, then patted Kelly's hand. "I've always told you I thought you should go to one of those baking conventions. I know you'll come back with a hundred new ideas."

"I hope so." *Here goes nothing.*

Mom's face lit up. "Is it in Atlanta? A bunch of them are there. That would be close enough to drive! Girls' trip. Your dad could hold down things here on his own." She turned to Dad. "Right, CB?"

"Sure," he said. "Anything for my girls."

This isn't going according to plan at all. Kelly scrambled. "This one is in Orlando. They're flying me."

"Oh, darn." Mom looked genuinely disappointed, then forced a smile. "I'm really proud of you for going. You never do anything for yourself." She hugged her tight. "Which recipe?"

This was exactly why she didn't lie. "I don't even remember."

"That's so funny."

As long as you believe it, and forgive me for the string of white lies when you find out what I'm really doing. I hope I'll be laughing all the way to the bank.

She promised herself right then that if she won, she'd treat her parents to some upgrades at the diner. Mom had talked about new countertops for as many years as she could remember, but Dad was never willing to splurge on the upgrade. And for Dad, a new commercial range, like she'd splurged on for herself. It would be the best surprise ever, and that made her want to win even more.

She'd better get out of here before Mom figured out she wasn't telling the truth. "I've got to get back. I've got to finish the cake for the Barco wedding." Kelly practically ran for the door, but before she could get there, she heard her name called from across the room.

She stopped and turned. Andrew was standing there, smiling. "Hey."

She stopped and smoothed her apron. "Hey there. I was just heading back over to the bakery."

"If it's not a sight for sore eyes," her mother shouted.

Kelly stood there dumbstruck by Mom's animated response. Yes, she'd told Mom they'd had a nice visit, but that didn't change the fact that he'd broken her heart. She was her daughter. Even if Kelly was having trouble staying mad, Mom shouldn't.

Kelly watched them hug. She felt the grimace on her face as she folded her arms. She quickly replaced it with a half-baked smile.

"It's great to see you, Mrs. McIntyre."

"You look good," Mom said. "So grown up." Mom flashed her a he-did-look-good glance.

"Have a cup of coffee with me," Andrew said to Kelly.

Mom was already racing toward the empty booth next to Andrew with two mugs. "Here you go. You have a few minutes to spare, don't you, Kelly?"

"Thank you, Mrs. McIntyre. Oh man, I'm going to need a piece of that cake too."

"Of course, you are. Kelly's practically famous for that around here."

"I am not," Kelly said, rolling her eyes and sitting down. "Moms. You know how they are."

"Quit being so modest. You're the best daughter a mother could wish for," Mom said. "She just won a big contest. She's headed to the big RBA event. Flying and everything."

Guilt hung in Kelly's throat. She was tempted to tell her parents the truth and swear them to secrecy right now. But just as quickly as that thought popped into her mind, she could picture Mom whispering to every customer who ventured into the Main Street Cafe, and at church on Sunday, the secret she was sworn to keep. Yeah, it would be around town so fast she'd be disqualified before she ever got on the plane to New York.

He looked impressed. "Kelly, that's great. Why didn't you say anything?"

"It didn't come up?" She shrugged, taking a sip of her coffee and trying to act as if it was no big deal.

"My baby girl's first plane ride," Mom gushed as she slid a whopping piece of cake in front of Andrew. "It's so exciting."

"It is," he agreed. "When do you leave?"

"Tuesday." She jumped to her feet. "And I've got so much to do before I leave town. It was good to see you. Enjoy your cake." She didn't wait for a response. She rushed over to the empty teacart and raced through the door to The Cake Factory, stopping only to whisper *"Mission accomplished"* to Sara as she passed by. Sara gave her a thumbs up and continued filling a box with pastries for the customer at the counter.

Kelly closed the door to her office and plopped into her chair. It would be just like Andrew to ask so many questions that he'd trip her up. She got out of there just in the nick of time.

Glad that was all behind her, she pulled out a legal pad. She turned the pad wide and started heading columns. Signature recipes. Undisclosed ingredients. Fast but Fabulous. Showdown original.

She started going through her recipe list, trying to figure out which recipes she should cite as her signature dishes if asked. She needed two in case one of the other rounds was perfect for the other recipe. Or, even more importantly, if she learned something from a judge in a round that made one of the recipes less appealing. Maybe she needed three signature recipes in her back pocket.

Being prepared for any scenario would make things a lot less stressful. Even if it might cause her to go bonkers now.

If she made it to the final round, she'd have to use a completely original recipe. That was easy. Her Triple-Layer Honey Almond Cake with Berries was hands-down her favorite dessert to make and the one most people were impressed by. She could make it in her sleep, the perfect situation for baking under pressure. Plus, the dish lent itself to something pretty and Valentines-y with the red strawberries and toppings. A winner for sure.

Sara poked her head in following a double-knock at her office door.

"Hey, come in."

"So, mission accomplished. The RBA convention worked?"

"It did. However, I moved it to Orlando. Hopefully she won't look it up." She pulled her lips together. "How bad is it if you get caught lying about your lie? She wanted to make it a girls' trip since Atlanta is close enough to drive. I had to do something. I told her I won a contest and they're flying me down."

Sara shrugged. "If she figures it out, just claim it's an exclusive one, by invitation only."

"I'm not sure if I should be impressed or worried by how quickly you can make up a story."

Sara giggled. "Impressed. I always wanted to be a novelist. Just can't sit still long enough to type all those words."

"That explains it."

"While you were working on your cover story, I worked on a little something last night to help." Sara fanned out a pile of orders.

"What is all of that?"

"Fake orders. Things you can practice with so no one notices what you're working on. Look. I wrote all the names in purple ink and highlighted the delivery stuff in pink. That's our code that they're fake orders just in case they end up lying around or fall into the wrong hands."

"This is a real battle plan." She nodded, impressed by the effort. "You've thought of everything."

"Trying to help. I made them tough too. So, good luck."

"I'm so ready. Bring it on."

Sara flipped through them. "Ahh. This one. Okay…you've got two hours. Go for it." She dropped the fake order on the desk and left Kelly scrambling. "The clock is ticking."

Chapter Eighteen

THE LONG BLASTS FROM THE oven timer pulled Kelly from her concentration on the four three-tiered mini cakes she'd just finished. With a *Red Hots* theme, she hoped the chocolate cinnamon combination held in proper balance once the frosting had been added.

She swept the back of her hand across her forehead, pushing her bangs from her face, then put down her piping bag.

Sara rushed in, shouting, "Time's up. Step away from the dishes."

"I'm ready," Kelly said. Lacing her fingers, she gave them a good stretch. It was crazy how this competition changed everything. If anyone had asked her just one week ago what her three best recipes were, she'd have rattled them off without hesitation. But now with all this on the line and knowing hundreds of thousands of viewers nationwide would be watching, she found herself constantly second guessing what the judges might like best.

She took a knife from the drawer and sliced a sliver of a wedge from one of the pretty cakes she'd just plated. The combination of the red frosting between the dark chocolate layers was flawless, and the white frosting on top was the perfect consistency, still holding its peaks. She inhaled the scent. Sweet and spicy. *So far, so good.* She took a bite, hoping for the best—the flavors mingled in a delicious union. She closed her eyes and smiled. *Nailed it.*

"Try it, Judge Sara," Kelly said, barely being able to hold her enthusiasm.

Sara pushed her fork into the cake and took a bite. "Oh. My. Goodness. This is amazing. I hope you wrote down this recipe."

"I'm going to. It is good, isn't it?"

"Too good." Sara took another bite. "Oh, yeah. Those cinnamon candies are perfect in the dark chocolate. Just enough spice."

Kelly relaxed. "It's anybody's guess what'll be thrown our way. It could be something as classy as an award ceremony dessert or a two-year-old's Halloween party."

"I think it's safe to say since it's the Valentine's Day show that it won't be Halloween, but it could be a kid's Valentine's challenge. We hadn't really brainstormed about that. Like the funny cards we all used to exchange in elementary school."

"True. Or it could be a timed event for something in an hour. You know hard that is."

"I saw one episode where they had liquid nitrogen cool things in a hurry."

"You're right. I remember that. I hope that's available." It wasn't going to do her any good to worry over things she had no control over. "I'm just going to have to trust they will."

"It's going to be fine," Sara reassured her. "Even ninety minutes is hard when it comes to cooling the cake long enough to do good work with the frosting and decoration. I bet they have all kinds of behind-the-scenes stuff going on. They'd have to, working under all those stage lights and everything."

"True. I've got to be ready for anything."

"You already are," Sara said. "This competition was made for you."

"I don't want to get caught flat-footed. I studied pastry terms online last night so I'd know what they were talking about if they threw any of that high-falutin' talk my way."

"Hadn't thought about that. They do that sometimes. Crème fraîche and all that."

"Right. We make that stuff, but we never call it that. I don't want to look silly."

Sara put her hands on Kelly's shoulders. "You won't. Don't try to be what you think they want you to be. Just be you. You're deserving of this opportunity. The only person worried about your lack of formal training is you. I promise you that."

"I hope you're right," Kelly said.

"You know desserts better than anyone, and you do sweet and savory all the time," Sara said. "It's why we have customers all over the nation. Something for everyone."

"I can do this," she said, trying to believe it.

"You've totally got this. Trust yourself. You know, you could sell these."

"Good plan." Kelly picked up a red marker and a bakery case card from the baker's rack and wrote Cupid's Red Hot Chocolate Cake. She lined up the other three cakes onto a narrow baking sheet and carried them out to the front case.

Kelly opened the case and slid the tray into place, then slipped the sign into the shiny metal clip.

"Those are beautiful." Mrs. Thompson, the town librarian, peered over her hot pink readers.

"Thank you. It's a brand-new recipe." Kelly caught the grin on Sara's face. "Thought I'd test out some new ones for the holiday."

"Add one of those to my order," Mrs. Thompson said. "And four forks. They're simply gorgeous. If they're even half as good as they look, they'll be to die for."

Kelly boxed up the cake, and then there were two.

They waved to Mrs. Thompson as she left.

"I thought I'd given you a challenge, but you handled that like nothing," Sara said. "I'd better up the difficulty on those orders I wrote up."

"Pickles. Sushi. Dirt!" Kelly rolled her eyes. "Okay, not dirt, but you know what I mean. Maybe edible flowers. And don't go easy. I mean crazy stuff. You've seen the show."

"I have. Okay, that's going to be challenging, but I can do that. I'll try to think of the toughest one I've seen them do, and flip it on its head."

"Great." Kelly grabbed two small buckets from the shelf—one red and one pink. "You can put the challenges in the pink bucket. And the random items in the red one. Then I'll just blindly pick one from each bucket and go for it."

"We only have two days." Sara grabbed a small mixing bowl and set it next to the buckets. "I'll put time frames in here. We'll do an hour, ninety minutes, or unlimited."

"Yes! That's a great idea." Kelly hugged Sara. "Thanks for putting up with me through all of this. I know I'm being a pain."

"Are you kidding? If I were in your shoes, I'd be one hot mess. You're just trying to be prepared, and I'm happy to help any way I can." Sara grabbed a notebook and pen. "I'm going to go back out front, but I already have an idea for the first challenge. Are you ready for it?"

"I hope so." Kelly slid the half-eaten cake to the side. "Whatever we bake that tastes good, we'll put in the case as a special."

"I think the customers will enjoy seeing your innovations. And they can always go next door to the cafe to get the good old standby flavors you always bake."

"Exactly. Okay. Good." She widened her stance and gestured to Sara. "I'm ready. Bring it on."

Sara held up a finger. "Baked dessert. Whatever you like."

"Easy."

"But…" She held up two fingers. "Your dessert must include

both of these ingredients. Old Bay seasoning and figs." Holding up three fingers. "You have forty-five minutes. Go!" She dropped her arm down to her side as if starting a race.

"Do we even have any Old Bay?"

Sara laughed. "Only because I picked some up at the store today for home. It's with my stuff. I'll bring that for you while you raid the pantry."

"Oh, man. Game on!" Kelly started the timer on the oven, and then raced to the stock room to gather ingredients. Hopefully the pantry on set would be close to the kitchen. Then again, she knew where everything was in her pantry. That would be a whole other challenge there. She'd eat up a good seven minutes just getting what she needed back to her kitchen here.

Kelly ran back into the kitchen with items on the rolling cart. She'd even grabbed a couple of extra things, still trying to come up with the dessert she'd make.

Racing against the clock, she shot a glance at the oven timer. She set the oven temperature to 350F. A safe temperature for just about anything.

She decided to go with something that would tickle the memories of whoever ate it. A savory twist on sweet potato pie. She went to work, encouraged by the preliminary tastes. She'd just plated the desserts and was dabbing whipped frosting stars to the top of each one when Sara got back.

Sara waved a flour sack towel in the air. "Time!" And just as she said it, the oven timer began to ping.

Kelly stepped back from the table and raised her hands in the air. "Got it!" Four dessert plates were filled with identical pastries. Picture perfect.

"Okay, let's see how you did." Sara lifted one of the plates and smelled it. "That Old Bay has a distinctive smell, doesn't it?"

"Yes. I hope I got the ratios right. It's either going to be amazing or awful."

"Explain what you've brought to us today," Sara said, doing her best Martin Schlipshel impression.

"I've made for you a savory twist on a fall favorite, sweet potato pie. I think the spicy Old Bay and sweetness of the sweet potato make for a light and wonderful accompaniment for summer seafood boils."

"Nice." She lifted a bite to her mouth, taking her time with a reaction.

"Come on already!"

"Well..." She looked to the ceiling, then took another bite before smiling broadly. "This is really good."

"You had me going there for a minute. The batter tasted good. Let me try it." She reached for a bite of the one Sara had set back down on the plate.

Sara smacked her away. "Get your own!"

"That's an excellent sign," Kelly said. "You never mind sharing with me." She grabbed one of the other plates and held it up, taking the time to smell it and touch it, looking for any flaw. Then she sliced it in half. The pie looked moist and held its shape. Finally, she took a bite. "This is surprisingly good. Why haven't I ever tried that before?"

"I don't know, but it's another keeper."

"I'll write it down before I forget." Kelly grabbed for a pen and paper.

"Can you imagine how good these would be with a low country boil out on the deck in the summer? You should send a box of these to Ned and Hailey for their Bed & Breakfast housewarming in Sand Dollar Cove next weekend since you won't be here."

"You'll have to take them for me. Did you see the pictures of the kitchen? I'd pay to cook there."

"I'm sure they'd let you cook for free," Sara teased.

"Wouldn't it be fun to do beach theme mini cakes? Oh gosh, and we could do kind of a sweet-salty, like the margarita cupcakes or salted caramel ones. And shells, starfish, even maybe some colorful flip-flops out of fondant on the top. It would be so cute."

"See? That's why you are going to win this thing. Hands down. There's no one better than you at this stuff. You're so creative."

"Don't jinx me."

"I'm not. I'm spreading good vibes." Sara skipped around as if tossing fairy dust. "Acting as if it's already happened. Don't you know the difference?"

"Apparently not."

Sara grabbed a whisk from the white stoneware crock and held it up to her mouth. "And introducing the winner of this round of Pastry Practice," she said in an exaggerated TV host voice. "The grand prize? The right to make me more fabulous treats to try, even though I'm going to have to double my visits to the gym next week!"

"Now to round two," Kelly said.

"I've already filled your buckets with ideas." Sara glanced at her watch. "I'm out of here for the day. Good luck with practice. I can't wait to see what you came up with when I come back to work in the morning."

"Me too." Kelly watched Sara leave. She was lucky to have such a good friend. It was perfect that she'd been here when the folks from the show had come. If she'd had to keep this news totally to herself, she'd have burst for sure by now.

It had been a busy work day, but even with the steady stream of customers and more than enough to keep her busy, Kelly's mind had wandered way too many times back to Andrew. She had a lot more important things on her plate than an old flame. Especially one who'd broken her heart. She wished he'd just leave town already.

She was able to try out another challenge after she closed for the night. With nothing better than baking to do on a Saturday evening, Kelly went to her office and pulled a challenge from the pink bucket to get her mind off Andrew. "Just my luck." The challenge she pulled was for a wedding mini cake.

She was tempted to pull another one instead, but if she could pull this off while she was trying not to think about Andrew, she could work under any pressure.

She pulled an obstacle from the red bucket.

"Peas?"

Sara was taking this challenge seriously. She could easily hide peas by mixing them into the batter, but how she integrated them was as important as just getting them into the recipe. And the judges were always less than pleased when an ingredient disappeared into the recipe and they couldn't taste them or recognize them at all.

She took a baggie and let herself into the cafe next door. Thank goodness everyone had gone home for the night. She went into the walk-in freezer and scooped a bag full of frozen peas, then went back to the bakery, feeling like a thief in the night.

She set the timer and got to work. She made the cakes and put them in the oven. That left twenty-seven minutes to get them cooled, frosted, and decorated before time was up.

She dropped the cakes in the deep freeze and got to work on the fillings.

Working as fast as she could, she made a batch of raspberry filling and another of chocolate. Then she swirled interlocking hearts on wax paper out of the white chocolate she'd colored with edible silver to use as cake toppers.

While the cake toppers hardened, Kelly took the cakes out and alternated sweet centers between the layers as she stacked them. Fondant was pretty, but in a hurry it could end up looking bad. A good thing to practice. Besides, she knew she could crumb coat and frost like a champ in a hurry with no problem.

She rolled out the fondant, then draped it over the tiered cakes. It laid smooth and perfect. She piped tiny thin vines of green ivy around the cake, then dunked the small green peas in shimmery edible silver glaze. She crossed her fingers and popped one into her mouth. "So good!"

Tickled with how they looked and tasted, she placed them around the bottom edge of each tiny cake to create an edible pearl-like ridge. Time was running out on the clock. She raced to the freezer and grabbed the cake toppers, popping them one by one on top.

The timer sounded, and she stopped and stepped back from the counter.

When all was said and done, she'd turned out four beautiful mini wedding cakes. Given a few more minutes, she'd have done a design on the plates to give it more of a finished look, but these were beautiful.

Chapter Nineteen

THE NEXT MORNING, RIGHT AFTER church, Kelly went straight to the bakery and took the baking sheet with the mini wedding cakes, and a pile of leftover edible decorations, aka silver chocolate peas, out to the bakery case.

"Good morning," Mom called out as she came through the rarely used door between the two businesses.

Kelly stopped mid-stride, feeling as caught as the day Mom had found her feeding cooked carrots to the dog under the table.

"Those are lovely," Mom remarked. "Bridal shower?"

Oh, how she'd love to lie and say yes. But only four? That would never fly. "No, ma'am. Just some samples for a client coming in tomorrow."

"I love the border around the bottom. So unique." Then her face brightened. "How'd you make them so perfectly round?" She pointed a manicured nail toward the pile of large silvered dots.

"Actually, I stole those out of your freezer last night on a whim. They're peas dipped in dairy-free dark chocolate and airbrushed with a silver glaze."

"Peas?" Mom looked at her like she'd lost her ever-loving mind.

Kelly flushed. "Yes. The bride is a very picky eater. Vegan. You know the type."

"Oh, heavens. I'm surprised she's even having a cake." Mom was teasing of course, being gluten-free and a vegan herself.

"A compromise, I'm sure."

Mom smiled gently. "When it's true love, compromise is easy."

The last thing she needed right now was a lecture on love. "Want to try one of the peas?"

She waved her hand. "I think I'll pass."

"Oh, come on. Let me know what you think." She lifted the tray in front of her face.

Mom picked one up like it was going to explode, hesitating before she put it in her mouth.

"Mom. Come on. Don't be so dramatic. I'd never serve something that tasted awful. You know me better than that."

"You're right." Her mom put the chocolate-covered pea in her mouth. With the pea still balanced on her tongue, she said, "You al-eady as-ed un, ight?"

Deciphering her words, she realized Mom was asking if she'd tasted one. "Of course I tasted one. You know I taste everything I bake. What are you doing?"

"Trying to forget it's a pea," she said in that open-mouth pea dialect.

"Stop it, Mom."

Finally she closed her mouth and chewed.

"Oh, gosh." Her eyebrows shot up. "This is really good. You'd never even know it was a pea. Let me have another one of those." She plucked one from the tray. "I like these. A healthy snack. You could probably just sell little bags of these."

"I'd say that's a win," Kelly said.

The front door of the bakery opened, and Andrew strode in. Before she could say a word, Mom was around the counter in front of him.

"Hi, Andrew. What are you doing here? Having a snack attack this early in the day?" Kelly asked.

"I was actually going to see if I could buy you lunch this afternoon." He shrugged, looking hopeful.

"I can't. I've got a lot to do."

"That's why I came early. So you could work it into your schedule. Even if you're busy, you have to eat."

Mom gave her a look of disapproval. What was she thinking? "Kelly, you should make him taste one of those peas."

"Peas?" Andrews's lips curled. "For breakfast?"

"Chocolate-dipped. I used them as decoration on a vegan dessert." Which probably sounded ridiculous to him.

Mom grabbed his arm. "They're so good. A little freaky when you know what they are, but so tasty."

She dragged Andrew closer to the bakery case.

Andrew said, "I don't know. That sounds like one of those crazy cable network food challenges."

A tingle of delight coursed through her. *Exactly what I was going for.*

Dad stormed into the room, muttering under his breath, "Of all the days. Kelly, I need to use one of your ovens. Ours is on the fritz. Again. And Colby is out of town. Wouldn't you know his sister would have to go and have her baby today?"

"How dare she," Kelly teased. "And on a Sunday."

"Hey, Mr. McIntyre," Andrew said. "What's going on with the oven?"

"Andrew?" CB laid the casserole pan on the counter, then walked over and cuffed him on the shoulder. "I didn't even notice you standing there. Good to see you. I heard you were in town. I guess you're a big-time chef now."

"Never would've happened without the start you gave me."

CB beamed. "You always were a great cook. Dependable too. Not like that oven. It's so temperamental these days. It's getting tired, like me."

"Why don't you let me see if I can fix it?"

"I couldn't ask you to do that. You're a fancy chef now."

"I'm still Andrew, and still handy. Let me see what I can do."

"That would be great. If you don't mind. I know you're only in town for a short time. I'm sure you've got things to do."

"Not a problem at all. I have a free afternoon, and your daughter just turned me down for lunch. Come on." Andrew followed CB back to the diner.

Kelly stood there steaming.

Mom turned and grinned. "I think he still cares about you."

"He's just being nice. Old friends. Don't push." Andrew York was a distraction Kelly couldn't afford right now.

"Wouldn't hurt you to be polite. You sounded like a grump."

"I did not." But even her tone just then sounded grumpy to her.

Mom shrugged. "Let's put this casserole in the oven for Dad. That old stove needed to be replaced a year ago. We've spent more fixing it than a new one would've cost."

Kelly didn't doubt it. Dad was frugal about stuff like that, wanting to get every last mile out of things. She preheated the oven to three hundred fifty degrees. "Forty-five minutes."

"That should do it."

"I'll bring it over when it's done," Kelly said.

Mom grabbed a handful of the vegan-friendly chocolate-covered pea rejects and left.

When Dad's famous corn casserole was done, she pulled it out of the oven, perfectly browned and bubbling on top. She let it cool long enough that she could carry it next door without burning herself.

The diner was a hive of activity. Plates clanked, and customers chatted over the first meal of the day. The smell of coffee permeated the air. She nodded hellos to neighbors as she walked between the tables with the covered dish.

The waitresses zipped to the order window and back out to the customers. Kenny was working the flat top in the kitchen with a row of order tickets hanging on the rack above him. She laid the casserole on the line counter.

It took her back to hear Andrew and Dad's voices in the kitchen.

"It's the thermocouple. I'm surprised you haven't had to replace that before," Andrew said. "They go out all the time."

"If it had, I'd have known what to look for."

Andrew stood and handed Dad the part. "If you find one locally, I'll be happy to install it for you."

Dad picked up the phone and made a call. "They've got the part." He must've noticed her standing there. "Hey, princess."

"Hi, Daddy. I put the casserole over there on the line counter. Did y'all figure out the problem?"

"Andrew did."

"That's great. What can I do to help until you get it fixed?" she asked.

"Could you go pick up the part for me?"

"Sure. Where is it?"

She could tell by the look on Dad's face it wasn't up the street.

"Is it in Raleigh?" *That would be my luck.*

"No. It's just over in Jarvis. Shouldn't take you too long. Here's the address." He handed her his credit card and the address on a slip of paper. "Thanks for saving me the trip."

She kissed him on the cheek. "Anything for you, Daddy."

"Thanks, Andrew. I owe you big time for this."

"Don't mention it. I'll go with her," he said, then turned to Kelly. "To make sure they give you the right thermocouple."

She wouldn't know a thermocouple from a thingamabob. No sense risking getting the wrong part and having to go back.

Andrew must've sensed her hesitation. "If it's okay with you."

"Of course. Let's go."

He washed his hands, then dug his hand into his pocket for his keys. "I'll drive."

"We'll be back shortly," she said, heading out of the diner with an extra skip to her step because he was going with her.

The bright yellow Mustang was parked right at the curb. She buckled her seatbelt and then put the address in her phone.

When he got in, she said, "This really is a nice car."

"It handles great too," he said, stepping on the gas to prove it. "I'm kind of impressed."

"What do you drive back in France?"

"A Lexus LC." He took the sunglasses from the console and put them on.

"That sounds expensive."

"It's my one extravagance since my great aunt insists I stay with her. I went a little wild on the lease of a fancy car."

"That sounds fun. Do you have a picture of it?"

"Sure." He pulled his phone out of his pocket and scrolled through the pictures.

"Not while we're driving," she said.

He handed her the phone. "Quit worrying."

"It's against the law to text and drive."

"I wasn't texting. I was looking for a picture."

"Same thing." The car was parked in front of a pretty white house with lots of flowers in front. "Nice. It looks fast sitting still. Is this in front of your aunt's house?"

"Mm-hmm. In front of the carriage house."

If she'd gone to Paris, she'd have been living in that pretty little place.

"What are you thinking?"

She moistened her lips. "Just how different your life must be there."

"What do you see next for yourself?" he asked.

"Wow. Good question. I think I'm doing everything I want with the business. I'd like to just continue to create a strong brand that'll solidify the jobs in Bailey's Fork. Stay on top of the trends. Maybe start spending some time going to some of the trade conventions. Travel a little."

"Do you still want kids someday?"

"Can't do that alone."

"You can. People do it all the time."

"I'd never. Besides, I have Gray. He's like having a permanent toddler in the house." But that wasn't entirely true. "I would like to have children of my own someday. It would be nice to have a family, and someone to carry on the business I've worked so hard to build."

Andrew nodded. "That makes sense."

"How about you? We used to always talk about having children as part of the plan."

"We did. I always thought that was a sure thing, but then I got busy, and I haven't thought about it much. Maybe with the right person." He turned and held her gaze.

"Right. The right partner is key. There are too many children in split homes these days. I'd never want that for my child."

"No one sets out to end up that way," he said.

"I know, but it seems like people quit easier these days too." No sooner had the words come out of her mouth did she find herself judging her own past actions. Just today, Mom was talking about how compromise was easy when you were in love. Had Kelly not been in real love? Or had she just given up too soon?

He'd gotten quiet too, but there was no way she was going to ask what he was thinking about.

She glanced down at her phone. "Turn left two miles ahead, then the building is on your right."

For the rest of the ride, there was an awkward silence. She stared out the window, but twice when she looked in the reflection of the side glass, she caught him looking at her, too.

"Here we are." He pulled into the parking lot of Carolina

Restaurant Equipment & Service, which took up nearly half of the warehouse-sized brick building.

They walked inside. It was even bigger than it appeared from outside. Rows and rows of appliances and equipment lined up under bright lights, taking up one side of the store. Just inside the door was the parts department, and rows of other supplies like linens and china.

"CB McIntyre called in about a part for Main Street Diner," Andrew said.

"Yes, he sure did. I've got it right here." The bearded man put the box on the counter. "You got lucky. It's not something we usually stock. I'd ordered it for another fellow, then he went and bought a new oven instead."

"That's probably exactly what my dad should be doing," Kelly said. Hopefully she'd win that competition and be able to buy him one.

Andrew compared the one in his hand with the one in the box. "Yes. This is the right one. Thank you."

The man rang up the sale, and Kelly paid with the credit card.

"I wish we hadn't been in such a big hurry," she said. "That looked like a neat store to browse around in. I can't believe I never even knew it was here."

"We could have wasted a day in there."

"Easily," she agreed.

As they walked back out to the car, Andrew said, "I should have your dad back and baking in no time."

"Thanks for looking at the oven. I really appreciate it."

He studied her. "I didn't do it for you. I did it for him." He got in the car. "Your dad wasn't only my boss when I worked at the diner. He was my mentor. I have a ton of respect for him. I'd do anything to help him out."

She'd never even considered that. "That's really kind of you."

"I'm a little put out that you're surprised."

"I'm sorry. I didn't mean to insult you."

He started the car and drove away. "I'm not insulted, really. I shouldn't have said what I did. I probably did do this a little bit because of you too. I did want to spend time with you."

As they crossed the county line back into Bailey's Fork, Andrew said, "I noticed the new fancy sign when I came in the other day. Is that our tree on it?"

The artsy rendering of a huge pine tree was encircled by pine roping and a pinecone border with *Welcome to Bailey's Fork* in forest-green and gold writing. Bragging rights of the tallest loblolly pine in the Carolinas and Established in 1801 scrawled across the bottom.

"It's not *our* tree. It's a landmark."

"Well, our names are on it. My heart used to race when I saw you standing under that tree waiting for me. The prettiest girl in town."

She didn't respond.

About two miles up the road, he pulled over on the side of the road.

"What's the matter?" she asked.

He turned off the car and turned in his seat to face her. "These past couple of days, have you thought at all about how things might've been if we'd stayed together seven years ago?"

"What kind of question is that?"

"That's not an answer."

She sat there, looking into his eyes. They held as many questions as hers did. "I have. I've wondered for seven years."

"I've never met anyone who made me feel the way you did. The way you still do. What about that 'if you love someone let them go' quote? Maybe there was a reason we were apart for a while."

"There was. You chose to pursue education and a career in another country instead of marrying me."

"That's not exactly how it was."

"Fine. I'll give you the benefit of the doubt. You may have only planned to go for a while, but in the end…you didn't come back."

"If I stayed, could we try to explore things between us?"

Her mind reeled. "You know I'm going out of town. I couldn't if I wanted to."

"But would you want to?"

"I can't think about this right now."

He took her hand in his and rubbed it. An unfair move. He knew how she loved having her hands massaged.

It was nice. She should pull her hand back and insist he take her home, but she didn't.

"You have somewhere you have to be too. Why are you asking an impossible question?"

"I'll cancel my trip to stay if it means I can have a second chance with you." His voice was soft. His eyes held hers.

"Andrew, this is crazy." But her heart wanted it too. "You've been gone seven years. You haven't even been back seven days."

"I know what I'm feeling." He lifted her hand to his heart. "I know it right here."

A single tear slid down her cheek. She didn't sweep it away, hoping he wouldn't notice. "This is all happening too fast. I don't know what I'm feeling." But she did know. Only the price of another heartbreak was more than she could risk.

"I'm sorry. I didn't mean to upset you. I know it's fast. Sudden. Crazy, maybe, but I couldn't leave without at least talking to you about what I know is in my heart. I'll stay longer."

"I'm leaving Tuesday," she said. She couldn't set her dreams aside for him. If she stayed she might lose both—the contest, which could mean the validation she'd wanted for so long, *and* him. "I don't know what to say. It's been too long. We've changed." The words seemed harsh, even to her. She opened the car door and got out wishing she hadn't said it. She mustered the strength to not take it back. "Thanks for helping Dad with the oven." Her lips trembled.

"You're welcome."

After he dropped her off, she hurried to the refuge of her shop, went to her office, and closed the door. In a way, Andrew York was responsible for all of this. She'd been so hurt, so angry, that she'd set out to prove she could make her dreams come true without him. The only thing missing had been him. She rubbed her temples. And for seven years, *good riddance Andrew York* had been her motto. She closed her eyes, her chest aching, unsure if what her heart yearned for could ever be true.

Chapter Twenty

T HE WHOLE TIME ANDREW WORKED on the oven at Main Street café, he'd hoped Kelly might show up and say something. Maybe she'd invite him to go with her, or at least ask him to stay until she got back. That didn't happen.

She didn't say she didn't have feelings too.

That has to mean something.

Monday came around a lot faster than he'd expected. He'd been worried when he scheduled the trip that he'd be chomping at the bit to get out of this little town, but that hadn't been the case.

He packed his suitcase, knowing he should be excited about the opportunities this New York trip could present, but honestly he'd have chucked it all to stay and give it a go with Kelly, had she given him an inkling of hope.

He zipped up his bag and rolled it toward the front door. Mom and Dad were talking in the kitchen. He left his suitcase at the door.

"Good morning. What are you still doing home, Dad? I thought you'd already be at work," he said.

"Couldn't let you leave without saying goodbye."

"I'd have stopped by to say goodbye. I promise."

"Now you won't have to," Dad said. "Your mom's making us a

nice breakfast. A family meal before you head out. Your sister is on the way."

"Sister is right here." Dawn announced as she came into the kitchen. "On time, even."

"Now this is a celebration," Andrew teased.

Breakfast was good, and Andrew was finding it hard to say goodbye.

"I guess I'd better get on the road."

Dad put his plate in the sink then gave Mom a kiss on the cheek. After over forty years of marriage, they still looked like they had that spark. Now that was special. He'd never thought much about how Mom and Dad got along. Dad was opinionated, and he had a lot of rules, but somehow the two of them had always seemed happy. There were never any arguments between them. She supported his dreams, and he supported hers, even putting up with all the horses when he didn't even ride.

Will I ever have that? Would there ever be anyone other than Kelly who really got him? Someone who understood his hopes and dreams the way she had? Had he missed out on the only true chance of happiness that he'd be offered in this lifetime?

The corner of Mom's mouth lifted, but her lips pulled tight, like she might cry. "I couldn't be happier." She clutched her heart. "This has been a long time coming—the two of you being civil again. I didn't think I'd ever see the day. All of us together for a meal, and it isn't even a holiday. See, sometimes things that seem impossible just take an open mind, and an open heart." She patted Andrew on the back. "Think about that. Anything is possible."

"You're right. I'm sorry I let it go on so long." He stepped over and gave her a hug.

"I can't believe you're already going," she said. "It's been so nice having you around."

"I'm really glad I came back." This trip had offered unexpected benefits. He looked over at his dad, his heart filled with pride. "I promise I won't stay away so long again."

"I hope not," Dad said.

Andrew hugged Dawn, then grabbed his suitcase and stepped out onto the porch.

"And drive careful," Dad said.

"Yes, sir. I was just checking on the weather," Andrew said. "Looks like things have cleared out since you came through Pennsylvania."

"Good. That was a mess. Text or call when you get to where you're stopping."

Mom jumped in. "Yes, please let us know you're okay."

"I can do that." He hugged Mom, then Dad. "Thank you both for everything. I love you."

They stood on the front porch, waving, as he put his suitcase in the car.

He pulled out of the driveway with an extraordinary void in his chest.

Andrew took the back roads toward Main Street, hoping he might catch another glimpse of Kelly walking Gray across the street like that first day he'd hit town. Customers were coming out of The Cake Factory when he drove by. He could picture Kelly standing behind the counter, a relaxed smile on her face as she greeted them.

He took a quick right and drove around the block. He had plenty of time to stop and say goodbye to the McIntyres and to Kelly. He slowed along the curb, then decided against it. He could send flowers, or a card instead. Maybe call while he was in New York after she got back from her trip. Valentine's Day was next week. Maybe Cupid would help him out.

He stopped and filled up his gas tank. As the gallons clicked off on the pump, he stared at the cars going by. There was a lot more activity in this town these days.

Rather than take the ramp up the street to get onto the

interstate, he took a left. There was one more place he wanted to stop before he left Bailey's Fork.

He timed the drive. Only seventeen minutes from the center of town.

The parking lot had seen better days. The asphalt was cracked, and dead grass had made its home there. He pulled in front of the Fresh Strawberries sign and shut down the motor.

This May, these acres would be lush and green and filled with ripe, red strawberries. Perfect for Kelly's Honey Almond Cake. He wondered if she bought fresh strawberries here.

He got out of the car and started walking. It was well over a football field-length to the barn. The outside was faded, but the pole barn structure was built to withstand time. Inside, the boards and beams were hefty, and sturdy. He stepped off the length and width, then climbed the ladder up into the hayloft. The double-doors in the loft had blown open at some point. The warped wood held them in place. From here the view was breathtaking. Tall pines lined the back of the property line, the brown-barked trunks skying to those deep-green needles gave the graying winter landscape hope.

He sat there in the loft, with his feet dangling out of the doors, feeling small against the vast backdrop. Kelly had given that old factory a second life, which in turn gave the town and its people a better life. Her success inspired him. For the first time, he was beginning to think how his skills, his talents, could be used to do more than give him a very comfortable salary and bragging rights.

His phone rang, breaking the silence. He dug it from his front pocket to see who was calling. Francois, again. He inhaled deeply, then sent the call to voice mail.

Andrew sat there for a long time; there was a fair amount of traffic that went down the road in front of this property in both directions.

He climbed down and walked back to his car, taking the route past the industrial park to the I-85 ramp in neighboring Farm City.

When Andrew got to Pennsylvania, snow had begun to fall. But at least it wasn't an all-out snowstorm like what his dad had driven through last week. Andrew's mind was still replaying the week. As he thought about the barn and the property his father had offered him, he remembered the phone call he'd ignored. He played the voice mail over the car speaker. Francois' voice boomed through the car. Had he ever heard Francois speak kindly of someone? Had he ever really said a heartfelt thank you the whole time Andrew had worked for him? The man was a genius in his field, there was no arguing that, but to be so celebrated as a chef doing what he'd always wanted, he sure didn't seem that happy.

There was nothing Andrew could do to change that. Even if he'd been back in Paris to defuse the situation of the day, Francois would only be bellowing about something else.

Wide awake, he decided to drive the last couple of hours into the city. On the plus side, at this time of night the traffic would be clear. He stopped for fuel and a cup of coffee to finish the trip. Took an extra minute to text his folks and let them know he was going to make the drive the rest of the way in tonight so they wouldn't worry.

The GPS took him right to the front steps of the hotel. He valeted his rental car and went inside.

"Good evening, I'm Andrew York," he said to the young lady behind the VIP Guest Services counter. "I was supposed to be here in the morning. I hope you have a room for me tonight. I drove straight through."

"No problem. We've been expecting you," she said in a hushed tone.

Why did he suddenly feel like he was on a secret mission, waiting on his orders and decoder ring??

"This is a...unique building," he said, taking in all of the stainless steel accents.

She glanced back at the clock. "Do you have a car?"

"I do." He handed her the valet ticket.

"Welcome to the Big Apple." She picked up a stack of papers and leaned over the counter. "Lucky for you, you won't have to drive yourself around again for the rest of your trip."

"That'll be nice."

"If you have a rental, we can get that returned for you if you like. No sense paying for it if you won't be using it. We have a free shuttle to take you back to the airport when you're done. I'm Gia, and I'll be your contact here at the hotel while you're filming."

"Thank you. That would be great."

"Is the rental agreement in the car?"

"In the console."

"That's all I need." She phoned the valet and arranged for the car to be returned while he stood there. "Any credit will go back to the card you used when you reserved it." She typed something into the computer. "Okay, Andrew, production is taking care of your stay, so I won't need anything from you except a form of identification."

He handed over his driver's license.

She typed in the details and slid it back to him. "Now, Lori will be your assistant for the show. Here's a packet of information she left for you." Gia handed him a bright orange letter-sized envelope with his name and room number on it. "If you'll just dial 18622 in the morning after eleven, she'll come over and get you all squared away."

"Thank you, Gia."

"Elevators to your left. Eighteenth floor."

He turned to leave.

"Oh," she said. "Good luck."

When he got to his room, he dropped his bag and turned in a

circle. "Holy cow. Mom would die if she saw this." He opened the curtain. The suite overlooked the hustle and bustle of the streets below. "I'm in New York City." With a fist pump, he spun around. "Amazing."

He unpacked his clothes and put all his things away. No sense acting like he was a temporary around here. He'd learned a long time ago that if he acted as if he'd already succeeded, he would. "I've got this."

The bed looked so inviting with the piles of stark-white linens. He took a quick shower and then climbed between the crisp sheets.

When he woke up, it was almost noon. He ripped back the blackout curtains to huge snowflakes falling, but they didn't seem to slow the traffic below.

He got dressed and dialed 18622. "Good morning, Lori. This is Andrew."

"Hello, Andrew. I'm so glad you made it in okay. I've got the adjoining room. Can I come over?"

"Absolutely."

He hung up the phone and met a blonde about his age at his door. "Come on in." He stepped out of the way and let the door close as he followed her into the sitting room of the suite.

"Not sure you've had time to really look around yet, but you'll notice a couple of things missing. No phone. No regular television. There's a long list of On Demand you can watch, though."

"I hadn't even noticed. No television? I'm here for a television show. What's that all about?"

"Just part of the sequestering process. I don't make the rules. I just make sure you follow them. It's just a few days. No one usually minds."

Lori's accent was southern, but more like Texas than the coast. "I'm fine with it. Just wondering. So this sequester thing, I thought that was hype for the show."

"Oh, it's the real deal. Hand over your cell phone." She put out her hand.

"But I might need to take a call."

"That's where this comes in handy." She took a form out of her leather portfolio. "Fill this out. Anything you deem as possibly critical should be noted here. Phone calls, or any other social media or messaging that might come through, like your parents, a girlfriend, boss, whatever, just list the important ones."

"I don't know the phone numbers. They're in the phone I just handed you."

"List them as they'll come up on the phone. I'll have it on me at all times."

He cut his eyes in her direction. "I'm not sure I like this."

"It's only a few days. Seriously, it's not that big of a deal. If any of those calls or texts come through, I'll help you screen through them and respond."

She was bossy for a little thing. "This is crazy," he said as he wrote down Francois Dumont on the list.

"It was spelled out in the contract you signed."

He wasn't really expecting a call from his parents or sister, but he added them to the list for good measure. "I didn't read the contract that close."

"I bet you cashed that first check with no problem."

That was true. He'd deposited it without a second thought. Since he was using his stacked-up vacation time, his time away was like getting a bonus with the stipend the show offered. He'd come out ahead—win or lose. "What else did I sign up for?"

"Guess you'll know when it happens," she said with a playful wink. "Don't worry. I'll have your back every step of the way."

"I'm all yours," he said, flirting a little more than was probably appropriate.

"Yeah, and strictly business. I'm here to help you stay on time, follow the rules, and hopefully win. Got that?"

He stifled a laugh. She was way too mouthy for him anyway. "Yes, ma'am." He playfully saluted her.

"We don't have to go to set until tomorrow, but if you'd like to check out the kitchen, I can arrange to take you over."

"I'd like that very much."

"I thought you might." She made a call to the producer. "Hi, yes, it's Lori. I'd like a time slot to bring Andrew over to see his kitchen on the Four Square set. Great, we'll be right over." She put her phone in her purse. "I'm just going to grab a couple of things, and I'll meet you in the hall in ten minutes?"

She left, and he rubbed his hands together. "Here we go."

He changed into a fresh shirt and went searching for his phone, almost in a panic until he remembered he'd had to hand it over. That was going to take some getting used to.

When he stepped out into the hall, Lori was already waiting for him. He liked people who were punctual. They went downstairs, and the doorman tipped his hat. "Miss Lori. Good to see you again. Your car is here."

"Thanks." She must've caught the look on his face, because she said, "I'm here all the time for the show."

The limousine was very nice. It still had that new leather smell. He could get used to this. A DVD of the Four Square Cooking Show ran on the flat-screen television. Someday somebody else would be riding in this limo, watching him on that show. His mouth pulled into a grin. Hard to believe.

He settled back into the seat, watching the people move along the sidewalks as if they were in a hurry.

Whoever had nominated him for this show, he owed them big, because he could get used to being treated like this!

The limo pulled to a stop.

"Hang on a sec," Lori said as she dialed her phone. "We're here. Thanks, see you shortly." She hung up and tucked her phone into her purse. The driver came around and opened the door for them.

He let Lori slide out first, then followed behind her.

The inside of the building had an industrial look to it, kind of minimalist and modern. Frosted glass doors blocked the view of most everything down the wide corridor. People were moving booms and cameras with purpose. A brunette wearing all purple sauntered by. Andrew nudged Lori. "Was that…"

She nodded. "Sure was."

"I never knew she was that tall."

Lori used a cardkey to unlock one of the doors with the Four Square Cooking Show logo on it. "This," she said, throwing her arms wide and backing into the room, "will be your kitchen."

It was a lot bigger than it appeared on television. White subway tiles made for a clean, sharp look and all of the equipment, like he'd seen online, was truly top-notch. Instead of a ceiling, above the kitchen was open with an abundance of grids holding lights and cameras. A microphone boom extended across the room. "There's a lot going on up there."

"You'd be freaked out if you knew how many camera, lights and mics are all over this space, and on you all the time. You'll want to remember you're always on camera and watch your mouth, because you never know what they're recording."

"Good to know." Now he was a little freaked out.

The kitchen was stocked with an industrial-sized mixer and two large ovens. The shiny silver wire racks that made up the pantry were nicely stocked and organized by type. One held nothing but bowls, tools, and baking pans, where another held spices and more sugary confections than he'd ever laid his eyes on in one space. The refrigerator had a glass front. He'd be able to quickly find what he'd need.

"What do you think?"

"I'm used to working in the finest restaurant in all of France, and this will do very nicely."

A man in the hall was talking about product-placement shots he needed in tomorrow's filming.

Andrew stared at the pantry, but his ears were totally tuned in to what was going on in the hall.

"…and Mark was just telling us that since they're not going to film another season of Charlie's show, they're thinking about picking up the winner of this for a special or two. It could work into something new."

"That would be good. Charlie was so hard to work with. I can't imagine having to drag that through another season."

"You and me both."

The door closed, and it was completely silent. The kitchen was definitely soundproof. Even the banging and squeaking of the equipment being moved up and down the hall had disappeared.

He'd been flattered to be invited to the competition, but things had just gotten way more interesting.

When he'd left Paris, he'd been thinking that if he won, he'd invest the $100,000 into Francois' newest restaurant. It was a safe investment that would surely make a nice return. Or he could invest in the one opening in Mykonos, and hopefully that would help ensure him getting to work in that restaurant for a while. It would be quite an experience to cook for the rich and famous, and play with them too.

But now, after his visit home, he had to really consider the opportunity to open a restaurant in Bailey's Fork and further foster his relationship with Dad. Was there any chance Kelly might let him back into her life? From what he could see, all she had was that pig. There hadn't been a single sign of a guy in her life. His mom's words replayed in his head. *Fight to get her back.*

Chapter Twenty-One

KELLY WALKED SARA ONE MORE time through all of Gray's
routines. "Thanks so much for staying here while I'm
gone."

"You'd do the same for me," Sara insisted.

"Except you have a well-behaved beagle. I have a pig."

"You've trained him better than most dogs," Sara said. "It'll be
fine. I'm not worried at all."

Am I crazy leaving like this? Her head swam. "I can't believe this
is happening."

"Believe it, and do us proud," Sara said. "Are you sure you don't
want me to take you to the airport?"

"No. Lyft will be easier. Besides, then they can *lift* this suitcase
and put it in the car." Kelly set her hand on the top of the large
rolling suitcase. She knew she'd overpacked, but she needed
wardrobe options, and she couldn't trust that the hotel would have
a decent hair dryer. That could be a real disaster.

"Did you get any sleep last night?"

Kelly shook her head. "Barely. I had the entire last season
of Four Square Cooking Show still DVR'd, so I ended up binge
watching them. At least I won't bake anything too similar to what's
been done on the show in the last season."

"Good use of your time, except you're going to be a zombie tonight."

"True, and it's almost time to go." Kelly checked her phone again. "My car will be here in two minutes."

"This is it!"

"Come here, Gray." The pink-and-gray pig ran into the room, sliding to a stop in front of her. "You be good for Sara."

He lifted his chin in the air, his ears flopping wide like he might take flight.

"I'm going to miss you." She scratched his chin, then put him back in his room. He raced right out the doggy door.

She balanced her carry-on bag on top of the suitcase and headed outside.

"Let me help you down the stairs," Sara said, rushing to her side. Between the two of them they were able to bounce the suitcase down a step at a time to the sidewalk.

A blue Prius pulled into the driveway.

"Hope your suitcase will fit in the back of that thing," Sara teased.

"Me too." Before Kelly got to the car, the driver, Josh, jumped out of the front seat.

"Hey, Kelly. I can't believe I'm running into you again so soon."

She hadn't even made the connection when the name Josh had popped up on the app. The picture was small, and she hadn't looked at it that close. Josh was a friend of Andrew's. He'd been at the party the other night. Of all the luck.

Luckily her bag fit in the car and they were off to the airport. She pretended to be doing something on her phone in hopes he would take the hint and not start a conversation on the forty-minute ride.

"Where are you off to?" he finally asked.

"Orlando. A work thing."

He nodded. "Are you and Andrew going to try to make things work again? He seemed pretty happy to see you the other night."

She shouldn't be surprised that people were speculating about her and Andrew, but her insides twirled just the same. There were still so many unanswered questions between them. She was afraid to trust her heart again. Either way, she didn't need those rumors running rampant in Bailey's Fork while she was away, so she shrugged nonchalantly and said, "Not a chance. Andrew is quite happy living abroad."

"Lucky me, then. Think you'd like to grab dinner sometime?"

I didn't see that coming. "You know, I don't really have much time to date. But thank you. That was really sweet of you to ask. Made my day."

His posture slumped a little.

Great. I hurt his feelings. Well, at least it might slow down the idle chitchat.

It had done more than that. He didn't speak another word all the way to Raleigh. "Which airline?" he asked.

"American."

He pulled in front of the American departure door and got her bag out of the car.

"Thanks for the ride. It was good seeing you again."

"Yeah, have a good trip," he said, although he didn't really sound sincere.

She lugged her bags into the airport. All of the machines and counters were a bit overwhelming. She made her way over to the American Airlines counter and stopped at one of the electronic kiosks. A welcoming message displayed on the screen. *Touch here to begin.* Easy enough. She tapped on the screen and fumbled through the instructions.

Finally, one of the airline associates came over and rescued her. "Sometimes these things are finicky. I can help you with this."

"Thank you so much. It's my first time flying."

"How exciting."

"I'm a little nervous, and confused on what to do and where to go."

"No worries. I'll get you all checked in here." Her bright red fingernails tapped in a clickety-clack against the keys of her computer. "Checking one bag to JFK?"

"In New York, right?"

The attendant smiled. "Yes. JFK is one of the New York City airports."

"Then yes. Thanks."

"Here's your license and boarding pass. I put your claim ticket for your bag on the back of your boarding pass for you. You're all set. Just follow the signs to security."

She looked over her shoulder and then trekked toward the escalator. The security line was long, snaking through a maze of webbing. She got in line, shuffling along in the crowd, like cattle on auction day.

By the time she got through security, her flight was already boarding. She took her seat, thankful when the pilot announced it would only be an hour and fifty minutes to New York.

She stepped off the plane, excited to share her first experience flying with Mom, but when she got into the terminal she was immediately overwhelmed by the size of the airport compared to their airport at home. People rushed by, and she got swept along as if she'd been caught in a riptide. She hoped the current was headed toward baggage claim.

In a panic, she pushed her way to the edge of the crowd and headed for help from a gate agent.

"I'm so sorry to bother you," she said. "This is my first time flying, and I don't know where to go to get my bag. Can you help me?"

"You're here at the busiest time of the day. Don't worry." She motioned to someone dressed in all blue. "Can you put her on the next cart with our young flier?"

"Sure. Here's the next one now. Follow me."

Kelly raced alongside them toward an extra-long golf cart gizmo. The attendant and the boy she was escorting sat in the middle seat, leaving one open seat on the back for her next to a well-dressed older woman. She scooched over as Kelly sat down. "Hi."

"Hello." The lady's bright red lipstick matched her nails. "Will you look at all these people rushing around? Do you hear a single excuse me or sorry?"

Kelly had to listen closely to understand her accent. *Awl?* All, she decided.

"No." The woman shook her finger in the air. "No. You don't. I've been sitting here watching them." She swung her head around and locked eyes with Kelly. "Where are you from?"

"North Carolina," Kelly said with a smile. "A small town. Bailey's Fork. Not all too terribly far from Raleigh. It's my first time to New York." *To anywhere.*

"My Henry owns the best diner in Manhattan." She rummaged in her purse coming up with a card and a tissue. "Tell him I said you have to try his cheesecake. It's to die for."

"You don't have to do that."

"I know. See, I'm just nice that way. Don't let people tell you New Yorkers aren't nice. That's just a nasty rumor some southerner made up." The woman shoved the card into her hand. "Seriously. Stop in. He's always there. I might even be there. Are you married?"

"No, ma'am. Not yet. I own a business. It's hard to fit in time for a relationship."

The woman cast her a look of judgment. "What kind of business do you have, dear?"

"It's called The Cake Factory."

The woman slapped her big shiny purse. "Oh. My. Word. Not The Cake Factory with the dinosaur egg cupcakes?"

A nervous giggle escaped. "Yes. That's me. You've heard of them?"

"You're practically famous. My daughter ordered your dinosaur egg cupcakes for my grandson's birthday. They were a hit. A huge hit, I tell you."

What are the odds in a place this big, hundreds of miles away from home, that I'd sit next to someone who'd heard of The Cake Factory?? "That's our bestselling kid's party item. I can't believe this." She proudly accepted her moment of fame. Hopefully, just a teensy test-drive before the big bake-off.

"I'll be honest, I was a little skeptical when I saw them. They were so cute I didn't expect them to taste like much, but your cakes are delicious. Ask my Henry, he'll tell you I went on and on about it. You and my Henry, you have to chat. You both love to cook. We were meant to meet. Karma and all that." The woman leaned in so close Kelly could smell the cough drop on her breath. "You know...I don't tell everyone this, but I'm a bit psychic," she whispered in her husky voice. "I don't know why you're in town, but I have a feeling that love is coming into your life while you're here. True love." She patted Kelly's leg and gave her a wink. "You take care."

The golf cart came to a stop. "Carousel one," the driver announced.

The old woman slid off the seat and grabbed her Louis Vuitton bag. "This is where I get off. So nice to meet you, dear. Come to the restaurant."

The airline attendant in the middle seat tapped her on the shoulder. "We're at the other end. You'll get off when we do."

"Thank you so much. I'd have been lost for sure."

The old woman waved as the cart took off.

Kelly waved, realizing she'd never even introduced herself. *Where are my manners? I didn't ask Henry's wife what her name was.* She looked at the card in her sweating hand. Henry and Candace Leary owned The Manhattan Original Diner. Right there on the card, they boasted the best New York cheesecake in the city.

Chapter Twenty-Two

WHEN THE DRIVER PULLED TO a stop in front of the baggage carousel for her flight, Kelly saw her suitcase coast by on the conveyor. She leaped off the cart, handed the driver a five-dollar bill for the rescue, then race-walked to catch up with her bag, but it was faster than she was in the crowd of people. She found an open spot and waited patiently for her bag to come back around.

She was just getting ready to pull out the piece of paper with the emergency contact information from Jennifer when she spotted a tall man in a black suit holding an iPad with the name McIntyre in bold capital letters.

He lifted his chin and mouthed, "Are you Ms. McIntyre?"

"I am." She nodded.

He crossed the space with long strides. "Excellent." He shook her hand. "Nice to meet you. I'll get your luggage."

"It's the green suitcase. It's already gone by once, should be coming back around any minute."

"No problem. Is it that one coming around now?"

"That's it." She waited while he scooped up her heavy suitcase like it weighed nothing and checked the tag. "Is this the only one?"

"Yes. That's it." She hitched her carry-on on her shoulder.

He pulled the handle up. "You're my kind of girl. My wife takes this size for an overnighter, and still carries a purse the size of Delaware." He led her out of the terminal to the parking area. He clicked a button on his keychain, and she saw the trunk lift on a long black limousine that nearly took up two parking spaces.

She started to sweat. "I think there's been a mistake."

"What's the matter? Are you okay?"

"I'm *Kelly* McIntyre. I...I guess I should have checked the first name too. I'm sorry."

He pulled out his iPad and touched a few things before turning the screen to her. "This is you, right?"

The screen had her name, address, and the TV channel contacts, even an outdated picture of her. "Yes." She breathed a sigh of relief. "Yes, that's me."

"Then we're all set." He held the door for her with a smile, and she crawled inside, unsure of where to sit in the roomy back.

"Wow."

"Never been in a limo before?"

"Never even seen one this close up." Even the funeral home only used Town Cars these days. She used to think they were pretty fancy. She ran her fingers across the smooth leather.

Certainly he was going to pick up some other people. The horseshoe-shaped seating pit could fit another ten people back here easy.

"There's ice and drinks. Help yourself."

She took a bottle of water and drank it straight from the bottle. No need to dirty a glass.

The drive to the hotel took almost a whole hour. The traffic was heavy, and they seemed to spend more time sitting still than moving.

"Is there an accident?" she finally asked.

"No, ma'am. This is pretty normal traffic for this time of day."

She didn't know what people saw appealing about living in a

big city. It was noisy, and loud, and the traffic would make her crazy. She'd take her sleepy little town any day.

Finally he pulled in front of a fancy hotel with lots of gold and two glitzy-dressed doormen. The bellman took her bag and put it on a cart.

"Thanks for the safe travel." She handed the driver a twenty-dollar bill.

"Production has taken good care of me. Save that and treat yourself to something fun in our city. It's been my pleasure." He started to get back in the car, then popped back up. "And good luck."

"Thank you." She hovered close to the bellman.

"You can check in over there." He handed her a tag. "Just give this to the desk clerk, and we'll be sure to get your luggage right up to you."

At the counter, suddenly everything seemed very real. She was in New York City! "Hi, I'm Kelly McIntyre. I'm checking in."

The woman tapped on the keyboard of her computer. "Yes. We have you right here. Your room is ready, and you have a message. Let me get that for you."

This is really happening. She swallowed back the emotion, hoping to keep her cool.

She came back with a folder and her room key. "You're all set. Elevators are to your right just past the columns."

Kelly couldn't believe how beautiful the massive lobby was. It was hard to take it all in. She imagined something in France or Italy looking like this. *Has Andrew ever seen anything like this in his travels? Probably all the time.*

The elevator doors were gold too. She fixed her hair in the reflection.

Her room was at the far end of the hall. She hiked down the long hall, glad she didn't have to lug her heavy suitcase all the way here. She waved the key in front of the door, and it unlocked. Inside the room was even grander than the lobby.

She took out her phone and started taking pictures of the room. "Mom and Sara are never going to believe this." It was so luxurious she imagined this could be a room at the palace. "I'm not in Bailey's Fork anymore." She looked out the window. Cars filled the streets, honking but barely moving, and people moved like little ants below. Across the way there were lights and a big electronic billboard advertising something new every few seconds. Suddenly, Martin Schlipshel popped up on that screen, arms folded with the Four Square Cooking Show logo. She snapped a picture of that too. Not that she could share them with anyone until after the show, but she sure didn't want to forget this.

The room was fancier than anything she'd ever seen even in a magazine. There were two king-size beds with headboards that reached almost to the ceiling. Why did anyone need two king-size beds in one room?

The comforters were a shimmery gold, and the way the fabric was ruched in alternating panels it looked like cake frosting. She ran her hand across the cool fabric, then climbed right into the center of the bed.

She took in a breath and spread her arms out wide. Suddenly she pictured herself as the cake topper on a perfectly frosted cake, like one of those princess doll cakes little girls love so much. She raised her phone, extending her arm and looking up and smiling. *Click.*

Crawling off the bed, she kicked off her shoes near the luggage rack. Speaking of which, why wasn't her suitcase here yet? What if that man didn't even work for the hotel and he'd just stolen her clothes? If she didn't have her hairbrush and curling iron, she'd be looking a mess when she saw the television people in the morning. She should have handled her bag herself. She was quite capable. That was what she got for acting like a prima donna. Served her right if it was stolen.

She wandered into the bathroom, where a plush robe and slippers had been laid out on the counter. She hugged the plush fabric to her cheek. She unwrapped a soap from the basket of fancy potions and inhaled the orange-gingery scent. She washed her hands and then ran a warm washcloth over her face, then dabbed her face dry.

A rapid knock came at the door.

"My bag!" She raced to the door, almost tripping over her shoes along the way. She pulled the door open, disappointed to see a tall redheaded woman standing with a fruit basket there instead.

"Welcome to New York! I'm Brenda, and I'll be your assistant while you're here. This is for you."

"Thank you. That was so thoughtful. Come on in." She hoped she sounded appreciative, but now she really was starting to get worried about her bag. "So, what exactly do I need an assistant for?" She'd seen in some of the competitions that there were helpers in the kitchen. "Do you bake?"

"Oh, no. I guess some people refer to think of what I do as a handler, but I like assistant better. I make sure you get everywhere on time and don't break any rules. That kind of stuff. If you have any questions, I can get the answers for you."

"Well, I'm a little worried about my suitcase. I've been here for a while, and it still hasn't come up."

"I can check on that. Sometimes they get busy this time of day with all the check-ins. I guess you noticed that you don't have a phone."

"No. I hadn't..." She scanned the room. "Noticed."

"There are no phone calls permitted unless supervised by me. And..." She motioned her fingers toward Kelly's phone. "I'll need that."

"I read that in the contract." She was glad she'd taken pictures before Brenda showed up. She handed over her phone. "Wait. Can we get a selfie together first?"

"Heck yeah." She took the phone and extended her long arm in front of them. "Smile!" She clicked the picture. "Nice way to start off a great adventure. So, I'll be in the room next door. Anything, day or night, come get me. For now, I'll run next door and call downstairs about your bag, and then I'll be right back."

Kelly's phone rang in Brenda's hand before she could even leave. "Your mom."

Kelly grimaced. "I have to talk to her, or she'll be worried sick. She thinks I'm in Orlando at an RBA show."

Brenda laid the phone on the bed and put it on speaker. "Nothing about the show, and keep it as short as possible."

"Hey, Mom. I just landed."

"That's great, honey. I just wanted to hear your voice. This is the first time we've been so far apart."

"I know. I just got here, but everything is fine."

"Were you afraid? You didn't sit next to anyone sick, did you? I've heard those planes are like one giant petri dish."

"No. The flight was really good. I wasn't afraid at all."

"I'm so proud of you. Well, you take care. I won't bother you. Have a wonderful time and learn a lot. We miss you already, honey."

"I miss you too."

"Kelly, I thought I'd better warn you before you get back." Mom's voice sounded strange.

"What's wrong?"

"Nothing really, but your dad's been talking about retiring for a while now, and I think he's actually ready to do something. I just didn't want you to be blindsided if you came home and he was talking about it or had gotten a wild hair and done something."

She agreed it was time for Dad to slow down a little. All that talk about throwing a party for Mom had probably stemmed from the whole retirement thing. Those surprises she was hoping to afford with her winnings for the diner might not be as good of an idea as she thought. "You know, there's nothing wrong with him letting Kenny handle the kitchen. He's a great cook, and he's dependable. I've told him that before."

"That's just it. Kenny gave his notice today. He's moving back to Georgia to be closer to his kids. Honey, your dad's talking about selling the restaurant. He said he's ready to throw in the towel and apron and relax a little. Go fishing. Take some trips. Do what retired people do. Whatever that is."

Kelly leaned against the bed for support. "I could take over the cafe."

"I knew that would be your immediate reaction, but I don't really think you want to take that on. The Cake Factory is doing so well. Main Street Cafe is just a little local restaurant. What you're building is the next generation of McIntyre legacy. We want you to take that torch and run with it."

"But—"

"Look, it may not even happen for a while. I just wanted you to have some time to get used to the idea in case anything really came of it. When he's ready, we'll do it. Don't worry. I'm sorry I even mentioned it now. I should have just kept quiet."

"Don't be silly, Mom. You can always talk to me. I'm sure this is weighing on your mind, and I'm sorry Kenny gave his notice. That's not good news at all." She didn't want the family business to close.

"We'll work it out. Thanks for telling me."

Her weak knees folded underneath her as she sat on the bed. She couldn't believe this. Sure, her parents deserved to retire, but she'd never once thought they'd actually close down the cafe.

"I'll talk to you when I get home," she said. A wave of nausea caught her on the last words.

"I'll try not to bug you. Bye, honey."

"You're never a bother. Love you, Mom." She ended the call a little homesick.

A knock at the door had Brenda rushing across the room. "Your luggage is here," she called out enthusiastically as she tipped the bellman. "One disaster averted."

"Thank goodness," Kelly said.

"Do you want to go out to dinner or eat in tonight?"

"I'm not that hungry. I can just eat in."

"I've got just the thing. Our craft service for the show has the best home cooking around." Brenda called down to Craft Service at the studio and ordered two of today's specials. "If it's okay with you, I'll prop the doors open between our room and I'll listen for the food while you get settled in."

"That would be great. I'm going to shower and change into some yoga pants."

When Kelly came out, a good-looking guy was standing in Brenda's room helping her unbox things.

"Oh good, you're out," Brenda said. "Dinner just arrived."

"It smells good. Suddenly, I'm very hungry." Kelly joined Brenda in the adjoining room.

"This is Tony Newmann. He works in catering, but he's also done some work on a soap opera."

Kelly recognized him. "You were Ethan! The casino owner who fell off the riverboat. You were really good. I can't believe I'm meeting a real actor. My mom will absolutely die."

"Thanks," Tony said. "I'll bring a signed picture for you to take to her."

"That would be so great. She'll never believe it."

He pulled a card out of his wallet and handed it to her.

She held the card between her fingers.

"When this show is all said and done, give me a call and I'll show you around the city if you like. I'm a great tour guide."

Is he flirting with me? Maybe Mrs. Leary was on to something after all. Is Tony my chance to find love?

Chapter Twenty-Three

AFTER SEEING THE SET, ANDREW was amped and ready to get this challenge started. On the way back to their hotel, he asked Lori, "Where can we get a good meal tonight? I was thinking maybe Le Bernardin, Chef's Table at Brooklyn Fare, or maybe Daniel. I've heard Per Se is amazing too."

"Our per diem is quite generous, but I can guarantee you none of those places are going to be in the budget."

"My treat."

"Even so, I'm fairly certain we can't place a pickup order from any of those places," Lori said.

Pffft. "Half the experience of the food is the plating and atmosphere in the restaurant."

"The only atmosphere you're going to be experiencing through Valentine's Day is here and on the set."

He'd talk her into it before the week was out. He had no doubt. There was no way he could be right here in New York City and not show up at one of the restaurants of the chefs he'd met when they'd visited his restaurant—well Francois'—in Paris. If he had to pretend to miss his flight to get an extra day in, he was going to get to at least one of those places.

A little disgruntled, he mumbled, "Happy Valentine's Day to me."

"Did you leave someone special behind?"

"No." He hadn't even left a plant. There wasn't anything personal in his apartment at all. Even the furniture had already been there when he'd moved in. He'd never made it a home. The thought of home made him think of Kelly. He could probably feel at home with her anywhere.

"Well, yeah," he said. "I guess I did leave someone special behind. I just didn't make it clear to her that I thought she was special."

"You're an idiot then. My ex was like that." Lori cocked her head and leaned away from him. "That's why he's an ex. Don't be like that."

Great. I would get the Dr. Phil of handlers. "You sound a little bitter."

"I'm doing you a favor by saying this. Don't screw up like he did."

The car pulled back in at the hotel, and they walked through the ground-level entrance to the elevators.

If only he could roll back the clock about seven years. It probably hadn't helped that Aunt Claire reminded him constantly how lucky he was to be working in one of Paris' top gourmet restaurants. He'd been highlighted in a magazine for being one of the youngest American chefs to ever work in a Michelin 3-star restaurant. And all of that had been awesome, but now he wasn't so sure he'd made the right decision. Maybe he'd known it wasn't the right one all along.

"Come on in over here," Lori said, unlocking her room next door. "We can figure out dinner."

"Sounds good." He sat on the couch in the sitting area of her room, which was exactly like his, except backward.

"So tell me about your baking experience. You're a pastry chef, obviously," Lori said.

"No. I'm really not a baker at all. However, I did study under the very best pastry chefs in France, and finished top in my class. I'm Chef de Cuisine for Francois Dumont. In his signature restaurant."

"But you're not a baker now?" Lori didn't look impressed. "So, why are you here then? You do know this is all about pastries, candy, and cakes right?"

"I do. I'm a good baker. It's just not my first love." The loblolly pine tree back in Bailey's Fork where he'd carved AY + KM popped into his mind. KM was his true first love. "I guess mostly I'm here because someone was kind enough to nominate me and the team here thought I'd be a good competitor. I'm not about to turn my nose up at a chance like this."

"I guess I can understand that. You're going to have some tough competition though. I know you went to some fancy schools, but if it's not in your heart, they're going to be able to tell."

I hope not. "About dinner. I'm starved. How about you get us a couple of street vendor hot dogs?"

Lori's face lit up. "Now you're talking my language. Chili?"

"All the way." He thought about the hot dogs he and Kelly used to make. They'd roast them on wire hangers over the fire pit in her folks' backyard. She loved hers burnt to a crisp. For someone who loved baking, she did have a peculiar palate, and that had made her all the more fun to cook for.

"You're in for a treat." Lori pulled on her coat and wrapped a scarf around her neck.

From the window he watched her jog across the street to the hot dog stand.

When Lori came crashing back into the condo, the onions hit him before she made it through the door.

"Dinner is served. Got you a pretzel too. May as well do it up right."

He'd pulled a bottle of wine out of the mini-bar and poured them each a glass. "Salut."

They both took a sip of the wine, then he bit into his hot dog. Chili ran down his chin. He swept at it with the napkin. "This is a darn good dog."

"Oh, yeah. We're known for them," she said through a mouthful.

"So are you going to be spending your Valentine's Day babysitting me?"

"If you make it that far," she challenged.

"That wasn't nice." He put his hot dog down and took another swallow of wine. "I'll make it to the end. Count on it."

"Good. It pays me a hundred bucks a day plus per diem for meals. Plus I get bonuses the farther you get."

"Not bad money. I guess you can always celebrate Valentine's Day the day after. Way easier to get reservations then anyway."

"I'm not big on roses and candy anyway, and there's no one special waiting for me at home. Remember the ex I was talking about?"

"Maybe he'll surprise you and call."

Lori balled up the paper boat the hot dog had been in and tossed it at Andrew. "What makes you think I want him to?"

He caught the paper wad in the air and leveled a stare in her direction. "Because you're mad." He pointed a finger at her. "That means you miss him. Which means there's still a chance." His ears tingled. If he listened to his own advice, then there was a chance for him with Kelly. She was still mad. Had even said so.

He laid down his hot dog, washing down the bite with another sip of wine. *Good news. There is a chance, albeit slim, for me after all.*

"I need to add another name to my important phone call list."

Lori pulled the list out of her tote bag and handed it to him. "Sure. Here you go."

He held the pen in his hand. This was totally wishful thinking, but if she did call…he wanted to know. He wrote Need Cookies on the phone list.

"Need cookies?" Lori asked. "Seriously? Is this a joke to get dessert?"

"No. It's a real person." Kelly was still in his phone under the nickname he'd given her in high school.

"This wouldn't happen to be the girl you should have told she was special, now would it?"

"Yeah. A nickname. We were in high school, and she'd been raising money to go to cheerleading camp. I'll never forget that day. It was the first time I'd noticed her as a girl, and not just a friend. We'd grown up together. You know how that is."

"Sure do. I'm from a small town too."

"I bought some of her cookies. They were amazing, but more amazing than the cookies was the sparkle in her eyes when she talked about baking them. Her eyes are as dark as milk chocolate. I was so taken by her enthusiasm that later that day I asked her for her number to *supposedly* help sell cookies. Really, I'd planned to call her for a date. I did, and that had been the beginning of a very good relationship."

"Until?" Lori had that judgmental look on her face, like she was going to give him unsolicited advice again.

"It's a long story, but if she calls, I definitely want to know." The thought of her calling made his mood lift. "And for the record, I want to take that call even if it means I have to give up my shot at winning this show to do it."

Chapter Twenty-Four

KELLY WOKE UP TO A lovely room-service breakfast in that swanky room feeling like the luckiest girl in the world. There'd even been a nice card from the studio on her tray.

She dressed in a pair of black slacks and a black V-neck T-shirt then finished putting on her makeup and fixing her hair. She'd been so excited to receive the Four Square Cooking Show chef's jacket, but now that she tried it on, it made her a feel like a bit of a fraud. Not being a trained chef, the jacket was a little off-putting. She preferred to wear a pretty apron.

Kelly straightened the jacket, then twisted to see how it looked in the full-length mirror. The fabric was heavy and constraining. It wasn't nearly as flattering as her apron either. This would take some getting used to. She only hoped it wouldn't pull her off her game.

Brenda knocked on the door. "It's me again. Are you almost ready?"

Kelly pulled open the door. "I think so."

"You look great." Brenda propped her hip against the door. "I thought I'd get you over to the studio early, so you have time to check out the kitchen you'll be working in. That'll give you a chance to get used to where things are and take a mental inventory of all the supplies, the pots and pans, pantry staples. I've never had anyone say there was something they needed that wasn't there, but there's always a first."

"That would be great. I can't wait to see it." Every minute counted on timed events, so knowing her surroundings would be key.

"Great. The car is already downstairs."

Kelly turned around and grabbed her purse, making sure she had her room key in the front pocket. "Then let's go."

Brenda put her purse on the seat next to her. "We're in the hotel closest to the studio. If it weren't for the weather today, we could've walked."

Traffic was lighter, and the ride was short over to the studio.

Brenda led Kelly inside and down the wide, stark corridors. They stopped in front of a set of double-doors with L2 written on it. "Here we are." She opened the door and let Kelly go in first.

When they walked inside, Kelly's breath caught. The space was really bright, and big. Much bigger than she'd expected, but then, most of the space was open so the camera crew had room to do what they needed. She was pretty sure once she got started cooking it wouldn't matter where she was. She wasn't picky. She could make do on a propane camp stove if she had to. She'd even made cast-iron Dutch oven desserts at the Pioneer Days celebration two years ago.

"I'm going to leave you to look around." Brenda put a hand on her shoulder. "Are you going to be okay in here for a bit?"

"Perfectly fine." Kelly roamed the room, taking in all the appliances first. Open silver racks held all the pantry items. She committed the unusual ingredients to memory in case the chance came up to integrate them. She couldn't think of anything she'd need that she didn't see here.

Even the refrigerator was well stocked. She had no worries about being able to bake here.

Two men entered her kitchen, one carrying a camera. "Getting settled in?"

"Yes, thank you."

"I'm Drake, and I'm going to be taking some publicity shots of you. Freddy here is going to touch up your makeup before we get started."

"Hi, I'm Kelly. What do you need me to do?"

Freddy whisked her to the edge of the counter. "Hop on this stool."

She did as she was told. He tipped her chin up and looked at her as if evaluating her. "Eyes closed."

She sat there with her chin up and eyes closed while Freddy brushed, dabbed, and sponged like an artist on a canvas.

"Eyes open. Good. Now look up." He swept her lashes with mascara. Then took her chin between his fingers and tilted her head back down. "Look right here." He tapped his chest bone. "Nice." A couple of quick fluffs of his fingers through her hair, a spritz of spray, then he yelled, "All set!"

He held up a mirror for her.

"Wow." Kelly barely recognized herself. "How'd you do that? My skin looks flawless. Thank you."

Freddy stepped back with a grin. "Makeup is my art, darlin', but you're a beauty all by yourself."

Drake walked over, fidgeting with the controls on his camera. "Okay, I need you to walk through that door and come straight toward me. "

She did as he asked, but it was like all of a sudden she didn't remember how to walk. Her knees were like Jell-O and her stride felt stiff and awkward.

"Great. Again?"

She ran through that short walk no less than six times before he finally seemed satisfied.

"Now," Drake said, "I need you to stand near the oven and look over your shoulder toward me." He snapped off a few shots. "Very good. Pick up a bowl. Smiling, and now serious." He glanced down at his camera. "Thanks. I think I've got all I need right now."

He and Freddy left as quickly as they'd shown up.

She stood there feeling a little awkward, so she meandered back over to the pantry shelves and tried to memorize everything on each shelf.

Brenda showed up with a bottle of water. "Okay, there's a shelf below the cabinet on the right side of the sink that's out of view. You can put your water there between shoots. Never leave it on the counter."

"Thank you," Kelly said.

"If the green light over that door says LIVE, don't mess with it or anything. That means that the camera is rolling. If it's not illuminated, you have a minute to readjust, get a sip of water. If it's flashing, get yourself ready because you're going live."

"Got it."

"Each soundstage is completely soundproofed. Yours may go completely quiet until they cut to you. So don't get freaked out. Just keep doing what you're doing. If anything gets out of sync, you'll see one of the production assistants signal to you from that spot right there."

"Okay."

"Don't worry. It sounds like a lot to remember, but if you be yourself and bring your heart to the show...that's how winners are made. I think you're going to do great." Brenda led her behind the fake frosted kitchen door. Really it was just a door inside the door where she'd make her entrance.

Kelly stood there in the shadows in her red chef's jacket. The theme music for the show started playing, and Martin Schlipshel was introduced. She turned and gave Brenda a shaky thumbs up.

"Welcome to our Four Square Valentine's Day Bake-Off! We're so excited to bring this special edition of Four Square Cooking

Show to you. Not only have we brought extra special pastry chefs in for this competition, but the prize is the largest we've ever awarded."

Kelly sucked in a breath.

"The Best Pastry Chef will walk away with one hundred thousand dollars. And now we'll introduce you to our four contestants."

Her kitchen went eerily quiet.

She stood there, unsure of what to do. The light over the door glowed green. Brenda had explained that whenever that light was green, you were being filmed. No bra adjusting, scratching your nose or talking to yourself.

Of course, her nose itched.

Suddenly her light switched on, and she heard Martin's voice come over the speaker.

"From Bailey's Fork, North Carolina, Kelly McIntyre. Owner of The Cake Factory."

She made her entrance and stood on the X like she'd been instructed.

"This self-taught baker has grown one of the most successful online cake shops around. If you haven't tried her desserts, you need to put them on your list right now. We're pleased to have her with us on this Four Square Valentine's Day Bake-Off."

She smiled, wishing she could see what she looked like on camera. Was she standing straight? Could they tell she was shaking?

"Okay, contestants. Go to your counters," Martin continued.

She moved to the spot in front of the counter. Another X on the floor. That made it easy.

"As always, this is a blind competition. No one knows who they're competing against."

The quartz countertop was so shiny that the lights made it sparkle as if it were under water. She folded her hands on the counter in front of her. A large wicker basket sat not two feet away from her.

Her hands left a foggy sweat print on the counter. She swept at the mark and put her hands behind her back.

Inside that basket was the first challenge. She'd seen the show enough to know that this was an invention challenge. She prayed her practice with Sara would pay off.

Right now it was her and her kitchen.

"Contestants. Please take your first surprise ingredient out of Cabinet One."

She opened the first cabinet and removed a bag of pastel-colored conversation hearts.

"The theme is love. All of you have the exact same ingredients. Open your baskets!"

Kelly took out the ingredients one at a time and placed them on the counter. Dark chocolate chips, whole raw almonds, and cayenne peppers.

"You have ninety minutes to make six servings of whatever you like, but you must use each of these ingredients to complete a dessert fit for a fiftieth wedding anniversary."

The theme music for the show began playing, and Martin announced, "It's show time, and the four contestants are being filmed on The Four Square Cooking Show set. The arena-styled soundproof kitchens keep the contestants out of view and earshot of one another, but the cameras are on them every step of the way. Your time starts...now!"

Thankful for the ninety minutes, and the digital clock that had begun the countdown in numbers twelve inches high in front of her counter, Kelly ran straight to the oven and turned it to 350 degrees, then ran for the pantry, pulling all the staples she'd need.

She made a fiftieth wedding anniversary cake for the Millers three weeks ago, but there was no way she could replicate that in ninety minutes. And she wasn't sure if she could integrate the cayenne and pull it off. Time was of the essence. At least six individual desserts would be much easier to manage on the clock, since both the baking and cooling times would be cut dramatically.

The traditional gift for the fiftieth anniversary is gold. Is that too obvious? She also knew the traditional flowers for this anniversary was yellow roses and violets. The leaves of the violet were small heart shapes. Maybe a small detail the others wouldn't know. Then again, she wasn't sure a few fondant flowers would make a big impression. She needed to take a risk. Her recipe needed to be something memorable that not just anyone would make.

Searching through the pantry, she loaded up with honey, cinnamon, chili powder, kosher salt, and the rest of the things she needed to get started.

Kelly decided to make a slight variation of her flourless chocolate cake, rich and moist and always a favorite. She knew she could integrate all the ingredients without fail.

On the shelf with all the decoratives, she spotted edible gold flakes and gold leaf sheets.

Keeping things organized, she lined up the ingredients on the counter, then ran back to pick out her place settings. She grabbed six black ramekins off the shelf and six small gold charger plates to set them on. Luckily, in the silverware tray there were six gold dessert forks. It would make for a classy display.

Dumping the almonds into the food processor, she set to pulverizing them into a light fluffy flour. She pulled out a few of the best sayings in the conversation hearts box to set aside for garnish, just in case.

Crazy 4 U, I <3 U, XOXO, Soul Mate, Best Day, True Love, and *Only You.* There were a lot she didn't remember seeing when she was a kid. Things like *Text Me* and *Tweet Me.* Times were changing.

She powdered the conversation hearts into a sugary mixture in a blender to use in the cake.

Melting the chocolate, her skin moistened under the heat of the lights above. The butter was soft before she even went to put it in the pan. She stirred until it was silky smooth, then whisked eggs in a big bowl and started adding the other ingredients, finally working in the chocolate mixture.

She buttered the ramekins, then filled each one and popped them in the oven.

They would take thirty-five minutes to bake. She glanced at the timer. Cooling the cakes to be able to frost them would be the trickiest part. She got right down to work on the frosting, first chopping the cayenne peppers. She beat the butter, then started creaming in the other ingredients. She tasted the frosting. The cayennes weren't quite adding the heat she needed to be sure the judges could taste them. She added a little more and tried it again. Another taste, and she was satisfied.

The timer went off, and she tested her cakes. The toothpick came out completely clean. Ready to go.

She pulled them out of the oven and put them on the cooling rack. While waiting for the cakes to cool, she piped six chocolate circles and put them in the freezer to harden.

Glancing at the clock, she took a breath.

She rolled out sculpting chocolate into an even quarter-inch thickness, and then cut precise 5's and 0's for the toppers to cover in edible gold leaf. The numbers turned out quite elegant. She set them aside by each charger plate to save time when she was doing the final garnish. She piped a swirl around each plate, then cut a cayenne in slices, removing the seeds to make tiny pepper flowers along the design.

The cakes finally cooled to the touch. She topped each one with a perfect swirl of frosting, then tucked a dark chocolate circle into the top of the frosting, followed by a gold leaf 50 in the center of each circle. She set one on the charger plate and stepped back, trying to see it from the judges' perspective. She could do more, but she didn't want to overdo it either. The dessert looked elegant as it was.

She finished the other five and plated them. On the show it always seemed as if the contestants were working to the very last second. She went back through the ingredients in her mind. She had incorporated each and every one of them. Everything tasted good, and the plates looked pretty. She was going to have to trust that her practice had paid off and that was why she'd finished a little early.

She washed her hands and tidied her kitchen.

"Contestants. Five minutes."

Her breakfast tumbled in her gut. To keep her nerves at bay, she concentrated on memorizing everything in the refrigerator and where things were in the pantry. Any time she could save would give her an advantage in the next round.

It was the longest five minutes she'd ever experienced.

"One minute."

She stood in front of her finished product, praying they were enough.

"Time's up. Please step away from your counters."

She raised her hands and stepped back.

The LIVE light went red, and she grabbed her bottle of water and took a long sip.

The desserts had turned out exactly as she'd hoped. Now it was up to the judges.

A woman wearing a white chef's coat came in with a metal cart and asked Kelly to place all six of her plated desserts on the cart, then left the room with them.

Kelly ran a shaking hand through her hair.

Brenda came running into the room. "You did great. You seemed so relaxed."

"I wasn't! I got done so early. It kind of freaked me out."

"You did fine. Don't worry. I watched for each of the ingredients. You got them all. I bet they taste amazing."

"I feel good about this round. I just wonder what everyone else did."

"You can take a little break while the judges get a look at each of the dishes. It'll be a while before you go in for your judging. When it's over, before you find out who's eliminated, you'll be able to see and taste the other three entries."

Butterflies jumped around in her stomach. She couldn't wait to see how her work stacked up against the competition.

"You'll be the last one to go into judging on this round. We probably have a couple of hours. Let's go get you some lunch."

Kelly followed her down the hall. "Those last five minutes were torture."

"It's out of your hands now. And if it's any consolation, I think yours is the prettiest and really fit the theme the best."

"Yes, that helps!"

Brenda laughed. "I might be biased, though. I want you to win, but that also means I have to keep you alive through all these rounds. Lunch is waiting in your dressing room."

"I can't eat. My stomach is spinning."

"Please try to eat a little something. I promise you it'll help with the nerves." Brenda guided her down the hall, talking on a walkie-talkie to be sure the coast was clear for her to move Kelly back into her dressing room. "Okay, we're good. Let's go."

Brenda used her key to unlock the door and let Kelly in.

"Where'd these flowers come from?" Kelly said. "They're beautiful."

Kelly leaned her head back and closed her eyes. One down, three to go…if she did her job right. It was so nice of the producer to send flowers for her dressing room. She reached over and arranged the fern that had drooped on one side.

A cold plate with more food than she needed for the whole day was on the table. She nibbled lightly, not really wanting to eat at all, but she tried.

Brenda rummaged through a basket on the counter. "Craft service hooked us up. Snacks, drinks, all kinds of goodies. Healthy and the good stuff. I never know exactly how long these rounds are going to take. We'll have something to snack on later." She moved the basket to the glass coffee table next to the flowers. "Do you know how you're going to describe your dish to the judges?"

"Yes. I've been practicing in my head." Kelly dug into the basket and took out one of the fruit and yogurt parfaits. Stress eating wasn't usually a problem for her, but right now it seemed to be doing the trick.

After two hours of excruciating waiting, Brenda's radio finally crackled back to life. "Go ahead," she said into the radio.

"We're ready for McIntyre on the judges' stage."

"On our way." Brenda clapped her hands together. Excitement made keeping up with long-legged Brenda easy.

They zipped right by the door where Kelly had finished her first round earlier this afternoon, then stopped in front of a set of double doors with the Four Square Cooking Show logo on them. A man with a clipboard checked off something on a sheet and let them in. Martin Schlipshel and the judges were already there.

I've got this. She raised her chin, set a smile on her face, and walked inside, but just as she did she caught a glimpse of two people rushing down the hall. For a second her brain told her she'd seen Andrew, but by the time she turned, they were around the corner. Her imagination had to be in overdrive. *No distractions. This is my big shot. Don't blow it now.* She balled her fists and then shook out her hands.

Chapter Twenty-Five

"I 'M KELLY. THANK YOU FOR giving me the opportunity to bake for you," she said to Martin and the judges.

"We've already introduced the judges for the show, so I'll just do an impromptu intro for you. We won't be filming that. Then I'll get you to stand on the blue X. They'll check the lighting and when they say action, we'll be rolling."

"Okay."

He quickly went through the introductions, and everyone was so relaxed and welcoming. It really put her at ease.

"Places, everyone," a voice came from above.

Kelly took her position on the blue X.

"Action."

Martin paused for a two-count then started with, "What have you prepared for our judges this round, Kelly?"

She clasped her hands in front of her to keep from using them when she spoke. "I've prepared a fiftieth wedding anniversary Flourless Chocolate Cake with a Spicy Mexican Frosting. I made almond flour with the almonds, and integrated the chocolate into both the cake and frosting. I pulverized the conversation hearts into sugar and used that in the cake as well. The cayenne peppers are highlighted in the spicy frosting and as flowers in the plate garnish. The golden fifty on top represents the traditional gift of gold for that wedding anniversary."

"Thank you, Kelly."

The three judges dove into the dessert.

She watched their facial expressions. No one seemed to be grabbing for water, always a good sign when it came to using peppers in food.

"Let's start with Chef Georgie," Martin said.

"Thanks, Martin." Chef Georgie pushed her long dark hair over her shoulder. "Kelly, you've given us a wonderful dessert that seems rich and special enough for fifty years of marriage."

The way Chef Georgie rolled her R's made "marriage" sound like the most beautiful thing in the world.

"The flourless cake is ultra-rich and delicious. I love the crunchy top, and I can taste the teeniest hint of the fruity conversation hearts in the chocolate. The frosting is perfectly spicy. It's lovely."

Kelly finally swallowed the breath she'd been holding. "Thank you, Chef." *One.* She held a finger behind her back. Then made it two, hoping for the best.

"Thank you, Georgie. Chef Abraham, what are your thoughts on Kelly's dessert?"

"I like it very much. It's much simpler in style than some of the others, but I like the balance."

Kelly's throat felt like it was swelling.

"You've used every ingredient successfully, and I love that you hand-carved the numbers for the topping. You show great precision. I would have like to have seen something a little more out of the box. Fancier, or unexpected."

Her smile wavered. She rubbed her thumbnail against that second finger, unsure if it had been a pass or fail.

"Good feedback from Abraham. And Chef Collin. What are your thoughts?"

Kelly's heart pounded so hard she had to concentrate on the

smolderingly handsome Chef Collin's mouth to make out the words.

"I disagree with Abraham. I think this dessert is out of the box." Chef Collin leaned over to eye his fellow judge.

Thank goodness. He must've liked it.

Chef Collin went on, "I don't know that I'd have baked a flourless cake in the first round. That in itself was a bold move, and we've got great, bold flavors to match." He turned and faced Kelly. "This cake is baked to perfection, and the frosting makes for an unexpected surprise. I'm not sure I'd want to eat chocolate flourless cake without your frosting ever again."

"Thank you, judges," Kelly said, trying to resist the urge to skip off the stage. As she'd been coached earlier, she turned and exited the stage to the left.

"Cut."

Brenda stepped through the door and grabbed her hand. "We'll just wait here for a second while they make sure they've got everything they need."

"We've got it," came over the speaker.

"You're done," Brenda said. They scurried down the hall toward her dressing room, and as soon as they closed the door, they both squealed. "You did so great, Kelly!"

"I'm afraid to get too excited."

"Well, don't be."

A minute later, a knock at the door sent Kelly into overdrive, but it was the woman who'd collected her desserts on the cart stopping by to deliver a sample from the three other entries. "Here you go. The competition."

"Thank you," Kelly said, jumping to her feet to get a first look at them. "These are gorgeous."

"Yours is beautiful too."

"Are you going to help me taste them?"

"You first," Brenda said.

Kelly took a seat and picked up her fork. She wasn't sure which one to start with.

There was an intricate layered dessert in a parfait glass. Layers of mousse and the thinnest almond cookies she'd ever had. There may have been a little hint of cayenne in the chocolate fudge layer, but if it was there, she couldn't taste it. The conversation hearts had been crushed and layered between the chocolate and cookie layers. On top, a dollop of thick-whipped icing with a conversation heart that read 4EVER YOURS.

"Try this one," she said, handing it off to Brenda.

The next dessert was a chocolate-almond petit four in a non-traditional rectangle shape. A bright red cayenne chocolate drizzle added the slightest hint of heat in contrast to the rich cake, and a chocolate disk lay flat in the center of the cake with a gold 50 dusted on it.

"This one is so good." Kelly loved the presentation too. "You have to try this one."

Brenda took it and pushed her fork into the cake. "You're right. This one is really good. Pretty too."

"I might be in trouble."

"You only have to beat one of these to stay in the round."

"True," Kelly said. "Okay. Then I can admit I love this one." She pointed to the petit four. "I'm begging someone for this recipe after the show." She picked up the third competitor's entry. Heart-shaped cookies. "These hearts are pretty, but they just don't seem enough to celebrate fifty years of marriage." She bit into one of the dark chocolate shortbread cookies. Frosted with a glossy chocolate icing that was spicy with not only the cayenne, but it tasted like paprika or some kind of seasoning salt too. "An interesting contrast."

"Interesting isn't always good." Brenda took a bite of that one. "I'm not sure of that one."

"It's not going to be easy though."

"Which one do you think you would eliminate?" Brenda lined

them up. "We're not even considering you in the elimination round."

"I think I'd probably eliminate the parfait. It was good, but I didn't get the heat from the cayenne at all."

"I think I'd eliminate the last one. The shortbread thingy. It had more of a Valentine's than anniversary look to it."

"Yeah, and that was tricky, because my mind kept wanting to go to Valentine's Day too. I mean, that's what the show is called."

"Right, but you need to listen carefully to what they're asking for. You don't want to be eliminated for that kind of mistake."

"I don't want to be eliminated at all." Kelly's hair was wet against her neck. She wasn't sure where she stood with this group, and that was amping up her nerves.

Kelly recognized the whistle ring tone she used for texts from Sara, then realized she didn't have her phone.

Brenda patted her pockets then looked at Kelly's phone. "Oh, gosh. You can see this." She held Kelly's phone out to her.

Kelly started laughing. "Aww. Sara knew I'd be missing Gray."

"That pig is yours?"

She nodded. "Sure is. He fit in a teacup when I got him. He's a lot bigger now, but I was already attached. He's really sweet. Sara works for me, and she's taking care of Gray while I'm here."

"I've never known anyone who had a pet pig." Brenda looked at the picture again. "He is cute though."

Brenda's radio came to life again. "Everyone back on set. Individual kitchens."

"Oh my gosh." Kelly's knees went weak. "This is it?"

"It is." She extended a hand to Kelly to help her stand.

"Wish me luck." Kelly headed to the door and tried to remember to breathe.

Brenda gave her a thumbs up.

Over the speakers, a voice directed the contestants to stand behind their counters on the green X.

Kelly located the green X on the floor and moved into place.

"Thank you. In five...four...three...two..."

The LIVE light went green, and Kelly felt like she was probably close to the same shade. She pasted a smile on her face.

She heard the welcome back from the commercial, and then the judges began talking about the desserts in this round.

"Not an easy round to judge," Chef Georgie said.

Martin's voice boomed. "Each of our contestants are back in their individual kitchens. We're watching them on the screen here in the studio audience. Chefs, in front of each of you is a covered plate."

Kelly's stomach churned.

"You'll each raise the cover and whoever doesn't have a Valentine on their plate...I'm sorry, you have been eliminated."

Kelly's hand shook as she placed it atop the shiny dome.

"Ready? Go!"

She lifted the plate, her eyes filling with tears of anticipation. Then she spotted the bright, funny Valentine on the plate. The kind you'd exchange in grade school. She picked it up and waved it in the air. "Yes!" She held her hand to her heart and leaned forward to catch her breath.

Judge Chef Abraham spoke. "I'm sorry, Frank. Your dessert was quite delicious. We enjoyed the dark chocolate shortbread, but the flavors were a little all over the place and since you left the conversation hearts out completely, we had to eliminate you in this round." The New York accent only made the message sound even harsher.

"I'm sorry. Frank Wells, you have been eliminated from this round," Martin said.

Frank said, "It was an honor to even be on the show."

Kelly lifted her chin toward the speaker with a weird sense of guilt for eavesdropping.

Martin continued, "You're the Executive Pastry Chef at the Elk Traxx Ski Resort in Colorado."

"That's right," Frank said.

"Thank you for being a part of this competition."

Kelly perked up. She couldn't wait to hear the rest, but then the mic went silent.

Four minutes later, the audio came back on in her kitchen. "And then there were three," Martin said. He made the closing announcements as the credits music began to play. "Join us for the next round of the Four Square Valentine's Day Bake-off. Next."

The LIVE light went red, and Kelly practically ran toward the door.

Brenda was there waiting on her. "I'm so happy for you."

"I can't believe it." She wanted so badly to be able to share the news with Sara or Mom. Someone who would truly understand how important this was to her.

"Believe it," Brenda said.

"You don't understand. I just beat the executive pastry chef at the fanciest ski resort around. They're known for their desserts. His bio must have four paragraphs of education and five of awards!"

"I can believe it. Your dish was amazing. I told you not to worry." She nudged Kelly with her elbow. "See, you're beating good competition." Brenda spoke into her radio, asking for approval to take Kelly back to the hotel. "Let's get you back so you can rest up for tomorrow."

She'd done what she'd come to achieve. She was as good as the other great bakers. "How am I supposed to sleep after this?"

Brenda clicked her fingers. "Oh, my experience is that as soon as you put your head down, this adrenaline rush is going to start wearing off. You'll sleep like a rock."

"I hope you're right." But she knew herself better than that. Her mind would be running through scenarios all night long. "Bring on the coffee in heavy doses tomorrow morning."

"I can do that," Brenda said, then her radio sounded again. "We're clear to leave. Let's go."

She led Kelly down the long hall to the back elevators. A black limousine waited outside for them.

"Would it be okay if we walked back tonight?" Kelly asked. "It's not but a few blocks and I sure could use the fresh air."

"Sure." Brenda held up a finger and called in the change, then rapped on the passenger window to let the driver know he could take the rest of the night off. She turned to Kelly with a wide grin. "Let's walk."

Chapter Twenty-Six

"**Y**ES!" Andrew punched a fist into the air.

When the other desserts came in, he knew he'd nailed this round. His dessert looked so refined compared to the others. Taste was another matter—they were all pretty tasty, but presentation he had. Only one other plate was a close second.

Lori rushed onto the set. "Congratulations!"

"Thank you." Energy coursed through him, only it was a bit anticlimactic to have no one to celebrate with. "Can we go somewhere and celebrate?"

"I'd have to get it cleared. Do you really think you should go out? You have another big day ahead of you. You need to be at your best."

"Heck yeah. We're in New York City, and I just won the first round of this competition. It's a meal. Come on. Humor me."

"I can ask. Anywhere specific in mind?"

He remembered Francois introducing him to the owner and chef at a place here in New York. "How about 2520?"

Lori laughed. "That place is booked at least four months out. We couldn't get in there if we tried."

"Tell them Francois Dumont's head chef is in town and would like a table."

"Let me clear it with production first. If they say it's okay, then I'll call the restaurant."

"Deal."

She called in the request to production, then hung up and dialed 2520 and spoke to the maître d'.

"Ah-ha!" Andrew was looking forward to this.

He could tell she didn't expect to get a table, but she dropped his name and Francois' like he'd told her to.

She hung up the phone and gave him the stink eye.

Maybe it hadn't worked.

"Son of a gun," she said. "I guess you *are* somebody special. Production laughed when I asked them if we could go there, but said if we could score a table we could go. You know this is on your dime, right?"

"Oh yeah, not a problem."

"Excellent. I've always wondered what that place was like."

"Tonight you'll find out."

She reached up and hit the button for the speaker to the driver. "We're not going to go back just yet. Please take us to 2520. It seems we have a reservation."

Andrew sat back in the seat as if on top of the world. He might actually be able to win this thing.

He stared out the window, enjoying the triumph.

Then someone on the sidewalk caught his eye.

"Whoa!" He slapped the window, and opened the door. "Stop!"

"What are you doing?" Lori grabbed his arm.

"Make him stop the car."

"Stop," Lori yelled to the driver. "You," she said to Andrew. "You calm down."

"I can't. Wait right here." He jumped out of the limo and cars honked as he raced to the sidewalk, dodging people. "Kelly!"

She turned around, her mouth dropping open. "Andrew?"

"I knew that was you," he said, huffing and puffing. "What are you doing here?"

The woman with her squeezed her arm.

"There…there was a fire at the resort down in Orlando," Kelly said. "My friend Brenda was there. RBA sent us up here as a consolation prize. It's been crazy. We just arrived."

"Hi," Brenda said, shaking his hand. "We were headed to dinner."

"You have to come to dinner with me. It's my only night off," he lied. "I can't believe you're here in New York. You should have called me." He wondered if she had. Maybe Lori wasn't passing along his messages.

Kelly patted her pockets. "You won't believe this, but I left my phone in the rush to get us out. I haven't been able to call anyone."

"Total chaos," Brenda agreed.

The limo must have gone around the block, because it was pulling up to the curb and Lori didn't look happy when she jumped out. "What are you doing?"

Andrew noticed the look on Kelly's face. Was she jealous? Just a teensy bit? "Kelly, meet Lori. She's my friend's fiancée. The one who's opening a restaurant this weekend. He's busy, so I'm taking her to dinner at 2520. It's an amazing restaurant. You and Brenda should come with us."

Kelly looked at Brenda and shrugged. "I don't know?"

"On one condition," Brenda said. "We don't talk about anything to do with cooking. This needs to be a night off."

"Deal," Andrew said.

Lori exchanged a glance with Brenda. "Yeah, I can agree with that. I'm so tired of my fiancé talking about recipes and his restaurant. All of that is off limits."

"You and I are on the exact same page, Lori. So, let's go," Brenda said. "It sounds like fun."

When they got to the restaurant, the maître d' took them straight in to a table near the fireplace. "Welcome. The chef asked if he can choose your menu for this evening."

"By all means," Andrew said.

"I'm feeling extremely underdressed," Kelly said.

"That's the nice thing about this kind of place. If you act like you belong, you belong. But Kelly, you look beautiful."

"Thank you." Her blush made him smile.

"Aww." Both Brenda and Lori reacted, and then he was the one blushing.

The sommelier came over and poured them both a glass of wine. Andrew swirled it in his glass, then took in the aroma. One sip later, he said, "Very nice."

The wine was poured. "To running into old friends in unexpected places," Kelly toasted.

"And new friends," Brenda added.

"Cheers." He took a sip of the wine.

Lori finished hers and poured another.

Dinner came, course after course, and the conversation was easy. Brenda and Lori seemed to carry most of the discussion, and that was fine with him, although they pretty much talked about nothing all night. That was okay, because being with Kelly made the evening perfect. She didn't know she was celebrating his win tonight, but it wouldn't have been the same without her.

"Andrew, this has been amazing." Kelly glanced around the restaurant. "I can totally picture you running an establishment like this. The food is wonderful, and the presentation was almost too pretty to eat."

"Yeah, it takes a lot to pull all this together. I love doing it though."

"So, you actually know the chef here?" Kelly asked.

"I do. We've met a couple times. He's dined in my restaurant. It's nice to experience his." He was proud of his work, and although this wasn't his restaurant or cooking, it was special to show Kelly the level of cuisine and ambiance that he executed on a daily basis in his real life.

The restaurant began to empty. Andrew hated to think about the night ending.

"Andrew York." The head chef of 2520 headed for the table. "It really is you. I'm so glad you made it to New York to dine with us. What brings you here?"

"Helping a friend," he said.

"Lori's fiancé is opening a restaurant in town," Kelly chimed in.

"Oh? Are you helping my competition?" he said to Andrew. "I may have to have you come here for a week or two and advise."

"Not even in the same ballpark," Andrew said. "No offense, Lori."

"None taken," Lori said. "My fiancé is opening a swanky pizzeria. Andrew is helping them bring on the swanky part. Totally different demographic."

Andrew appreciated the rescue Lori had offered. That girl was quick on her feet.

"New York is a great city. I'm sure I'll be back. Everything has been magnificent. It's been our pleasure tonight." He gestured to the three ladies. "Please meet my dearest friend in the world, Kelly. And new friends Lori and Brenda."

"Fine food and even finer ladies. You're living high on the hog tonight."

"It's been a pretty good night," Andrew agreed.

"Give my best to Francois."

"Will do."

Kelly offered an impressed nod that made him smile.

Brenda pushed back from the table after dinner. "I'm afraid Kelly and I need to get back to our hotel. We've got a busy day tomorrow. Thank you, Andrew, for the very generous night out. This has been the most amazing meal I've ever had."

He stood and helped Kelly from her chair. "I'm so glad I saw you. You made my night."

"It's been a perfect day. Thanks for being the cherry on top," Kelly said, placing a hand on his arm. "Really perfect." Then she hugged him for a beat or two longer than was probably considered friendly. "Thank you so much."

"You're welcome. I hope there will be more nights like this for us."

She pulled her lips tight, then turned and left.

The waiter brought coffee and dessert for him and Lori.

"This was totally worth it, right?" He spread his arms out. This restaurant was an experience in itself.

"Absolutely delightful, and somehow you managed to do it without breaking your contract. I'm shocked."

"Thank you."

"That wouldn't happen to have been 'Need Cookies' Kelly would it?"

"Was I that transparent?"

She laughed. "Sort of. Thank you for treating me to dinner. This had to have cost you a fortune."

"Nothing but a generous tip. I've done the same for him in Paris." It was nice to be able to show off a little. Having this kind of night out on the town was a nice perk.

Lori lifted her phone. "The driver is out front when you're ready."

He stood and pulled out her chair. "After you."

They got in the car.

Andrew asked the driver, "Do you think we could stop in one of these little souvenir shops and pick up a couple of postcards?"

The driver glanced toward Lori.

He'd forgotten about his short leash for a moment there. "Guess that's your call, huh?"

"Sure. I'll run in for you unless you want to pick them out yourself."

"No. Something touristy, I guess, and stamps, please."

The driver pulled over to the curb, and Lori jumped out of the car.

Andrew pushed the door open for her as she came back out of the shop. "Thanks, what do I owe you?"

"This is on me," she said. "The least I could do after that dinner."

"Well, thank you."

About fifteen minutes later, the limo pulled into the unloading zone underneath the hotel. Lori swiped her key in the elevator to access their floor.

"I'll make sure you're up on time," she said. "How much time do you need to get ready?"

"I'd like to have about forty-five minutes to shower and drink some coffee before I have to talk to anyone. Including you."

"Me too. I'll knock on your door. Let me know if you need a follow-up knock."

"Sounds good. Thanks for celebrating with me."

She waved her key in front of her door. "Now get some sleep, or I'll be in trouble."

"Yes, ma'am. Wouldn't want that to happen." He closed the door behind him and took out the postcards from the small paper sack. It had seemed like such a good idea when he'd asked her to stop. Now, it seemed kind of cheesy. She'd gotten him an I ♥ New York pen and magnet too. That was sweet.

He laid the postcards on the nightstand and took a shower to try to relax so he might get some sleep. The dinner had been amazing. He hadn't had a meal that good that he hadn't had a hand in cooking in a very long time.

When he got out of the shower, he towel-dried his hair and put on a pair of sweatpants, then flipped on the television to the permitted on-demand channel and stretched out on the bed. He picked out the postcard with the New York skyline at night, then turned it over and began to write.

Dear Kelly,
Seeing you tonight was wonderful.

He held his pen over the card. He wanted to write, *wish you were here*, but somehow that didn't seem appropriate with their past.

Instead he wrote,

New York was even more amazing with you in it.
Hope to see you again soon.
Andrew

He laid the card on the bedside table, unsure if he'd actually ask Lori to mail it or not. Then he turned off the light, and the television, and lay back onto the pillow. A few minutes later, he turned on the light and reached for the postcard and pen. He inserted the word "very" between again and soon.

That was more like it. He put a stamp on it and sat it on the nightstand.

He drifted off to sleep.

"Up and at it, Andrew." For a second, he was back home in Bailey's Fork on a school morning, then he realized where he was and that it was Lori from the show pounding on his door.

"Yes?"

"It's time to get up. You've got forty-five minutes."

"Thanks."

"Need a snooze alarm knock?"

He hopped out of bed and opened the door. "No, thanks. I'm getting up."

"Here's your call sheet for the day in case you want something to read while you're dosing caffeine." She handed him the printout. "I'll knock when they're here to get us."

"Thanks." He let the door close behind him and headed for the coffee pot.

He made two cups of coffee and then pulled back the curtains. A light snow had already begun. He probably should've packed warmer clothes, though. Being surrounded by the three seas, Paris rarely got more than a dusting, and anything that fell melted immediately. It was pretty much the same back in Bailey's Fork, except for maybe once a year. He did remember once having a fairly significant snowfall in France, and just like back in North Carolina, it had been utter chaos.

The call sheet itinerary showed his scheduled arrival, hair and makeup, and first lighting checks. The actual show wouldn't begin filming for hours after they arrived. It took a lot of people and a lot of time to put together a short television program.

He tossed the call sheet on the nightstand and pulled his black pants out of the drawer. They hadn't fared too well on the trip, so he pressed them before putting them on. A black T-shirt was all he'd need under his chef's coat. It wasn't like he'd really be walking around outside anyway. They rushed him in and out of every building.

Three quick knocks came at his door.

"Coming." It felt weird to not have his phone or keys to keep track of. He tucked his room key into his wallet and joined Lori outside.

"Ready for round two?"

"More than ready."

They went downstairs and got in the car.

"Where's the call sheet?" Lori asked.

"I left it on my nightstand. I'm sorry. Do we need it?"

"Give me your key. I'll run up and get it." She made a dash for the elevator.

A few minutes later, she jumped back into the limo. "Let's go," she said, and the driver took off.

Round two went much like round one except that it seemed to take longer to finally get to the actual challenge. Between long periods of sitting and waiting, they shot a few stills and did some interview questions.

He was impatient, probably because he was tired. If he hadn't stayed out so late after that heavy meal last night, he might be in better sorts today. But it was too late to change that. *It is what it is.*

Finally they were called to their kitchens, and hair and makeup did one last sweep before they were put back on their mark for the opening.

He eyed cabinet two.

What did they have up their sleeve today?

Andrew closed his eyes and inhaled. He had an excellent sense of smell, and whatever was in that cabinet had a flowery aroma.

Martin's voice boomed over the speakers. Andrew's mind wandered as Martin went through the setup for the show and ended with the explanation of the ingredients in the cabinet behind each chef, along with the reminder that they were expected to use every item in the basket.

"Before we get started with round two, this begins a double elimination. That means a chef has to lose two rounds to be eliminated. So no one will go home tonight. Hopefully that takes a little bit of pressure off our contestants."

Andrew liked the sound of that. No matter what, he'd be in for a third round. If he made it through with a win this round, he was practically guaranteed to be in the final two.

"Today's theme is *Puppy Love and Paper Roses* for a kid's Valentine's Day party."

Andrew's mind went blank. *Kid's party? What does that even mean? Puppy love? Paper Roses? Wasn't that a Marie Osmond song from eons ago? Don't overthink it.*

"Alright, chefs, open your cabinets. Inside you've got a tin of fresh rose petals. Today the other two mystery ingredients are your choice of any nut, and any fruit. You have three hours. Have fun with it. Your time starts now."

Andrew watched the clock start ticking down hours: minutes: seconds.

Kid stuff? All he could remember about Valentine's Day from when he was a kid was heart-shaped suckers and cupcakes with red frosting in homeroom, and he wasn't going to flaunt his mad kitchen skills with either of those.

After a couple of missteps, he finally decided to make his Sesame Apricot Rose Nougat. It would showcase the fresh rose petals beautifully, and he always got compliments on the delicate combination of flavors in that recipe. Apricot would fulfill the fruit requirement. Sesame was technically a seed, so he'd have to integrate a nut of some kind. Not hard.

He gathered the ingredients for the nougat. Thoughts reeled like a tilt-a-whirl in his mind. *How can I make this kid-friendly?*

He moved a heavy saucepan to the stove and began stirring the sugar mixture. He hooked a candy thermometer to the side of the pot and watched it while he beat his egg whites until they formed stiff peaks. As he mixed the ingredients, it finally came to him.

Rather than squares or drops, he'd make long pretzel-type rods. Kids loved things they could hold. Each of the six servings would contain two rods. One would have a rose decoration, rose petals at the top with pistachios as the stem. The other, he'd grind the rose petals and pistachios together and make puppy paw prints down the long rectangular rod.

This would work. The Italian recipe was a versatile one, and he could get this done in the time they had with no problem.

Happy with his decision, he laid a piece of parchment paper on an eighteen-by-thirteen baking sheet then quickly turned out the mixture on the pan. Once the nougat was firm, he'd cut them to create nine-inch rods one inch wide. Plenty to spare in case the decorating didn't go as planned, or better yet, he came up with something even more kid-friendly to decorate them with before the clock ran out.

While the nougat cooled, he began preparing the rose petals and pistachios for the toppings. With extra time on his hands, he set rose petals aside to sugar for a garnish.

He sliced the rods and then went back to the pantry to find something to plate the challenge treats on for presentation to the judges. The two rods would look skimpy and probably way too fancy on a plate unless he did something playful on the plate with drizzle. He rummaged through the different plates. With the rods being nine inches, his choices were limited, but then he noticed a shelf of tall, thin-footed glasses across the room, only about two inches in diameter. He could put two in each one and they'd look fun, and also show off the rose design standing lengthwise like that.

Delighted with his choices, he went back to his station and finished decorating the Sesame Apricot Rose Nougat Rods and began plating them.

"Five minutes to go."

He had plenty of time, but hearing that announcement set his competitive edge into overdrive.

Taking great care to make sure each of the six desserts were exactly the same, he tucked and tilted the rods into a glass. Unhappy with the presentation, he pulled them out and tucked sugared rose petals in the bottom of the glass, then repositioned the rods. A much more fun and colorful display.

"One minute to go, chefs."

Andrew placed the last two pieces into the glass, then double-checked his entry. Rose water was in the recipe. His fruit, apricot, also in the entry. Pistachios in the garnish on all pieces. Check. Check. Check.

"Time!"

He raised his hands and stepped back from the counter. He'd serve them in his restaurant any day. In fact, they were lovely enough for a wedding reception, or a nice alternative to a cake for the rehearsal dinner.

Chapter Twenty-Seven

MARTIN'S VOICE CAME OVER THE speaker with a boom, making Andrew jump. "This round, the judges will be coming to you, Chefs."

His desserts were picture perfect. He was pretty sure they'd stand up to anyone's.

The door to his kitchen opened, and cameras moved across the framework above Andrew's head.

"Good afternoon, Andrew," Martin said with a dip of his head. The judges filed into the kitchen and lined up across the quartz countertop, facing him. Georgie, the beautiful Latina chef who'd made dessert burritos a thing around the world. Then the dark-haired Collin, every housewife's fantasy with his dark hair and smoldering eyes. And finally Abraham, whose head was as smooth as well-done fondant with that unforgettable raspy New York accent that got people's attention. These judges represented the best in the baking world. All very different, but just as celebrated.

Martin Schlipshel took long strides around the counter and stepped next to Andrew. "What have you made for us this round?"

"Hi, Martin. Chefs." He was at ease in front of them, considering himself their peer even if his expertise was on the cooking side. "I've made a unique pretzel-rod-shaped candy for the kids. Sesame

Apricot Rose Nougat with a rose petal and pistachio decoration on each. Rather than plating them, I chose to present them in a fun glass with a couple of sugared rose petals in the bottom."

Martin looked impressed. "Very interesting." He shifted his attention to the judges. "See what you think."

The judges each took a footed glass. They examined his entry from all sides and then took generous bites. Abraham nearly ate his whole serving. That had to be good.

Martin gave them a moment to taste the dish, then said, "Let's start with Chef Abraham this time."

"Thank you, Martin," Abraham said. "Well, this is a beautiful dessert. I like the idea of a long-shaped dessert as being interesting to a child, but I'll tell you there's no way my kid would eat this."

Andrew's heart fell.

"Don't get me wrong. It's delicious, and gorgeous. I could eat both of them right now. But the tastes are mature. You've given us a complicated combination. It works from a dessert perspective, but I'm afraid you've totally missed the mark for *Puppy Love and Paper Roses* this round."

The words cut like swords. "Thank you, chef." Andrew heard his heart pounding in his head.

Chef Georgie laid one of the nougat rods down on the napkin in front of her. "I agree. It's as if you didn't listen to the challenge at all. I think these are lovely. I'd love to have them at my next restaurant opening or gala, so let's definitely talk. But to serve to children? This would never fly. Not to mention that you served them in a thin glass." She tapped it with her fingernail. "You don't have kids, do you?"

"No, ma'am." Andrew regretted the mistake.

"I didn't think so. One of these would get broken for sure. What if someone got hurt?"

He hadn't even considered the glass being a problem for kids. His mind flickered to the days when there were kids' parties at

Main Street Cafe. The running. The laughter. She was so right. He'd blown it.

Andrew's T-shirt clung to his body under the heavy chef's jacket. He ran a finger under the collar.

"Chef Collin. What are your thoughts?"

Chef Collin straightened. "Okay. It's an elaborate dish. It might be a little too over-the-top frou-frou for a kids Valentine's Day party, but I know my kid would eat it. It's good. The technique was on point. The paw prints are playful. I'd give you this to take away with you. Listen carefully to the theme of the challenge."

"Yes, chef," Andrew said. "Thank you." He turned and walked off stage as the theme music played.

When he exited the stage door, Lori led him back to his dressing room. He was angry with himself for making the stupid mistake.

"It'll be fine," she said.

"Thank goodness it's a double elimination, or I'd be going home right now."

"But you're not. It's one so-so round. Be flawless the rest of them. I have a feeling you've got it in you." Lori flung the door open to his dressing room and then spoke into her radio. "We're in the dressing room."

Over her radio, a crackled voice commanded, "Thank you. Next contestant. Come forward."

"What was I thinking? I'd have been better off making a simple cupcake." *My training is more mature than this. I'm not going to be able to just pull old recipes out of my hat and execute.*

"They just couldn't appreciate what you made," Lori said, trying to be supportive.

"No. They were right." What did it matter anyway? He had a great trip home, and he was earning a nice stipend on top of his vacation pay to be here. So what if he got eliminated? He'd go back to Paris and step right back into his role at the restaurant. Not a darn thing wrong with that. Or call Kelly, get his whole life back. His phone. His freedom.

If he got the boot today, he'd drive back down to North Carolina and spend the rest of the time there with Kelly. Those RBA things weren't usually more than a few days long. She might even be back already.

Lori's phone rang. She spoke quickly, then headed to the door. "You ready to go back to the hotel?"

"Absolutely." He followed her to the limousine. The ride back was quiet. He was glad she respected him enough not to force conversation.

When they got up to their rooms, she asked if she could come in. "You're mad," she said as she closed the door behind her.

"I'm disappointed. I thought they wanted excellence. I didn't know I was supposed to be making school cupcakes. I mean, who can't make those?"

"Trust me, not everyone." She raised her hand slowly in the air. "Like me."

He snickered. "You can't cook? Really?"

"Not a lick."

"How'd you get a job here?"

"I'm studying journalism. This internship was on the list, and it sounded way more interesting than the others. And it is. I loved it so much I stayed on. That was three years ago. It's pretty cool. I meet people like you." She sat down on the couch in the sitting area of his room and called in a pizza. "You made it to the next round. Don't be so hard on yourself."

"Everyone is making it to the next round."

"So, nothing to worry about. Let it go. Your Sesame Apricot Rose Nougat sticks were delicious. All three judges said so."

"They also said a lot of other things. Weren't you listening?"

"I was, but trust me, anything can happen in these rounds. Relax."

"Relax?" His voice rose a note. "I practically burned a bridge with the man who mentored me for the past seven years to be in this stupid contest." He swept a hand through his hair. "What was I thinking, coming here for this?"

"That you wanted to showcase your skills. Maybe that you want to use that money to fulfill your dream of having your own restaurant."

He plopped down on the other end of the sofa. What he was really thinking was he wished he'd ditched the contest and followed Kelly. After seeing her at the restaurant, he believed more than ever that they were meant to be. Who bumped into someone in New York City? It was meant to be.

He glanced over where he'd left the postcard on the nightstand in the other room.

But it wasn't there.

He got up and walked into the bedroom and flipped on the light.

"No way."

"What's the matter?" Lori asked.

"Maid must've stolen my postcard."

"The one to Kelly in North Carolina?"

He peered around the corner. How did she know? "Yeah."

"I saw it when I picked up the call sheet this morning. I dropped it in the mail slot in the hall on my way down."

"Oh." He wasn't sure whether to be mad or thank her. It wasn't really the worst thing that could happen. He wasn't sure he'd have had the guts to send it himself anyway. "Okay. Yeah. Thanks."

"Andrew you're being way too hard on yourself. Relax. Your skills are going to shine no matter what you make. Don't try so hard. Let your personality come through in your desserts, not just your culinary acumen. Have a little fun with it. Smile. That goes further than you think. They're watching you all the time."

"I'm sorry I was short with you."

"It's okay. On another note, not to re-stress you out more, but that chef in Paris is blowing up your phone. How important are those calls? Can they wait until after we're done filming?"

"I don't know."

"We can listen to them together."

The pizza arrived, and Lori jumped up and paid for it on her corporate card. "Smells good."

They both dove into the pizza, and Andrew opened the mini-bar. "Beer or soda?"

"Water's good."

He tossed her a bottle of water, then grabbed a soda and popped the top. "Let's hear the messages."

"Here we go." Lori put the phone on the coffee table and pressed the button to play on speaker.

Three messages. All from Francois Dumont. With his heavy accent, it was almost hard to understand them, but Andrew had been face-to-face on these rants enough to know that Francois had been red-faced and practically spitting his words. He was in an all-out ego-driven tirade over one of the chefs.

"What is wrong with that guy?" Lori's face twisted into a grimace. "Did the guy he fired work for you?"

"No." Andrew handled his own kitchen. If there was a problem, he'd have taken care of it long before Francois ever caught wind of it. "I'm Chef de Cuisine in a different restaurant he owns."

"Then why is he calling you?"

"He's mad and wants to rant. Probably wants me to do the dirty work, or clean up after he created a mess by firing someone on the spot." It was truly exhausting. "Happens all the time."

"So Chef de Cuisine translates to babysitter? Plus he gets *all* the glory for your hard work? That doesn't sound fair at all. Then this is your time to shine." She took a bite of pizza and raised the slice in the air. "You need to rock the rest of this competition."

Seeing Francois through someone else was eye-opening. Andrew's phone rang again.

"It's him," Lori said. "You can take it, but don't mention the show. If you do, my hands are tied. I have to report it, and you'll be disqualified."

"I'm clear on that." Andrew pressed the speaker button and answered. "Francois. I just got your messages."

"I have fired that miserable excuse for a chef. I will not tolerate him changing things on my menu without my prior consent. It's the last straw. I need you to come back and cover for him. They are in chaos in that kitchen. They are waiting on you."

"I can't be there tonight, Francois." His excuse to leave wasn't buying him the time he needed.

"What?" Francois became even more agitated. "What is it that could be so important that you can't come back and take care of this tonight? You are my right hand. You are here to keep things running smoothly. Things are not running smoothly."

"Francois, I told you I'd be gone. I wish you had let things lie until I got back. That's not even my restaurant you're having a problem with."

"Your restaurant. None of them are yours. They are all mine. And you work for me. Where I need you."

Andrew glanced over at Lori, who'd turned her head. He was embarrassed, and for the first time realizing how poorly Francois treated him for all he did for him. And had since the day he'd started working for him.

"Francois. I haven't been totally honest with you. I'm off dealing with important personal affairs, and I'm back in the United States. If I could, I'd be there. As I've always been. But it's not doable this time." In five years, no matter what happened, when Francois called in a tizzy Andrew had dropped what he was doing and shifted gears to dig Francois out of a bind of his own doing.

"I had no idea," Francois said.

He seemed to calm down a little bit.

If Andrew forfeited the contest and went back now, he'd be right where he'd been. Not such a bad place at all. But if he stayed, and he won, that would be one nice chunk of change toward starting his own restaurant. No matter where he decided to open it. Of course, if Francois fired him, Andrew may have no choice but to stay in the U.S. to do it. Once Francois had blackballed a chef, it took a long time to earn his way back into the circle.

Andrew tried to keep his voice calm. "I'm sorry to let you down. I promise you, Gillian is ready. Give her the chance, Francois."

"You know how I feel about women in charge of my kitchen."

"Trust me on this, Francois. I've never steered you wrong."

A long, guttural moan came from the phone. "I'll handle it," he grumbled.

Andrew could imagine the wrinkle in Francois' forehead, the one that creased so deeply it made his eyebrows seem to meet and curve into devil-like horns on the ends.

"We'll talk when you get back."

"Yes, sir."

He hung up the phone and let out a long breath, dropping his forehead into his hands. "Not good." With his eyes closed, he saw the same scenario play out in his head a dozen times, and that was just in the past two years. Francois had a short fuse. He ran though chefs like they were day-old bread.

Andrew had never, until now, considered that he was the only constant around Francois since he'd been in France. And yet, would he ever reach the heights of his own career in the shadows of Francois?

"Well played," Lori said.

"I hope I haven't just closed the door with him. He's not forgiving," Andrew said. "At all."

"Well, the right thing will happen."

"You're one of those, huh?"

"One of what?"

"Those look-on-the-bright-side types. Kelly would've given me the exact same advice. Only I don't think that's always true. Lately, I've been thinking my life would be a lot different in a better way if I'd never gone to Paris."

"She must have been pretty special in your life at one time."

"That doesn't begin to describe her." He wondered where she was tonight.

"I hear melancholy in that statement. You really did love her."

He nodded.

"Fine, I'm not sure listening to those messages was the best way to get you to relax, but it certainly was exhausting. I'll wake you in the morning."

The following morning at the studio, they started with the announcement of who took the loss in the second round. Since it was double elimination, everyone was still in play for the $100,000 prize.

Andrew stood in front of his covered plate in the kitchen on set, waiting for the music intro and lights to go live.

"In three…two…one…"

"Welcome back. We're ready to show who lost one life in this two-round elimination to the one-hundred-thousand-dollar Four Square Valentine's Day Bake-Off. Chefs, prepare to lift the covered plate in front of you. Like in the last round, you're looking for a Valentine card. If your plate is empty, then you lost this round."

Andrew readied his hand over the handle of the silver cover plate.

"Now."

He lifted the cover, almost afraid to look down, but there on the tray was a brightly colored Valentine card with a bright green frog leaping into the air right in the center of a field of green grass and flowers made of red hearts. It read, You Make Me Hoppy!

He practically fell to his knees with relief.

A buzzer rang, and the hair and makeup people came in to change things up a little to make it look like the next day. Martin started the announcement of who got eliminated, but of course the mic cut out and Andrew was left in silence.

He'd eked through. *Thank goodness.*

Lori walked in, carrying a bottle of water. "Congrats!"

"How did that happen? I saw the other entries. Mine was ridiculously off the mark. Almost embarrassingly so."

"I told you anything could happen. Dishes are undercooked, burned, and I can't tell you how often someone flat-out forgets to integrate a mandatory ingredient. Or time runs out and they don't get everything on the plate."

"I'm thanking my lucky stars right now."

"Good, because we'll be moving to round three now, and these count," she reminded. "You're halfway there."

They went through the same drill as in rounds one and two, and it did seem to get easier. Andrew was much more relaxed, letting Lori and the team shuffle him around.

Martin announced the theme of round three. "Black-Tie Affair. In your cabinets, chefs, you'll find the mandatory ingredient."

Andrew listened and opened the cabinet when he was instructed to do so.

All that was inside was a pomegranate and Pom juice.

Lori's advice ran through his mind. "Relax and concentrate on the challenge. Let the baking skills show themselves naturally. Don't flaunt them."

Black-Tie Affair.

He pictured a swanky black-tie affair at his restaurant. He'd hosted many there with the rich and elite.

Pomegranate brought a beautiful color to the table, but the taste could be tart.

At this kind of party, things were small. Elegant. A smile played on his lips.

He'd make vanilla-coconut almond panna cotta with a pomegranate jelly layer in a tall shot glass. He'd layer the panna cotta at an angle until it set long enough to then spoon the red transparent layer of jelly on top.

The recipe itself wasn't complex, but the collision of flavors should delight the judges while perfectly meeting all of the expectations of a Black-Tie Affair.

The precise execution of layering the flavors and colors into the thin tall glasses required a steady hand and years of practice, which he had. Not a smear or shaky line was to be seen on any of his six entries.

His ego was recovering a bit from the last round.

He relaxed, and for the first time in a long time, seven years maybe, he enjoyed creating a new recipe. He examined the finished product. Almost right, but missing something. *What would Kelly have done differently?* He grabbed a handful of ripe pomegranate seeds and sprinkled them atop each of the desserts. *You're my secret ingredient, Kelly, and you don't even know it.*

Chapter Twenty-Eight

I N ROUND THREE, KELLY HAD made a layered shot glass dessert of gingerbread crust, a pomegranate-infused gelatin, and a light almond cheesecake, with sugar-glazed pomegranate seeds on top. She'd been so surprised to see another shot glass dessert, one even prettier than her own with the pomegranate jelly. Perfectly clear. With no bubbles, it was almost like red liquid suspended.

But it hadn't mattered that they'd been even a little bit similar, because those two *Black-Tie Affair* entries were the two that had made it to the finals.

She actually had a chance of winning this.

"And then there were two," Martin Schlipshel said over the speakers. "Welcome back to the final round of our Four Square Valentine's Day Bake-Off. Four of the best pastry chefs around have been vying for our biggest award yet. And we're down to the final two. The grand prize? One hundred thousand dollars and the title of Best Four Square Bake-Off Pastry Chef."

Music filled the air, and then her kitchen went silent. It was the long lulls that made the whole thing feel like an out-of-body experience.

"Tonight's show is in front of the live studio audience."

Kelly could picture the big screens on either side of the stage as Martin played puppeteer with the contestants, including herself, from the stage in front of the audience.

Kelly's arms shook all the way up to the elbows. She shifted on her feet. Somewhere she'd heard if you bent your knees slightly you wouldn't pass out, and that would be a plus, because she could hardly bake in this final round if she was laid out on the floor.

This was the longest she'd ever gone in her life without talking to her parents. She hadn't even been allowed to watch television. She felt so isolated. But it was only one more round.

I can do this. I can do this. I can do this.

"Hello, finalists," Martin said.

She smiled and said, "Hello."

"Are you ready for the final round of Four Square Valentine's Day Bake-Off?"

"Yes, sir."

Wouldn't it be nice if whoever was in the other kitchen just tossed their white flour sack towel into the air and said, "Nope. Think I'm done." And then Martin awarded me the winner without the next grueling eight-hour task?

"I thought so," he said.

A girl can dream.

"Here are the guidelines." As Martin began to explain, two men in black chef jackets wheeled in a whiteboard with the details printed on it. "You'll have eight hours. Each of you has been assigned an assistant. Your assistant is an accomplished sous chef from our own Four Square Restaurant here in Manhattan. They're here to assistant you in any way you see fit."

Kelly heard the door open to the studio, and in walked a young man in a white chef's coat. "Hi, Thank you so much. I'm Kelly."

"I know. I've been watching you. I'm excited to be here to help. I'm Randy."

"So nice to meet you. Thank you."

"The dimensions of your entry," Martin continued, "from the

table to the top of whatever is tallest on your masterpiece can be no shorter than twenty-three inches, and no taller than forty-seven inches. Any original recipe will do, so bring out a twist. You'll display your whole entry as one. Afterward, we'll pull eight servings. Six for the judges—our three judges from the previous rounds and three celebrity judges. One serving for me, in case of a tie, and one piece for the competition to try."

Kelly was already doing the math in her head. She knew from experience that her multi-layer cakes she made every day of the week measured a whopping eight inches tall. The height was what everyone commented on, and no matter how thin you sliced that cake the customer felt like they'd gotten a whopper of a piece. She'd need three of those to get to the minimum height.

Was taller better? Probably more impressive.

"The theme this Valentine's Day is…"

A drum roll vibrated through the studios.

"Marry Me."

The audience applauded, and through it all Kelly heard a laugh that reminded her of Andrew's. She shook the interrupting thought. Surely it was the Marry Me theme taunting her memory, since Andrew was the only man to ever say those two words to her. Her nose tickled, and for a fleeting second she thought she might tear up. *He's in town. Is it possible he'd come to see the show being taped live? He'd be shocked to see me standing here on stage.*

Until recently she thought she was living their dream, but now seeing him again, in her kitchen, in her house, then here on the street in New York—it was like he'd been the missing piece all along.

The clock that rose above the white board at the front of her kitchen lit up.

08:00:00

And then it began to count down.

She turned to Randy. "I have to win this."

For all the moments she'd ever missed Andrew. For the money

to put aside to help keep Main Street Cafe a part of Bailey's Fork. She'd buy it and figure out how to make it all work. Her team could keep The Cake Factory going. She could hire a chef to run the cafe if she had to. Or maybe just expand the factory into the old Main Street Cafe space and serve light fare during the lunch hour. But now wasn't the time to waste brain cells on that.

Kelly turned to Randy. "There are five hundred ideas rolling through my head right now."

He smiled. "You'll impress them no matter what you do. I'd suggest you create the cake proposal you'd want. Start with one decorative factor, and let it go from there."

"A Tiffany blue ring box. It seems like the most romantic thing in the whole world to me. You see that blue box and you know it's special."

"Yeah. I'm still saving for one of those. My girl thinks the same thing. Okay. What is your knock-'em-dead cake?"

"Oh gosh, traditional wedding cake is amazing, but if I were making this for me, I'd go with my favorite recipe. One I created myself over weeks and weeks of practice to come up with the right balance of flavors. Triple-Layer Honey Almond Cake with Berries."

"I think I just drooled."

"It's so good, plus it's a nice upgrade from the traditional almond cake." He'd unstuck her flow. She started sketching out the design on the parchment. "We alternate a light, fluffy mascarpone crème fraiche with fondant-covered cake layers. So, four layers, and the ring box topper."

He ran his finger along the sketch. "Fondant at the bottom, then whipped, fondant, whipped, and the ring box?"

"Yes."

"I like it."

"We'll do an edible white chocolate card hanging from the box with Will You Marry Me? in red with interlocking hearts to tie in the Valentine's Day part of this theme."

She held the pencil to her lips. "Oh. I know! Then conversation hearts in Tiffany blue, white, pink, and yellow with YES on every one of them, like he's stacking the deck."

"Clever. I like it." He nodded and got right to work. "I'm great with modeling chocolate. Want me to make the box?"

"Yes. Larger than life—let's make it about six inches. We'll make the ring too. We can do edible sugar glass for the big diamond. I'll get the cakes going."

In a flurry of activity, and a mist of flour, the final round was under way.

Chapter Twenty-Nine

A NDREW WAS NEARLY IN ANALYSIS paralysis, trying to decide which of the fancy recipes he'd mastered over the years he should bring to the table.

Andrew's helper, Victoria, stood by as he rattled off different cake ideas. "We could do a pink champagne cake with a raspberry mousse. That would be easy to pull in Valentine's Day colors." Then he jotted down three more. "Oh, or a salted caramel toffee crunch cake. We could color the toffee red and do three tiers, but no frosting on top or the sides, just loose frosting poured across the top dripping down. It could be really pretty."

Victoria was a young lady, wearing a 3/4-length sleeve chef coat and a wedding band.

"I think," she said, "take the competition out of the equation for a second. If you were proposing to the girl of your dreams tonight on Valentine's Day, what would you want to bake? I mean, something dripping down the sides doesn't sound like it's going to sweep a girl off her feet."

He stepped back. "You're right." It was essentially the same advice Lori had been giving him. *Keep your eye on the theme. Don't worry about the complexity of the recipe. That'll come naturally.*

The only woman he'd ever asked to marry him was Kelly. There was no question in his mind what he would bake for her. The Honey Almond Cake they'd created while they'd been dating and he'd worked in the café slinging hash in the evenings. Simple in taste, but he could make the presentation elegant.

Andrew shook Victoria's hand. "If there's anything you're not comfortable with that I ask you to do, let me know. We'll divide and conquer to your skill set."

"I was top of my class. Don't you worry. I've got your back," she said proudly.

"Awesome." He folded his arms across his chest. He hadn't made a tiered cake since culinary school, but this wasn't a wedding cake competition; the theme was Marry Me. A proposal cake. "So, I'm thinking a proposal cake can go a couple of ways. If you're confident of a yes, it could be a big party cake. Not so sure of the yes, then it could be just the two of you."

"Somehow I find it hard to believe you've ever had an unconfident day in your life."

"I'm going to take that as a compliment." He laughed. He liked her confidence too. Like Kelly, she spoke her mind.

"Just brainstorming here for a few minutes to be sure we've got a solid plan," he said. "We could do a Croquembouche. Kind of tie to France, where I live. Or we could do a tower of petit fours with *Marry Me?* written on them. I do great petit fours." He grabbed the pen from his shirt pocket. "Or..." he sketched out a large round cake, "...frost in a quilted pattern with tiny diamonds between gold-colored piping, like engagement rings. I saw a conical layer tray in the pantry room. We could make macarons and stack them on their edges on that tray towering above the cake like a topiary. On the top, the words Will You Marry Me? Two rows—WILL YOU, over MARRY ME?—in bright-red candy glass. "

"That sounds beautiful. That's totally it."

"We can do two different flavor macarons. One for yes, and one for no." He shook his head. "No. We don't want any nos. We'll do passion fruit macarons, strawberry for a nice red color, and good old almond, and we'll stamp with edible ink YES on one side and I DO on the other. Hopefully we'll have some gold back there for that. I think I saw it."

"Good thinking. It sounds fabulous. And doable."

"Let's see what we can find in the pantry for the display." After fifteen minutes of rummaging through their options, they had to nix the topiary idea. The display wasn't sturdy enough to place on top of the cake, and attaching the *Will You Marry Me?* topper was going to present too many opportunities for mistakes. Instead, Andrew found a four-tier wedding cake form. He'd use the three widest layers for the custom macarons, then at the top layer he'd place the cake and cake topper.

"Can you calculate how many macarons we'll need to make for those three layers?" he asked Victoria.

"I'm on it."

He wrote out a list of the steps they'd need to take, in what order, with times next to them to be sure they stayed on track. This wasn't his first rodeo. He could make anything happen as long as he had a plan.

Andrew redrew the final idea, marking the colors and tools needed for each step.

He wrote down the recipe for the cake. "We'll use a passion fruit curd in between the layers. It'll be bright and fresh," he said, mostly to himself.

On a separate piece of paper, he began listing the recipe steps for the macarons. "You've made macarons before?"

"Every week."

"Thank you for being my partner."

"You have someone very special in mind as you're making this cake, don't you?" Victoria said.

He remembered Lori saying the cameras and mics were always on. He held back the truth. "Actually, no. I was just trying to pick something that would be both elegant and yet different."

"Oh, sorry. The way you seemed so excited…I thought maybe this was almost a practice run for someone."

"I wish it was," he said quietly.

She shrugged. "No offense, but who ever said men were smart wasn't a woman."

He laughed. "Probably true."

"If you wish it was, make it so. It's really pretty simple," Victoria said.

He walked over to the counter then came back. "You know what, I'm going to switch something up here."

She stopped mid-motion. "I've got the strawberry macarons started."

"That's cool. No change in the macarons at all." He whipped past her. "It was what you said about this cake being special enough for that special person. I know exactly what cake is most important to her."

"Now you're talking! Cooking with your heart. I'm telling you from experience, that's the secret ingredient in every great recipe."

The words played in his mind. The secret ingredient? It was true that the recipe had never come out quite as perfect as when he and Kelly had made it together, but if she saw the show, she'd know he was serious. His love for her was still as strong as it ever was.

"Thank you for saying that. I think a few things just fell in place for me."

"My work here is done then," she said with a laugh.

"Hardly. We've got a lot to do over the next few hours."

"We've got this."

He prepared the cake pans and set them aside, then got right down to work on the one cake recipe he knew meant the world to Kelly McIntyre—the Triple-Layer Honey Almond Cake.

Chapter Thirty

"ONE HOUR TO GO," MARTIN Schlipshel announced, then made a visit to each of the kitchens, which only made Kelly want to chase him out with a rolling pin. She had things to do. He traipsed around her kitchen with his microphone, murmuring comments, but she didn't let him get her off her game. She continued frosting her cakes. All of the elements were coming together just as she'd pictured them, and Randy was an excellent baker in his own right.

"How's your sous chef working out?" Martin asked her.

She'd hoped he'd do his little recon mission and disappear without pulling her into a conversation. "I couldn't have asked for a better partner."

But that really wasn't true. She'd had the best partner once. She knew exactly what that was like. It was more of a collaboration than giving orders. And there was a silence in the movements, neither having to ask the other for anything—one fluid creation. She still had a box of all those handwritten recipes she and Andrew had worked on. She'd always thought they'd eventually have a cookbook together. One they'd sell in their restaurant. *Focus. This isn't about Andrew.*

"Thirty minutes left. Start bringing it home."

She and Randy started stacking the completed pieces. Everything fit right into place. The open Tiffany blue box was the perfect cake topper.

"Ten minutes."

She and Randy made a slow walk around the finished cake.

"It looks great," he said.

"I'm really happy with it. The edible glass diamond is perfect." She tapped the tag to shift it a millimeter. The words in red, *Will You Marry Me?*, made her heart stutter. If someone ever asked her to get married with something as elaborate as this, she'd break down in joyous tears.

Martin announced, "One minute."

"I'm satisfied." She took a step back from the counter, and Randy took her hand and raised it in the air.

"Time's up!"

She and Randy turned toward each other and high-fived with both hands.

A moment later, the LIVE light went out, and Brenda came in to get them. "You two worked great. It was like you'd been baking together forever."

"She's a great talent. I learned a few things," Randy said.

"Thank you."

Brenda said, "This is where you and Randy will say goodbye. We'll be taking you back to get freshened up, then to hair and makeup while the judges deliberate."

"Oh, gosh. Randy, thank you so much. I appreciate everything you did. You went the extra mile. That ring box is so perfect."

"You're so welcome. You know my girlfriend is going to expect a cake like that from me now."

"Sorry."

"No. Thank you, and thanks for letting me be a part of it. I just got my fifteen minutes of fame. My mom is in the audience."

"No way!"

"Yep. I'm going to go sit with her and watch to see who wins." He raised his crossed fingers. "I hope everything you ever wanted comes true for you."

He turned and left, and she felt lonely for a moment. She wished her mom was in the audience too. Or Sara. Someone.

"That's so sweet," Kelly said. "I'm so glad for him."

Brenda hugged her. "I've got something sweet that came over your phone earlier for you. I think it'll add to this perfect moment."

"From Sara?"

"Sort of." Brenda handed Kelly's phone to her. There were two pictures, one right behind the other. The first was a postcard of the New York skyline at night, the other a note from Andrew on the reverse side. "That was so sweet."

"Is this the same Andrew on your call list? The one we went to dinner with?"

She nodded.

"Seemed like a nice reunion from what I could tell at dinner the other night."

"It was, and I'd give anything to be sharing this experience with him. There's a lot of history there. Not all of it good."

Brenda gave her a sly wink. "Not all of it bad either, from what I saw." She led Kelly to the dressing room. "You've got ten minutes to freshen up and get changed." An identical uniform hung on the back of the door. "I'll be back to get you."

Kelly stretched her arms over her head, then slowly bent to the side. Her limbs felt heavy. If she sat down now, she might never get back up. Eight hours of competitive baking was a long day. Her muscles ached, and her eyes burned from being under the bright lights all day.

The judges were judging her entry right now. Her stomach knotted.

She grabbed the change of clothes, raced into the bathroom and turned on the shower. She put a shower cap on her head and jumped in, letting the hot water pour over her. She silently counted out the seconds to one hundred eighty, then stepped back out of the shower. Her body relaxed a little as she quickly changed into the clean clothes, then threw away the shower cap and ran a quick brush through her hair.

Brenda hustled her down the hall to hair and makeup.

Kelly sat in the chair, and three people came from different angles around her all at the same time.

Then Brenda's phone rang. "Yes. Okay. Right. In Studio A?" She put her phone in her pocket. "Slight change in plans." She grabbed Kelly's hand. "Come on, we're going to the stage."

"Not the kitchen?"

"Nope. Not sure what's going on." A line creased in Brenda's forehead. "They're going to do an on-stage interview. They want you to walk straight out. You'll see your cake there on a table. There's a blue box taped on the stage to the right of the cake. Stand in the box."

"To the right of the cake. Blue box." Kelly nodded. "Got it."

"Good luck."

Chapter Thirty-One

FROM HIS SPOT JUST OFF stage, Andrew could see the judges seated behind a long table covered in a formal black, long tablecloth with a white runner. Glass vases of red roses separated each judge.

The stadium seating on this sound stage was filled with people, and there was a thrum of nervous excitement building.

Martin paced the set in front of the judges. "It's the first time in all of our Bake-Off history that we've encountered this during a competition." He turned toward the judges.

Andrew could see both cakes, but from here he couldn't make out much detail.

"Our judges are stumped," Martin continued.

The crowd cheered. Andrew's insides churned. He'd been so sure his entry would blow any competition away. It had turned out perfectly.

"Both of these Marry Me entries are unique in their own way, but equally as lovely in presentation," Martin announced. "The uncanny thing is that both cakes taste nearly the same. For the first time, we have a tie."

A tie?

"But we can't have a tie, can we?" Martin was dramatically building excitement with the audience.

"Noooo," the crowd yelled.

"We measured both cakes." Martin moved around the stage with great animation as he led the contestants and the audience on. Still not revealing the competition, he said, "Madam, your cake came in one inch shorter than the maximum height."

The audience applauded.

"Sir, your cake is obviously shorter." He moved to that side of the stage in front of Andrew's cake. There was an audible groan from the audience. "The macaron layers are thin, but the cake layer is significant. Thank goodness you have that tall declaration of love on top, because if you'd left off the 'Will You Marry Me?' cake-topper, you'd have been below the minimum height. You're both within the limits."

The audience applauded wildly.

"I'm the tie-breaking vote," Martin said. "So let's bring out both of our pastry chefs."

The theme music filled the room, and applause rose.

Lori prodded Andrew to the stage door. "Go!"

He headed straight for his cake, located the tape outline on the floor behind it, and stood facing the judges and Martin.

The music continued to play.

Movement in his peripheral vision caught his attention. He saw the other cake and couldn't take his eyes off it. Someone had definitely brought their A game.

He blinked against the bright lights, then turned to face his competitor and almost choked.

Her mouth hung wide.

"Before we talk to our two finalists, I want to bring out the other two contestants in this Four Square Valentine's Day Bake-Off."

Music played, and Frank walked out on stage.

"Welcome back the first chef to be eliminated, Frank Wells. Frank is the Executive Pastry Chef at the Elk Traxx Ski Resort in

Colorado." They shook hands. "His wife, Danica, nominated him. She's in the audience tonight."

Danica stood and waved.

Frank said, "I promise it's the only time I've lied to you, honey."

"I'm so proud of you," she said, blowing him a kiss.

Martin walked a few steps to the right. "Our second contestant to be eliminated was Kacey Nugent. Come on out, Kacey."

She walked on to the stage, waving.

"It was a close competition. Kacey is known for her New York cheesecakes around here. She owns Kacey Cakes here in the city, and was nominated by a customer."

Kacey smiled and clapped. "Who?"

"We'd like to share with you and our studio audience who nominated you for this show." The camera scanned the audience, then settled on a New York City police officer in uniform. "Do you recognize him?"

Kacey's hands flew to her face. "Oh. My. Gosh! I do. He's one of my best customers. *You* nominated me?"

"I did, and I'd like to take you out to celebrate if you'll let me."

She pulled her lips in, showing a dimple in her left cheek.

"I think you've just been asked out on a date on national television," Martin said. "Are you going to answer his question, or do we need to take this off-stage?"

"Yes. Yes, of course I'll go out with you. How can I say no to that?"

Martin shrugged dramatically. "Apparently, you can't. In our Valentine's Day Bake-Off we're not just baking, we're making happy-ever-afters."

The audience cheered.

"Come on over here." Martin motioned to the two couples. "We loved having you on our show. We'd like to send you out on a very special Valentine's Day dinner on us. There's a limo waiting outside. Everyone give them a big round of applause."

Martin marched over to Andrew and Kelly as the others left the stage.

"This might be the best match-up we've ever had on our show." Martin walked to Kelly. "Do you have any idea who may have nominated you to be on the show?"

"No, sir. I've thought about it a lot. At first I thought maybe it was my friend Sara, but she seemed as surprised as I did when you walked into The Cake Factory that day."

"You're right. It wasn't Sara."

"Have you kept being here a complete secret?"

"I have," she said. "Completely."

"I bet you were surprised to see a familiar face on the stage then."

She glanced in Andrew's direction. "Yes. Very surprised. I saw him for the first time in seven years last week. He said he going to New York to help a friend open a restaurant. I didn't suspect a thing."

"Good one," Martin said, giving Andrew a nod as he moved over with the mic to talk to him.

"Andrew York. Executive Chef, or Chef de Cuisine shall we say, for the infamous Francois Dumont. You flew in all the way from France for this competition."

"Yes, sir. I did."

"And you've kept this under wraps as well?"

"Yes, but it hasn't been easy." He glanced over at Kelly. "I don't like lying to the people I care about."

"Well, I'm sure everyone will understand when they see where you've been the last few days. So, tell me, Andrew, any idea who may have nominated you?"

"I'm pretty sure it was my Aunt Claire. She was the one who got me into pastry school in France. She's been instrumental in paving the way for me to garner experience with the most celebrated chefs of all types."

"No. It wasn't your aunt, but it was someone you know very well." Martin walked out on stage, closer to the audience. "You might be surprised to learn that the same person nominated both of you."

Kelly and Andrew looked at each other.

He shrugged. It made no sense at all.

"Now, the two of you haven't yet tried each other's entries, is that right?"

"Correct," Kelly said.

"Right," said Andrew.

Georgie, the head judge, got up and carried a tray over to them. She came to Kelly first and gave her the piece from Andrew's entry, which consisted of a sliver of cake and a macaron. Then she took the other plate to Andrew.

He recognized the cake immediately. She'd made their recipe too. A warm glow flowed through him, and this time it wasn't the stage lights. *Could it possibly mean she's been thinking what I've been thinking all along?*

"Go ahead, give them a taste." Martin watched them both take a bite. "I bet you can see why we're having such a tough time judging this final round."

They exchanged another look.

"Kelly, what is the cake that you baked for us?"

"Triple-Layer Honey Almond Cake." Her mouth pulled into a rigid smile, but he knew her real smile. That wasn't it. His mood sank. She was mad.

"Andrew?"

He glanced over in Kelly's direction. "The same. With a tower of macarons in passion fruit, almond, and strawberry with 'yes' on one side and 'I do' on the other."

"She had a similar concept. With the chocolate conversation heart answers. I guess great minds think alike," Martin said. "We're going to take a quick commercial break, and we'll be back."

The cameras pulled back, and the commercial aired on the screens at the edge of the stage.

Martin walked over and spoke to them. "Filming in front of a live audience creates a lot of challenges as it is, but this is the first time we've had to punt on the rules."

Kelly's jaw pulsed as she turned to Andrew. "That's my recipe."

Chapter Thirty-Two

NO LONGER SEQUESTERED, KELLY AND Andrew were escorted off the stage into one of the green rooms, although it wasn't green at all.

As soon as the door closed behind them, Kelly spun around on him. "Why would you use my recipe?"

"Wait a second," he said. "That wasn't *your* recipe. We worked on it for weeks and weeks together."

"Excuse me, so then your Lobster Risotto is also my dish? I helped you with that, I seem to recall."

"I guess so. That is your favorite cake. At least, it was. I mean, a lot of time has gone by, but I know how much you loved it, and we had so many great nights working on that recipe together in the kitchen at your parents' house while they were at the restaurant."

"That's true."

"It was my idea to add the strawberries," Andrew reminded her.

The edge of her mouth quirked at the edge. "It was better than the fresh blackberries I tried at first."

"But it inspired your recipe."

"See?" Her eyes danced. "You admit it. It's my recipe. That cake has been one of my best recipes for years now. I'm known for it."

Her head lolled to the side. "Andrew, you're privy to recipes from the finest restaurants. Why on Earth would you use that one?"

"First off, don't underestimate your talents, Kelly." He tipped his fingers under her chin. He wanted to pull her into his arms, to put everything behind them and turn back the calendar. "Second, my sous chef made a comment about putting my heart into the work, and something clicked. I realized at that moment that if I were making the proposal cake for anyone, it would be you. That's why I made that cake. Your cake."

He paused.

"Kelly, you're the only woman I've ever asked to marry me. The one person I could ever imagine sharing my life with. That Triple-Layer Honey Almond Cake represents us to me. The weeks we worked on it were the best in my life. We burned it, we over-spiced, under-spiced…remember when we tried it with the coconut?"

"And when we tried it with marzipan instead of almonds," she said. "Totally different."

"You knew what would work. It wouldn't have happened without you. It was your project, and I loved being a part of that. It's one of my best memories."

Her eyes glistened. "Mine too." The words were barely audible.

"When I was at my mother's, I was in the attic getting some stuff and I came across a box of our things. That recipe was in the box. I never would have remembered how to bake it if I hadn't just seen that. I tried to make it a few times when I first got to France. It never turned out."

"The judges clearly loved it tonight." She pressed her lips together. "What were you leaving out before?"

"I don't think I left out anything. I think the missing ingredient was us. It's our love that makes that cake so perfect."

Her eyes softened. "I never stopped loving you." Her chin trembled. "You're the one who didn't come home."

"I know. I'm so sorry." He brushed her hair back from her

cheek. "This cake was more than an entry, it was my heartfelt...I don't know...my feelings for you coming out. This isn't coming out right."

She cocked her head and looked confused, but at least she wasn't fuming like she'd been a few moments ago.

He took her hand. "Kelly, if I were asking you to marry me again, that's the exact cake I'd have baked for you." He rubbed his thumb across the top of her soft hand. "Would you have said yes?"

She pushed her hair back over her shoulder, then touched her hand to her mouth, but she didn't answer.

"I really wish you would."

She closed her eyes. "Don't say that."

"It's the truth. I felt it as soon as I saw you again."

"Don't throw me off my game. We aren't done here yet. One of us is going to win."

He shrugged. "I kind of already did."

"Excuse me?"

It took him a minute to realize she thought he meant the bake-off. That he was a sure thing. "Not the contest," he hurried to correct himself. "I mean showing up back home first. It was a good visit. With my family. My dad."

"Really?"

"Yeah. Amazing visit with him. But most of all, you."

"It was good to see you again." She shook her head. "You're the last person I expected to see here."

"I know. I can't believe I didn't put two and two together when I saw you on the street."

"Your cake out there, it's gorgeous. I love the way you used the macarons on the other layers. Texture and color. Very clever."

"Thank you. Yours is beautiful too. You know I like the real frosting layers. Never have been a fan of fondant."

She laughed. "I remember. This way, it was the best of both worlds."

"You nailed it," he said. "I guess I'd better decide what other recipe I'm going to bake. Technically, that cake really is your recipe. You wrote it down, you started the whole idea. I just helped refine and garnish it. It's yours. It's only fair that if they're going to make one of us bake something else that I do that."

She lifted her chin. "I hope they don't disqualify us both."

"They won't do that," Andrew said. "It's not like either one of us knew the other was here or what was being baked. We've followed all the rules. We could have just as easily both made chocolate cake."

"I guess so. Since we never knew who else was competing, we couldn't second-guess what might separate us from the others. A simple go-to like chocolate might have been a better idea."

"Keeping the show a secret from you was the hardest part. That night at your house I wanted to tell you about this so badly," he admitted.

"I was dying to tell you too, because I knew you'd understand how exciting this is, but I couldn't risk breaking the rules."

"I know." He took both of her hands in his and squeezed them. "I have to wonder how things would've turned out if I'd never left."

"Don't have regrets."

He pulled his hands together, then put one on her leg. "But maybe we—"

A production assistant came into the room. "Back on the set in two minutes. I need you both right here."

He and Kelly both sprung to their feet and ran to the door.

She ran her hands through her hair and straightened her jacket. When she turned to him, she raised her hand in a high five. "Good luck."

"I'm going to need it," he said, slapping her hand mid-air, holding it there for an extra second. "I want you to know that I don't care who wins. For once in my life, this isn't about me or what I want. I want you to have what you want and deserve, and I honestly think you're the best baker in this competition." He laced his fingers through hers and pulled their hands to his side.

He pulled her closer, but they were interrupted.

"Follow me." The production assistant rushed them back to the set. "Right here." She raised her hand, showing three fingers, then two, one. "Now."

They took their places back under the hot lights. His cake looked like it could use a little refrigeration right about now. He hoped the WILL YOU MARRY ME? topper wasn't going to go toppling onto the stage and break into a million pieces on national television. That wouldn't be a good omen at all.

Martin Schlipshel faced them.

The studio audience cheered.

Andrew's heart pounded. Right now. All of this. He couldn't imagine being here with anyone but Kelly. He turned to her and extended his hand. What a magical moment to share together.

She laughed that incredible laugh of hers, her nose crinkling as she smiled, then leaned in and whispered to him, "Break an egg."

Chapter Thirty-Three

THE ENERGY OF THE STUDIO audience amped Kelly as she walked back out on stage with Andrew right behind her.

The applause seemed to wrap all the way around them in a dizzying fashion. She looked at her cake. She was proud of what she'd put together. But looking over toward Andrew's, she couldn't be angry if he took the prize home. The cake he'd made was the perfect proposal.

"We've been so impressed by your culinary skills. Both of you. Your execution and presentation have been toe-to-toe throughout this competition," Martin said.

The audience cheered again, setting off a nervous giggle in Kelly.

"Meet Andrew York," Martin said as he walked over to Andrew. "How long have you been baking?"

"It's a long story, but the short version is that I went to pastry school." He glanced over at Kelly. "Honestly, I never intended to be a pastry chef, but my first culinary school exposure was an exclusive session in Paris under Pierre Hermé, known as the 'Picasso' of pastries."

"Indeed," Martin said, looking impressed. "That explains the amazing macarons too."

"Yes, I definitely learned how to make them from the best. I now work with Francois Dumont. It's been an amazing journey, learning new techniques all the time."

Andrew continued, "Chef Gordon Ramsay once said, 'If you want to become a great chef, you have to work with great chefs.' That's what he did, and so that's what I did too." He flashed his 1000-watt smile toward the audience, and a couple of girls squealed.

"Excellent. And you work for Francois Dumont in Paris now?"

"I do. I'm the Chef de Cuisine in his signature restaurant."

"Impressive," Martin said. "I've eaten there. It's an experience."

"Oh, yes. You don't come to our restaurant for a quick meal. It's a nine-course experience."

"That it is," Martin said.

"Now over here we have Kelly McIntyre from Bailey's Fork, North Carolina." The audience applauded and cheered. "They love you, Kelly. How are you feeling?"

"Nervous. Excited." She looked toward Andrew. "Shocked that I'm standing here next to someone I know...or knew...so well. Until last week, we hadn't spoken in seven years."

Martin stepped next to Kelly, blocking her view of Andrew. "We'll talk about that in a minute."

An ooooh rose from the audience, and things began to seem a little Jerry Springer-ish.

"Tell us about your training, Kelly."

She blushed. "I'm self-taught. I've never been to a class or traveled to France. Haven't trained professionally. I learned through spending hours at my grandmother's side in the kitchen. She was an amazing baker, and I loved helping her. I've been creating my own recipes since I was old enough to use the oven, and still writing with crayons. Sometimes when I get an idea I still write with the first thing I can find. Markers, crayons, in frosting if it's all I have."

Martin laughed. "You own your own bakery, and I have a feeling many of our viewers aren't strangers to your business."

"I do. I have a bakery in Bailey's Fork called The Cake Factory. We ship fresh and tasty cakes and cupcakes all over the nation."

"We've been to your shop. It's beautiful. Crisp, clean, whimsical, and yet you have a full factory in the building attached."

"Yes sir. We employ sixty to a hundred employees, depending on the time of the year. Of course, some of the holidays bring a wave of orders. From Valentine's Day to Easter and late in the year between Thanksgiving and Christmas. I'll be honest, this is the first time I've ever worn a chef's jacket. If y'all ever come to my place, you'll see me in my black-and-white apron."

"Well, apron or chef's jacket, these two can bake," Martin announced with a dramatic pause as he moved toward the audience with both arms out to his side while they cheered.

Martin stopped at the edge of the stage and turned back toward Kelly. "Kelly, do you know who nominated you?"

"No." She shook her head and shrugged. "I don't."

"Well, we want to share with you both who nominated you. But first, did I just see one of Cupid's arrows whiz across the stage?"

Kelly wasn't following what Martin was trying to say.

"So, I'm not sure if you've picked up on the secondary theme in this year's special bake-off," Martin said. "We had a married couple. A first-date couple." He turned to Kelly and Andrew. "And these two."

Andrew shot a look toward Kelly. Her vision narrowed. *What's going on?*

Kelly looked at Andrew. He looked confused too.

"This person," Martin continued, "completed the online form and said that you two had been the best cooking team she'd ever known. That before your job took you halfway across the world, Andrew, the two of you had plans to partner your talents. She thought bringing you together in this competition would be a wonderful way to reunite you. And since you're both so competitive, a fun way for you to both showcase your skills. In her mind, it's a win-win no matter which of you wins." Martin laughed. "Say that three times fast."

A drum roll pounded, filling the air with chaos as the lights dimmed.

"Could it have been your mom?" he whispered.

"Not in a million years."

The huge screen on the side of the stage broadcast the audience shot. The spotlight panned across the room and then stopped in the middle of the second row.

The camera focused on the woman, and her smiling face filled the screen.

"Would you mind reading your letter for us?" Martin climbed down the stairs to the audience and sidled up to the woman. "Mrs. Dawn York Redding nominated you both."

"Dawn?" Andrew dropped his head back. "You?"

"I knew why you were coming to New York the whole time, brother," she said with a smile.

Kelly was confused.

"Dawn, I took the liberty of bringing a copy of the letter with me. Will you?" He handed the piece of paper to her.

"Sure." She held the paper then looked toward the stage. "I hope y'all are going to forgive me for this."

Martin said, "One of them is going to go home a hundred thousand dollars richer. I think either way, you're going to be forgiven by at least one of them."

The studio audience laughed.

Dawn began to read,

"Dear Martin,

I love your show. Even the bakery in our town, The Cake Factory, schedules their breaks around the viewing schedule of your show so their employees can stay motivated and proud of the work they do. I'd love to nominate not one, but two people to compete in your special Valentine's Day edition. Now, I'm not the husband or wife or fiancée as the call-out at the end of the show on December fifteenth stated, but I know two people who were once so in love that no one expected to ever see them apart. Kelly grew up in our hometown of Bailey's Fork, North Carolina. She's such a good person. Hard working and caring, a great part of our community. She built The Cake Factory in our hometown. Not only is it the bakery everyone goes to for every special event, but she also brought jobs to our community as her online company has expanded. Now people all over the nation are enjoying her recipes right out of our small town."

Kelly couldn't see a thing for the tears welling. She didn't dare brush them away, hoping no one would notice.

"My brother was engaged to Kelly when my Aunt Claire arranged for him to go to France to a very elite pastry school for six months. The whole time he was gone, he and Kelly worked on recipes from thousands of miles apart."

An awww crossed the audience like the wave.

Dawn continued, "Careers and opportunities have kept them apart, but neither has found that special someone. I think both of them are worthy of the title of Best Four Square Valentine's Day Bake-Off Pastry Chef, and if it brought the two of them together, then it would be the icing on the cake."

Someone in the audience whistled.

Kelly swept away the tear that fell to her cheek.

Andrew tapped his heart with his right hand. "Thanks, sis."

Dawn pulled her hands to her mouth and blew kisses toward them.

"She's right. We've never had talent so closely matched." Martin waved toward her. "We might need to hire you to do some casting."

"I'm available," she said.

Martin turned back to them. "It was shocking for us to get almost the same dessert from you both."

Kelly clicked her thumb against her fingernail.

"Our hidden cameras caught you two talking about the last round backstage."

Kelly's mind reeled in an attempt to rewind to what they'd said. The show had been quite open about filming and recording throughout the whole process. She hoped she hadn't said anything she'd regret. Over the past few days, she'd gotten so comfortable she'd kind of forgotten the cameras were even around.

The big screen suddenly filled with footage of the two of them talking in the green room.

Martin led Kelly and Andrew off to the side of the stage where they could see better.

She watched the two of them talking. His body language echoed her feelings—leaning in toward each other. Him touching her hand so gently. Her giggling as he pushed her hair back from her face. The tilt of her chin as she looked at him. There was still something there, and it wasn't one-sided.

As they got to the part where she said they might get disqualified, her hands clenched.

"Don't you two worry," Martin said. "There's no disqualification, but we are going to get down to a winner. Only one of you can win the hundred-thousand-dollar prize."

Kelly's lips quivered as she smiled.

Andrew probably wanted the money to open his restaurant. She just wanted validation. She hoped he won.

"We were going to have you both bake something, but instead we've decided to let the audience help choose the winner of this round. After all, we do have two huge desserts here."

Whoops and whistles poured from the audience as a team of twelve people dressed in white chef jackets made their way out on stage to begin serving cake.

They split into two teams, six on each of the cakes.

Martin explained how things were going to be decided. "Our team of bakers will begin passing out cake to everyone in the audience. While they're getting that going, everyone will find a controller under their seat. Once all of the cake has been distributed, we'll have a countdown, and you'll select your favorite pastry chef."

The white-coated bakers carried trays with plates of cake out to the audience, making short work of it.

"Those who choose Andrew's as being the most creative, most applicable to the proposal theme of Marry Me, and of course, taste, will choose A. Simple, A for Andrew. If Kelly's entry meets those three points—creativity, theme, and taste—then you'll be voting B on your controller."

The two cakes on stage had quickly dwindled, the beautiful creations now reduced to what looked like the aftermath of an earthquake.

Excitement built in the room as the audience took to the task with fervor.

Chapter Thirty-Four

A S THEY STOOD THERE NEXT to each other on stage, Andrew reached for Kelly's hand. She smiled and let him take it.

He gave it a squeeze. His heart pounded so loud he wasn't sure if she'd said anything when he'd taken it. As the cake was distributed to the audience members, the noise level rose significantly.

Andrew said to Kelly, "I don't think any of the original recipes I've created since I left have been as good as anything we created together."

"I know that's not true. You're a culinary artist," she said. "I'm just doing what I love."

"I want to do what I love too." He never took his eyes off her. "With *who* I love."

She rewarded him with a smile broader than the one in his heart. "Me too." She moistened her lips. "So much," she whispered.

"Are we ready?" Martin asked. "Help me count down from ten…nine…eight…seven…six…five…four…three…two…one. Cast your votes."

The audience held their controllers, and on the big screen a graph began calculating votes. The bar chart shifted as the votes were counted. Andrew's votes jumped higher, and then Kelly's overtook the lead. The numbers stayed close, but as the last few votes registered, the winner was Kelly.

She stood there dumbfounded.

"You won," he said, and with all his heart he was happy for the outcome.

Martin walked over to her. "Our winner of the Four Square Cooking Show Valentine's Day Bake-Off! Kelly McIntyre."

Like a Miss America beauty queen, her eyes filled with tears and her hands went to her face. She looked, wide-eyed, toward Andrew, shaking her head.

He stepped over and pulled her into his arms and swung her around. "Congratulations!"

Confetti in red, pink, and white began falling from the ceiling.

Her hands shook as Martin held a huge cardboard check in front of her.

"Our one-hundred-thousand-dollar prize winner."

"Thank you," Kelly said. "Thank you so much." She turned to Andrew. "I can't believe this."

He pulled a macaron from what was left of his entry and handed it to her. "You deserve this."

She read the word *Yes* on one side, and then turned it over and saw *I Do*. "Was that a mistake, or were you hedging your bets?"

"It was no mistake."

"I know, I know. Everything you do is intentional."

He pulled her into an embrace. "Except when I broke your heart."

"Let's never talk about that again."

He tilted his head back. "Best thing I've heard all day. I really am the winner. You can have that check and title."

She laughed. "I worked hard for that. You were tough competition."

He reached for her hand and laced his fingers through hers.

"Best day ever," she said.

Dawn rushed over to them. "I knew you two were perfect for this show. I'm forgiven, right?"

"Yes, I can't believe you did all of that," Kelly said.

"I'd do anything to make sure my brother finds the happiness he deserves, and I've always thought you two were perfect together," she said.

"I owe you big time, sis. In a good way."

"Just be happy. I've got to run. My flight leaves in less than two hours. It's going to be tight as it is. I'll talk to you both soon." She blew them a kiss and ran off.

The PR team tugged Kelly from one stage to the other, shooting photos to go with the morning show spots and other promotion materials that would go out over the next few days. Then Martin came over.

"We've got a special Valentine's Day dinner for you two as well. Your ride is ready for you," he said. "I'll take you."

They followed him to the elevator. Martin pressed a button and stood in front of the panel while Andrew and Kelly stepped inside.

Kelly wobbled and reached for the wall. "Is this elevator going up or down?"

"Drunk on victory," Andrew teased, but when the elevator doors opened, they weren't in the parking garage, they were on the roof, and there was a helicopter waiting for them.

"No way," Kelly said.

Martin swung his arm out to the rooftop. "Your ride is here to take you for a quick tour of our gorgeous city and then to dinner. Afterward, Brenda will meet you and take you both back to your hotels."

"Thank you, Martin," Kelly gushed. "I can't believe all of this."

"You earned it. Our ratings are going to be through the roof. I just know it." He grinned. "I feel good about this."

Andrew and Kelly jumped in the helicopter and put on the

headphones as they were told. The ride over the city was exhilarating. The pilot pointed out some of the main attractions.

"The Statue of Liberty," Kelly said. "I can't believe it. I've always wanted to see it." She giggled with excitement.

How had I forgotten how much I loved that smile of hers? Kelly is what I've been missing in my life. If I can get her back, I'll never risk losing her again.

Andrew grabbed her hand and pulled it into his lap. "This is amazing."

The helicopter dipped and then lowered on top of a building. A man in a black suit helped them out of the chopper and whisked them off to the side as it took off without them.

"I can't believe we were just flying in that thing," Kelly said. "Crazy."

"Your dinner is ready," the man in black said, taking her by the elbow.

Andrew put his hand on the small of Kelly's back, and they followed their host to the other side of the rooftop. A pergola was covered in what must've been two thousand twinkle lights. Beneath it there were tall heaters and a small round table for two.

Andrew pulled out the chair for Kelly. "Wow. They're really treating you right."

He lifted his glass of wine. "To the Four Square Valentine's Day Champion."

She lifted hers. "Thank you."

"Wait. I'm not done."

"Oh?"

"To the only woman I'd want to be with on Valentine's Day. I miss you."

She caught a breath.

"I want to be a part of all of your tomorrows. Will you be my Valentine tonight?"

She lowered her eyes, then smiled and nodded as she touched her glass to his.

After a perfect dinner, Brenda came to the table. "I hope you've enjoyed your night."

"It's been wonderful," Kelly said. "The most romantic dinner I could ever imagine."

"The fun is just beginning," she announced, waving a folder. "Let's go downstairs so they can clean up here."

"You knew the whole time, didn't you?" Kelly said to her as they walked to the elevator.

"Yeah. Lori and I both knew. We were so worried when Andrew saw you on the street that you'd blow it at dinner. I can't believe you made it through the night with no slips."

"Man of my word," Andrew said.

"I'm a rule-follower," Kelly said. "But it wasn't easy."

They went into Kelly's dressing room and sat together on the couch. Brenda reviewed the commitments Kelly needed to fulfill over the next two days.

"I'm going to be very busy," Kelly said, glancing over toward Andrew.

"It's going to be great," he said. "I'm so happy for you."

Kelly cocked her head then turned to Brenda. "Could Andrew come with me?"

"I don't see why not." Brenda smiled. "In fact, it might be a real plus. Sit tight." She pulled out her phone and made a call. When she came back, she wore a huge smile. "I have good news. You should see all the posts on social media about you two. You're the darlings of the Internet tonight. I asked the show about extending Andrew's stay. They approved it." She turned to him. "If that's okay with you. Don't be surprised if they drag you on stage too, though."

"Will you come?" she asked.

"This is your win. All you."

"I want to share the experience with you. Come on. We'll have fun," she said. "Please?"

"Then I wouldn't miss it for the world." Andrew kissed the inside of her hand.

She pulled her hands together, wanting to hold that kiss forever close to her heart.

Chapter Thirty-Five

A FTER A TWO-DAY WHIRLWIND OF interviews and a segment on the network's morning cooking talk show, It was time for Kelly to get back to the real world.

Brenda was waiting for her at the car. "This is where I say goodbye. Here's your cell phone back, and the hotel will shuttle you to the airport when you're ready. It's been such a treat working with you."

"Thank you for everything. I couldn't have gotten through this without you."

"Thank *you*," Brenda said. "I get a bonus for you winning, and you've been the easiest contestant I've ever worked with. I'm so glad you won." She glanced over at Andrew, who was talking to someone on the phone. "He's great too. Both of you. I'd love to hear what's going on with the two of you in a few months."

Kelly let out a nervous giggle.

"He's pretty awesome," Brenda continued.

"I'm afraid. He broke my heart once, you know."

"Don't be afraid. He's sweet. Cute. Generous. A great cook. What more could a girl want?" She pulled a large envelope from her portfolio. "These are a few mementos from the show I thought you'd enjoy."

"You didn't have to do that."

"I wanted to. I won't be surprised if they have you both back very soon. If they do, I hope they call me in to assist."

"I'll request you," Kelly said as she got in the car.

Andrew finally hung up from his call and stopped to chat with Brenda before he got into the car.

"Ready to go?" he said to Kelly, patting her on the leg.

"I don't want this to end." She stared with longing at him. "My flight leaves at nine tonight."

"I know." Andrew massaged her neck. "You've got to be exhausted."

"I am." She rolled her neck side-to-side. "That feels good."

"Why don't we drop you off at your hotel first? Get a nap in, and I'll come back over around five."

"That sounds good."

Andrew leaned in toward the driver. "Can you drop Kelly off first?"

"Yes, sir."

When they pulled up in front of her hotel, Andrew slid out and held the door for her. "Sleep well."

"I know I will. I'll see you in a little while?"

"Definitely."

She waved as she walked away.

"Kelly. One more thing." He jogged over to her side. "I've made some big mistakes, but I want to make that up to you. I know I'll have to earn your trust again, and it's a long row to hoe, but I'm up for the task."

She held her hand up like a traffic cop. "Let's just enjoy this time and leave the past where it belongs."

His jaw relaxed. "I like the sound of that."

Kelly went upstairs and sprawled out across the bed. She flipped through the messages on her phone. Practically everyone she knew had texted her. "All of this really did happen." She laid back on the bed and closed her eyes.

She rolled over onto her stomach and dialed home. "Mom?"

"Kelly! We're so proud of you. The show called and told us everything. We taped it so you can watch it again with us." Mom was talking faster than a gunshot.

"CB! Kelly's on the phone. Pick up the line in the kitchen."

"How's my winning girl? I'm so proud of you." Dad's voice was as chipper as she'd ever heard it.

"Thanks, Daddy. I'm so sorry I couldn't tell you about it. It was in the contract. I felt like the worst daughter in the world, leaving like that."

"Don't be silly. They explained everything. You were so brave, Kelly! I could never go to that big city alone."

"I can't wait to tell you all about it."

"And about Andrew," Mom said, with a hint of accusation.

"Am I crazy, Mom? Dad, what do you think? I didn't even know he was in the competition, but before I left, we had some nice time together…and here, things have been so good."

"Like old times?" Dad asked.

"Even better. Because I'm stronger than I ever was. I think it's good I've been on my own and have found success. I'm not sure I'd have believed I could do everything I've done by myself had all that not happened."

"You're a remarkable young lady, Kelly," Mom said. "I don't think you're crazy at all. I told you before that I thought you still missed him. I had a feeling love was coming back into your life."

An odd sense of *déjà vu* filled her, and then Kelly remembered that was almost exactly what the woman at the airport had said. She reached for the card she'd left on the nightstand in case she got a chance to go. "I'll see y'all in the morning. My flight gets in pretty late. I can't wait to see you."

"Come to the diner for an early breakfast," Dad said. "I'll make your favorite."

"You're on." She hung up the phone and made short work of packing her things. With her bags packed and next to the door, she set her alarm on her phone and then laid down to rest.

Kelly woke up and scrambled for her phone. Thank goodness it was still early enough. She went downstairs, checked her bags with the bellman, and asked them to hail a cab to take her to Andrew's hotel.

Inside, she asked the front desk clerk to ring his room for her. "Hi, Andrew."

"Hey. What's up? Couldn't you sleep?"

"I did, but I need you to come downstairs right now."

"Are you okay?"

"I'm great. I want to take you somewhere." She couldn't hide the excitement in her voice.

"Uh-oh. You're worrying me. You've never been to New York City. Where could you possibly think I need to go?"

"Are you going to come with me or not?"

"On my way."

It seemed like forever before the elevator doors opened and he stepped off.

He took her hand. "I think I like this take-charge side of you."

"You'd better get used to it." Kelly raced to a taxi waiting at the front door. She dug for something in her purse, then opened the passenger door and leaned in. "We need to go here." She thrust the business card toward the driver, then slid in.

Andrew got into the car. "Are you going to tell me where we're going?"

"I have a special invitation from a very nice woman for what's supposed to be the best cheesecake in the whole city."

"Really? In the whole city?" He shifted his glance. "You do realize New York is known for its cheesecake."

"Yep."

They drove across town. Kelly hoped Mrs. Leary would be there. She wanted to thank her for her words of wisdom and kindness.

The taxi pulled to the curb, and Kelly peered out the window. "This is it." She jumped out first, bouncing with excitement as Andrew stepped out of the car in front of The Manhattan Original Diner.

He followed her inside.

Kelly waved down a waitress. "Hi, I'm hoping Henry Leary is here. His wife, Candace, told me I had to come and try his cheesecake."

"Grab that booth over there. I'll check and be right with you." The waitress snagged two menus from the counter. "Here you go."

"Thanks." She scooted into the booth.

"Oh. My. Gawsh. Who knew I'd ever really see you again!" The tiny woman slid right into the booth next to her.

Kelly slid over. "How could I pass up your offer?"

"You're a good girl. I knew it." She shook a finger in her direction. "You can't pass up my Henry's cheesecake. He'll be here in a minute. He's bringing it out personally."

"Thank you," Kelly said.

"You should've told me you were going to be on my favorite television show! I almost dropped my dentures when I saw you on there. I cheered for you the whole way. No offense," she said to Andrew.

Mrs. Leary leaned her forearms on the table. "And this, Kelly. This man. He's the one. I knew it before they even revealed that you two had been a couple before the show. I just knew it." Mrs. Leary tapped the side of her head. "I have special gifts. I just know things."

"I'm glad that was in my favor," Andrew said.

"Oh, yes." Mrs. Leary leaned in close to Kelly, but her whispering skills lacked. "Trust the happiness that's coming your way, my dear."

Kelly blushed. "Yes, ma'am."

"I could listen to you talk with that little southern accent all day."

Y'all are the ones with the accent, Kelly thought.

A robust man wearing white came toward the table, carrying two huge plates of cheesecake. One with cherries on top, one plain. "For my new friends. I saw you both on the Four Square Bake-Off. I'm so glad to meet you. Candace told me all about you, young lady." He slid the plates onto the table—the cherries in front of her, and the plain in front of Andrew. "Eat up."

Andrew and Kelly locked eyes, then with a laugh she switched the plates. "Just like old times," she said.

"Even better."

They dug into the cheesecake, and when both plates were clean, Henry asked, "So, what do you think?"

"You're right. This is the very best cheesecake I've ever had."

"Fabulous. Hold on. I need to get a picture of us together. You'll sign it for us!" Henry ambled over, carrying an old Polaroid camera. "Franny. Come take a picture of us. This lady won the Four Square Bake-Off!"

Franny squealed and came racing to his side. "I lawwwve that show. I can't believe you're in the diner. I'm Franny. My mom and I watched. I was almost late for work because of you."

"Oh no, I'm sorry," Kelly said.

Henry, Candace, and Kelly stood together. "Get over here, boy," Henry said to Andrew.

"Me?"

Candace pulled Kelly closer to her. "Yes, you. I want the four of us together in the picture."

Andrew stepped in close to Kelly. She leaned back against his chest, then tilted her chin back to him with a broad smile. "This is great," he said.

Three pictures spit out of the camera at an alarmingly slow rate with a buzzing that sounded like a big bumblebee.

Candace grabbed them and started flapping her arms, stopping every few seconds to see if the picture had come in to view yet. "These are going to be so good."

Henry walked over to the cash register and came back with a marker. "How'd we do?"

Candace eyed each one. "This one goes on the wall." She shoved it toward him. "You two sign this."

Henry handed him the marker, and Andrew signed along the very bottom, leaving the rest of the white cardboard-framed border for Kelly.

She wrote, "Best cheesecake I've ever had!" Then signed above his name, finishing with a curly ampersand.

Kelly & Andrew. Seeing it written like that brought back so many memories.

"Can I have one of the other pictures?" Andrew asked.

"Of course." Candace handed them both to him. "Take your pick."

Andrew tried to pay for their cheesecake, but Candace and Henry insisted it was on the house. It was like a family goodbye of hugs and handshakes as they left the diner.

"That was amazing, but we'd better get back to the hotel and pick up your things to go to the airport," he said.

Kelly's mood softened. She hated for this to end. "When do you fly back out?"

"I've got something to tell you."

She closed her eyes, bracing herself.

"I'm coming back to Bailey's Fork. We're on the same flight."

Her head jerked up. "We are?" Her heart was full of hope, but then she paused. "For how long?"

"All the way. You were right. Home can only be one place. I want to make my home in Bailey's Fork. I hope it'll be with you. It's where we belong. With our families. That's home."

"I—"

"Please let me finish." He placed his hand on her arm. "I know I messed up. I know we have a long way to go to repair the damage I've done, but with all that said, if I'd asked you to marry me on that stage, tell me…would you have at least for one tiny second considered saying yes?"

She sat there trying to not hyperventilate while gathering her thoughts.

Andrew sat quiet, almost looking defeated.

She grabbed her purse and pulled out the macaron he'd given her on stage. "Yes." She handed it to him. "Yes. I'd have considered it. I've thought about it so many times since you've been back."

"You scared me for a minute there." Laughing, he pulled her in for a kiss. "Please tell me this means you'll give me a second chance. I love you, Kelly. I've never loved anyone but you."

"Me too. Well, I was really mad with you for a long time, but no one could get to my heart. It's always been yours."

"I'm coming home," he said.

"Home. That sounds so good." Her brows pulled together. "Wait."

"What's wrong?"

"We have a problem. It's Gray."

"That's not a problem." Andrew's smile was broad. "I love Gray. I think that pig is cool."

"We're going to need a new name for him."

"Why?" Andrew sat back. "I was only teasing about it being a weird name. It suits him."

She shook her head. "No. It's a long story, but I'm thinking maybe we need to call him Whay now."

"Okay, I have no idea what this is all about, but you can call him whatever you like as long as we can be together. What's the big deal about Gray anyway? I think he kind of looks like a Gray."

She bit down on the left side of her lip. "It stood for Good Riddance Andrew York."

"Ouch." He winced. "Really?"

She shrugged. "I could have gone the burn-all-our-pictures route, or there was talk of a voodoo doll. Or a rebound guy. Instead I got a pet pig."

"Okay, so why Way?"

"W.H.A.Y. Welcome Home Andrew York. I mean, since you really are going to come home and stay home, right?"

"I am. My home will be wherever we are together. I think maybe part of why I never came home was that I knew I wouldn't be coming back to you. I never want to feel that way again."

"We won't let that happen." She placed her hands on either side of his face and kissed him. "Welcome home."

Chapter Thirty-Six
One Year Later

ANDREW HAD THE ARCHITECTURAL PLANS finished and was ready to break ground for his new restaurant on the property his father had given him. Farm to Fork, named for its location between the towns of Farm City and Bailey's Fork, would open in time for the Christmas holidays if all went according to schedule.

Until then, The Main Street Cafe had kept all the same home cooking on the menu, but now the place had enjoyed a makeover. The updated booths made it a comfortable place to grab a quick bite, but the additional white-tablecloth seating in the new section off the back, including an outside area under a pergola with ceiling fans and heaters for year-round dining, had added a touch of class Bailey's Fork had never had before. Andrew trained new chefs who would help carry on this cafe and cook in his new restaurant.

The old Main Street Cafe sign had been retired and replaced with a new one. The New York Cafe. A play on words. The town that had brought he and Kelly back together, and the last name he hoped they'd soon be sharing.

Whay didn't seem to mind his new name, and Andrew had found someone to make a tiny piggy tuxedo jacket and bow tie for him for the big day.

As the last customers were being served their Valentine's Day celebration dinner, Kelly and Andrew sat outside next to the fireplace, enjoying their own special dinner.

"It's hard to believe it's been a year since we got back together."

A waiter came outside with a plate carried high above his head. He then set it down right in front of Kelly. A slice of Triple-Layer Honey Almond Cake like the one she'd made on Four Square, but a miniature version, and this time the Tiffany Blue box wasn't made out of fondant. It was the real deal.

"I hope I got this right." He reached over and opened the box.

She pulled her hands to her chest. "It's beautiful."

"Like you." He lifted the ring out of the box and got down on one knee. "Kelly McIntyre, will you marry me?"

She picked up the macaron that sat on the side of the plate and turned it over to yes. "Yes. Yes, I will."

His hand shook as he slid the ring on her finger. "I missed seven years that we could have been together."

"Don't be sorry. We've both done a lot of great things over that time. We've matured, and our love withstood it all. That has to mean something."

"It means we're meant to be together." He paused. "Can we get married in front of the tree in front of your house where we first carved our initials?"

"I like that idea," Kelly said. "Just close friends and family?"

"Of course. I'm all for that. Pick the date."

"That's easy. June fourth. The same date we originally picked."

"Just a few years later than we'd planned."

"Right." She leaned in and kissed him. "I'll love you forever."

He held his hand gently to the curve of her cheek. "I'll never let you down again."

"I'm not worried. I think we finally know the recipe for a good marriage."

He raised his hand. She slapped it in a high five, and he laced his fingers through hers, tugging her in close then spinning her around. "A recipe to treasure."

Honey Almond Cake with Berries and Mascarpone Crème Fraiche

A Hallmark Original Recipe

In *The Secret Ingredient*, Kelly and Andrew were once engaged and dreaming of opening their own restaurant. But life took them in different directions, and those days are far in the past...or are they? One very special recipe turns out to be a sweet reminder of how perfect they are together. For a truly special occasion—or no occasion at all—this dessert is a showstopper.

Recipe:

> **Yield:** 1 Three-Layer Cake
> **Prep Time:** 60 minutes
> **Bake Time:** 30 minutes
> **Total Time:** 90 minutes

INGREDIENTS

Almond Cake:
- 1 cup plus 2 Tbsp. buttermilk
- 2¼ cups granulated sugar
- 6 large eggs
- 1 tbsp. vanilla extract
- 1½ tsp. almond extract
- 2¼ cups all-purpose flour
- 1 cup almond meal flour
- 1½ tbsp. baking powder
- 1 tsp. kosher salt
- 1 cup plus 2 tbsp. canola oil

Vanilla Honey Glaze:
- 1 tbsp. honey
- 1 tsp. vanilla extract
- 1 tsp. lemon zest, fresh
- ½ cup confectioner's sugar
- 4 tbsp. half and half cream

Mascarpone Crème Fraiche
- 3 (8-oz.) packages mascarpone, room temperature
- 1¼ cups crème fraiche
- 1 cup confectioner's sugar
- 1½ tsp. vanilla extract

- As needed, whole strawberries
- As needed, sliced toasted almonds
- As needed, fresh mint sprigs

DIRECTIONS

1. To prepare cakes: preheat oven to 350 degrees. Coat three 8-inch cake pans with nonstick cooking spray. Place a round of parchment paper on the bottom of each pan; spray with cooking spray.

2. Using a handheld or stand mixer fitted with a paddle attachment, combine buttermilk, sugar, eggs, vanilla extract and almond extract in bowl and mix until fully blended. With a rubber spatula, scrape down sides of bowl.

3. In a large bowl, combine flour, almond flour, baking powder and salt. Add to buttermilk mixture and beat on low until fully blended. Scrape down sides of bowl.

4. Slowly add oil to buttermilk/flour mixture and beat on medium-low until fully blended.

5. Divide batter evenly between prepared pans. Bake for 25 to 30 minutes, or until a toothpick inserted in the center of each cake comes out clean. Cool in pans for 10 minutes; invert on wire rack to release cakes.

6. To prepare glaze: combine honey, vanilla extract, lemon zest, confectioner's sugar and half and half in a bowl and whisk until smooth. Brush tops and sides of warm cakes evenly with glaze. Cool cakes completely. (If making cakes ahead, wrap tightly and freeze.)

7. To prepare mascarpone crème fraiche: combine mascarpone, crème fraiche, confectioner's sugar and vanilla extract in a large bowl and whisk until smooth.

8. To assemble cake: place first cake on cake pedestal or serving plate. Spread about ¼ of mascarpone crème fraiche over top of cake. Top with second cake layer. Spread about ¼ of mascarpone crème fraiche over top of cake. Top with third cake layer. Spread about ¼ of mascarpone crème fraiche over

top of cake. Spread remaining ¼ of mascarpone crème fraiche on sides of cake to make a light crumb coating. Using a bench scraper or cake spatula, lightly scrape top and sides of cake to remove excess mascarpone crème fraiche forming a smooth surface.

9. Top cake with strawberries, toasted almonds and fresh mint sprigs.

10. Chill thoroughly before serving.

Note: Find prepared crème fraiche in the dairy aisle of your grocery store. Crème fraiche is easy to make if not available in your area. Combine 1¼ cups heavy cream with 2 tbsp. buttermilk. Cover and let sit at room temperature for 12 hours or until thickened. Refrigerate until ready to use.

Thanks so much for reading *The Secret Ingredient*. We hope you enjoyed it!

You might like these other books from Hallmark Publishing:

Love on Location
Sunrise Cabin
Christmas In Evergreen
The Christmas Company
A Timeless Christmas
At the Heart of Christmas

For information about our new releases and exclusive offers, sign up for our free newsletter at hallmarkchannel.com/hallmark-publishing-newsletter

You can also connect with us here:

Facebook.com/HallmarkPublishing

Twitter.com/HallmarkPublish

About the Author

USA Today bestselling author Nancy Naigle whips up small-town love stories with a whole lot of heart. She began writing while juggling a successful career in finance and life on a seventy-six-acre goat farm. Her many books include *Christmas in Evergreen*, the heartwarming companion novel to the Hallmark movie, and *Christmas Joy* and *Hope for Christmas,* which were adapted into Hallmark movies. Now happily retired from a career in the financial industry, she devotes her time to writing, horseback riding, and enjoying the occasional spa day. A Virginia girl at heart, Nancy now calls North Carolina home.

DISCARD

DISCARD

CPSIA information can be obtained
at www.ICGtesting.com
Printed in the USA
LVHW031703160119
604161LV00001B/40/P

9 781947 892378